MINE

*Just when Brooke and Remy need each other the
most, she is torn away from the ringside.*

"STEAMY, SEXY, INTENSE, AND EROTIC, *MINE* IS ONE
THAT WILL HAVE YOU HANGING OFF THE ROPES.
AND BEGGING FOR MORE."
—Alice Clayton, *USA Today* bestselling author of *Wallbanger*

"Wow—Katy Evans is one to watch."

—*Wicked Little Pixie*

REMY

*What moves a man as complex as Remington
Tate? Let him tell you in his own words. . . .*

"SEDUCTIVE, WILD, AND VISCERAL."

—Christina Lauren

"Reading this book is like the best foreplay ever. The sexual tension was incredible. . . . I'll follow Remington Tate to the ends
of the earth."

—Emme Rollins

BOOKS BY KATY EVANS

Katy Evans's *USA Today* and *New York Times* bestselling series strips away everything you've ever believed about passion—and asks the dangerously enticing question, "How REAL is what you feel?"

Praise for Katy Evans and

REAL

Remington Tate, the unstoppable bad boy
of the Underground fighting circuit has finally
met his match . . . in Brooke Dumas.

"I loved this book. As in, I couldn't stop talking about it."
—*Dear Author*

"Kudos are in order for Ms. Evans for taking writing to a whole new level. She makes you FEEL every single word you read."
—*Reality Bites*

"Remy was complex and his story broke my heart . . . made me cry! Katy Evans had me on the edge of my seat through the whole story. . . . Without a doubt I absolutely fell in total LOVE with Remy."
—*Totally Booked*

"Edgy, angsty, and saturated with palpable tension and incendiary sex, this tale packs an emotional wallop. . . ."
—*Library Journal*

"Unlike anything I've ever read before. [A] love story that has to be experienced because until you do, you just won't get it . . . one roller-coaster ride that you'll never forget!"
—*Books over Boys*

"Some books are special. . . . What a rare gift for an author to be able to actually wrap your arms around your readers and hold them. Katy Evans does just that."
—*SubClub Books*

ROGUE

katy evans

Gallery Books

New York London Toronto Sydney New Dehli

G

Gallery Books
A Division of Simon & Schuster, Inc.
1230 Avenue of the Americas
New York, NY 10020

First Gallery Books trade paperback edition July 2014

GALLERY BOOKS and colophon are registered trademarks of Simon & Schuster, Inc.

For information about special discounts for bulk purchases, please contact Simon & Schuster Special Sales at 1-866-506-1949 or business@simonandschuster.com.

The Simon & Schuster Speakers Bureau can bring authors to your live event. For more information or to book an event contact the Simon & Schuster Speakers Bureau at 1-866-248-3049 or visit our website at www.simonspeakers.com.

Interior design by Davina Mock-Maniscalco

Manufactured in the United States of America

10 9 8 7 6 5 4 3 2

Library of Congress Cataloging-in-Publication Data
Evans, Katy.
    Rogue / by Katy Evans. —First Gallery Books trade paperback edition.
        pages cm
1. Man-woman relationships—Fiction. I. Title.
    PR6105.V3495R64 2014
    823'.92—dc23

                                        2014017210

ISBN 978-1-4767-5561-8
ISBN 978-1-4767-5564-9 (ebook)

to dreams coming true
and to CeCe, a dream come true

Rogue:

noun
Someone without principle; a person, esp a man,
who's not what he seems. A scoundrel.

verb
To deceive
Destroy
Act like a rogue

adjective
Not belonging, such as a man who doesn't belong.
Renegade, with savagery, and unpredictable, such as one
who deviates from the norm; example, a rogue cop. Or
maybe even a rogue prince charming . . .

ROGUE PLAYLIST

"WAITING FOR SUPERMAN" by Daughtry

"THE HAUNTED MAN" by Bat for Lashes

"STORY OF MY LIFE" by One Direction

"MILLION DOLLAR MAN" by Lana Del Rey

"DARK HORSE" by Katy Perry

"GRAVITY" by Alex & Sierra

"HOME" by Daughtry

"XO" by Beyoncé

"SAY SOMETHING" by Alex & Sierra

"THE LAST SONG EVER" by Secondhand Serenade

"THIS IS WHAT IT FEELS LIKE" by Armin Van Buuren

THE ONE

Melanie

At a very young age I was taught that there were no certainties in life. Life itself is not a certainty, nor is friendship, or love. But given the first, you have the certainty of an opportunity to chase after your friendships, live your life, and search for love.

It's been twenty-four years and I'm still searching. I know what they say about love: how it hits you when you least expect it, how it's not all it's supposed to be. But I know exactly how it will be. I await it like a thunderstorm sweeping over me. I am prepared for it to take me away and, at the same time, embrace every pore of me. I am prepared to fall, and fall hard, if only I would just find him. This faceless, nameless man who will make all the others feel like little boys to me.

Sometimes I see his face in my mind, and though he's in a haze I can feel him, strong and solid as I hoped he would be, and

I wait because I know this with a certainty: I will never stop living my life, loving my friends, and looking for love. I know with a certainty that when I find him, he will be all that I dreamed he would be, perfect in every way.

The perfect man for me.

ONE

ZERO

Greyson

I've got my dick buried inches deep in a mewling woman's cunt when I first become aware of the click of my front door. I pull out and grab a handful of bedsheets, toss them over to her, and she moans in protest over being without my dick anymore.

"Cover up, sugar, you have three seconds . . ."

Two.

One.

The first to materialize in my door is Derek. "Your father wants you." Next to him is my asshole half brother, Wyatt, and he looks none too pleased to see me. What can I say? It's mutual. I jump into my jeans. "He sent two of you?" I ask, almost laughing. "If I were a girl, I guess this would be the part where my feelings get hurt."

Both men walk into the room, checking out the territory with quick flicks of their eyes. They don't see me coming. In less than a second, I've got Derek pinned up against the wall and I've got Wyatt in a choke hold. I spin them to face the door as I watch the rest of the men shuffle in. Seven of them, plus the two squirming in my hold. The nine-member squad composes the Underground enforcing committee led by my father—every man here with a different level of skills. None, not a single one of them, as skilled as *I*.

"You know damn well if it involved you, it'd be a nine-man mission," Eric Slater, my father's brother and right hand, says as he steps inside. Eric is stern, silent, and dangerous. He's my uncle and the closest thing to a dad I had growing up. He taught me to live among my father's private little mob—no, not live. He taught me to survive. To take my circumstances and thrive. Because of him, I grew smarter, stronger, meaner. I learned whatever there was to learn, multiplied by the billionth power. The power of kill or be killed. *Doesn't matter if you'll use the skill, it's an insurance. Ever heard of insurances, boy? People who have insurances rarely use them. It's those who don't have shit who end up needing one. See that arrow? Use it. See that knife? Wield it, fling it, learn how to use the least amount of effort to do the most amount of damage. . . .*

I've got all kinds of insurances. My entire mind is a computer programmed to think the worst of a situation, all in less than a second. Right now, I know for a fact all these men are armed. Some of them carry two weapons, under their socks, at the small of their backs, or in the front flaps of their jackets. Eric watches my eyes scan each and every one of them, and he smiles, clearly proud of me. He opens his jacket and looks down at the gun on his hip. "You want to touch my piece? Here you go, Grey." He pulls it out and extends it, the barrel in his hand.

I let go of the two men in my grasp when I sense Wyatt is about two seconds from passing out. I pull them back, then with a shove send them smashing against the wall. "I don't give a shit what he wants to say to me," I state.

Eric looks around my bedroom. My apartment is perfectly clean. I don't do mess. I have a reputation and I like hearing a pin drop . . . the reason I heard these assholes enter my studio loft in the first place. "Still banging these whores? With that fucking face, you can get a goddess, Grey."

He eyes the woman in my bed. She's no masterpiece, true, but she looks just fine pressed down against the mattress with her ass in the air, and she expects absolutely nothing of me except money. Money I can give. Money and cock, both of which I have in abundance.

I grab the dress on the floor and toss it to the whore. "Time to get out and go home, sweetheart." Then to Eric: "My answer is no."

I peel off a couple of bills from a stack on my nightstand and push them into the whore's extended hand. She makes a big show out of rolling them into her bra, and the men part to let her pass, some of them whistling while she flips them off.

Eric comes closer to me and lowers his voice. "He's got leukemia, Greyson. He needs to pass on the reins to his son."

"Don't look at me like I can feel pity anymore."

"He's got the act cleaned up. No more killing. All the businesses are strictly financial now. We've no more open enemies. The Underground is quite a successful enterprise, and he wants to officially pass it on to his son. Are you that cold blooded you'd deny him his last request?"

"What can I say, his blood runs through my veins." I grab a black T-shirt and jerk it on, not out of modesty, but so that I can start loading up my babies. My Glock, a Ka-Bar, two smaller knives, two silver stars.

"Boy . . ." He steps to me, and I meet his lone dark eye—not the fake one. I haven't seen him in several years. He's the one who taught me how to use a .38 Special. "He's dying," he stresses meaningfully, curling his hand over my shoulder. "It won't be long. He's got six months, if not less."

"I'm surprised he thought I'd care."

"Maybe when you're done womanizing, you'll start to care. *We*"—he points at the men in the room—"want *you* to be the one who takes control. We'll be loyal to you."

I cross my arms and look at my half brother, Wyatt, the "Whiz"—my father's pet. "As long as I'm his lapdog and do as he says? No thanks."

"We'll be loyal to *you*," he stresses. "Only you."

He jerks his head toward the guys. One of them cuts the center of his palm. Soon they all follow.

Blood starts dripping on my floor.

Eric ducks his head and slices his own palm. "We're pledging to you." He holds out his bleeding hand.

"I'm not your leader," I say.

"You will be our leader when you realize your father is finally willing to reveal your mother's location."

Ice spreads through my veins, and my voice hardens as Eric mentions her. "What do you know about my mother?"

"He knows where she is, and it'll die with him if you don't come with us. Morphine makes him delusional. We need you back, Greyson."

My face reveals nothing of the turmoil I feel. My mother. The only good I remember. I'll never forget the look on her face when I made my first kill. Right in front of her, I lost my humanity and let my mother see that her son had turned into an animal. "Where is he?" I growl out.

"He's flying to a fight location; we have a plane ready to meet him there."

I shove things into a black duffel. A laptop. More weapons. When you deal with my father, you can't deal with him straight. My father taught me to be crooked. Guess I learned from the best. I grab my Leatherman tool knife, cut deeply into my palm, and slam it into Eric's hand, our bloods meshing. "Until we find her," I whisper. The other men come over and shake hands with me.

I search their eyes and make sure they meet my stare. There's a threat in my gaze and I know that if they know me, they'll heed it.

No matter what words are spoken, what acts are committed, I never, ever take my eyes off someone else's. The way they flick to the left or to the right, a tiny flicker, tells me more than when I hack into someone's computer. But I do that too.

I trust no one. My right hand does not trust my left. But as the most powerful of the nine men I'm faced with, the one I least trust is Eric Slater. As it happens, he's the one I most care about too. He and my friend C. C. Hamilton—but C.C.'s been visiting me even after I left, secretly helping me track my mother. I trust him as far as I could ever trust a human being. Which still means I interrogate the crap out of him every time he comes in. I can never be sure if my father knows he's meeting me.

Hell, even with the blood oath, I'm going to have to test each and every one of these men's loyalties before they can get any semblance of trust from me.

❤ ❤ ❤

NOW, AN AIRPLANE flight later, we find my father in a closed room wired with cameras, in the Los Angeles Underground. The Underground is our livelihood. A place where fighters square off against each other every season, two or three times a week. We organize events, sell tickets, program the fights in warehouses, bars, parking lots—wherever we can get the people in and get a good deal. The tickets alone make us a fortune. But the gambling on the side makes us ten times more.

Tonight, we're in a warehouse-turned-bar crammed with screaming people and rowdy fights. I used to enjoy strategically planning the locations where the fights would take place, which fighter would face who next, but it's all being taken care of by the rest of the team. Everything from the organizing, to the fights, to the gambling.

I head down with Eric as the fights are under way, my eyes

scanning the crowd, gauging the number of spectators, the location of security cameras, the exits.

We access a small dark hallway and then stop at the final door before Eric jerks it open. "I take your presence here tonight as acceptance of my offer?" my father asks the moment the door swings open and I step inside. I check the room for the exits, windows, the number of people.

He laughs, but it's not a strong sound.

"When you're done wondering if I have a sniper around ready to hit you, maybe you'd come closer. One would think my mere presence offends you."

I smile coldly at him. Julian Slater is called "Slaughter" among his enemies; he's been suspected as a man who silences his problems the old way. Even weak and in a wheelchair, I will never underestimate the damage my father can do. In a world measuring one's destructive capabilities, my father would be the nuclear bomb, and wouldn't you know it? Bastard's already throwing verbal vomit my way. "You look fit as a bull, Greyson. I bet you still turn tires for fun and do a couple of cunts in your sleep. I'd give more than a penny to know what your thoughts are right now, and you know how stingy I can be. Hell, you know what I do if a single penny is stolen from me."

"I remember clearly. Being I've done the dirty work for you. So let's spare you that penny. I'm thinking, why bother to wait for you to die? I could smash your oxygen tank right now and take care of you nicely." Slowly, I hold his gaze with a cold smile, pull out my black leather gloves from the back pocket of my jeans, and start sliding one hand inside.

He glares at me for a quiet moment. "When you're done disrespecting, go and clean up, *Greyson*."

One of the guys steps forward with a suit.

I calmly slip my hand into my other leather glove.

"As before, no one will know your name," my father begins in a softer tone. "You can have money and the life you want as my son—in fact, I demand you live like a prince. But I need your head and heart in this. The job comes first, and I'll have your word on that."

"I have no heart, but you can have my head. The job is all there is and all that's ever been. I AM my job."

Silence.

We survey each other.

I can see the respect in his eyes, even, maybe, a little fear. I'm no longer a thirteen-year-old, easily bullied by him.

"For the past five years of your absence, my clients . . ." he begins, ". . . they've seen no weakness from us at the Underground. We can't forgive a single cent owed or we'll be seen as weak—and right now there are many collections left to be done."

"Why not have your minions do it?"

"Because there's no one as clean as you. Not even the fighters know who you are. Zero trace. You're in, you're out, no casualties, and a hundred percent success rate."

Eric pulls out my father's old Beretta and offers it to me as some peace symbol, and when I find it in my hand, slightly over two pounds of steel, I find myself flipping it around and aiming it at my father's forehead. "How about instead I take your Beretta Storm and encourage you to start telling me where my mother is first?"

He looks at me icily. "When you get the job done, I'll reveal your mother's location."

I cock the gun instead. "You can die first, old man. You're well on your way already and I want to see her."

My father's eyes flick to Eric, and then to me. I wonder if Eric will really be "loyal" to me while my father sits there, pretty as you please.

"If I die," my father begins, "her location will be safely revealed in an envelope, already in a secure location. But I won't reveal *shit* until you prove to me, through the collection of what every name on this list owes me, that you are—even after these years apart—loyal to *me*. You do that, Greyson, and the Underground is yours."

Eric walks over to a nearby chest and produces a long list.

"We won't be using your real name," Eric whispers as he hands it over. "You're the Enforcer now, our Collector; you go by your old alias."

"Zero," the rest of the men in the room say, almost reverently. Because I have zero identity, and leave zero traces. I run through cell phones like I run through socks. I am a nothing, a number, not even human. "Maybe I don't respond to that alias anymore," I mutter, curling my fingers inside my leather gloves before I stretch them out and open the list.

"You will respond to it because you're my son. And you want to see her. Now get changed, and work your way down the list."

I scan the names, top to bottom. "Forty-eight people to blackmail, scare, torture, or simply rob in order to get my mother's location?"

"Forty-eight people who owe me, who have something that belongs to me that needs to be retrieved."

A familiar chill settles deep in my bones as I grab the suit by the hanger and head to the door, trying to calculate how long getting pertinent information about each of these debtors will take me. How many months it'll take me to meet with them, try to bargain the nice way—then the hard way.

"Oh, and son," he calls, his voice gaining strength as I spin around. "Welcome back."

I send him an icy smile. Because he's not sick. I'd bet this list on it. But I want to find my mother. The only thing in my life I've ever loved. If I have to kill to find her, I will.

"I hope your death is slow," I whisper at my father, looking into his cold slate eyes. "Slow and painful."

TWO

HERO

Melanie

Sometimes the only way to stop a pity party is with a real party. Expectation hums in the air as warm bodies jostle, my body straining in between the other dancers. I can feel the fun around us spinning like whirlwinds at my sides, intoxicating me.

My body's slick from dancing, my silky gold top and matching skirt clinging to my curves in a way that tells me I should've probably worn a bra. The brush of damp fabric only causes my nipples to poke into the silk and draw several discerning male eyes in my direction.

But it's too late now, and the crowd is high on the music, the dancing.

I stopped by tonight when one of my clients, for whom I decorated this small little bar/restaurant, invited my boss and all my colleagues over. I said only one drink, but I've had a couple extra, and the one half empty in my hand is now *seriously* the last one.

A guy approaches.

I can't miss his sudden, I-want-to-bang-you smile. "Want to dance with me?"

"We already are!" I say, moving a little with him, swinging my hips harder.

The guy wraps an arm around my waist and pulls me closer. "I meant if you want to dance alone with me. Somewhere else?"

I look at him, feeling a little high and dizzy. Do I want to dance with him?

He's cute. Not sexy, but cute. Sober, cute is *no way, Jose*. But drunk, cute is completely doable. I try to find the answer in my body. A tingle. A want. And nope. Today I still feel . . . hopeless.

Smiling to ease the blow, I edge away from him but he presses close to my body and blatantly whispers in my ear, "I really want to take you home."

"Of course you do." I laugh, declining the drink he offers with a playful, but firm, shake of my head.

I think I'm a little too drunk already, and I have to drive myself home.

But I don't want to aggravate a possible client, so I kiss his cheek and say, "But thanks," and head away. He takes me by the wrist and stops and turns me, his eyes hot and lusty. "No. Really. I want to take you home."

I give him another once-over. He looks rich and just a little bit entitled, the kind who always uses me, and I suddenly feel even more hopeless, more vulnerable. In less than a month, my best friend is getting married. The effect of that wedding on me is not bad, it's worse. Far worse than anyone could have imagined. My eyes burn when I think about it, because everything my best friend, Brooke, has—the baby, the adoring husband—has been my dream for so long, I cannot remember having another dream.

Here's a man who wants to have sex with me, and once again I'm tempted to fall. Because I always fall. I always wonder if he, maybe *he*, is the one for *me*. The next thing I know, I wake up alone with a bunch of used condoms around me and feeling lonelier than ever, and I am once again reminded I'm only good for one-night stands. I'm no one's queen, no one's Brooke. But god, will someone just tell me, *when do you stop kissing frogs?* Never, that's when. If you want that prince, you have to keep trying until one day you wake up, and you're Brooke, and a man's eyes are shining on you and *only* you.

"Look, I've done you a thousand times," I whisper, sadly and hopelessly shaking my head.

The guy lifts his brows. "What are you talking about?"

"You. I've done *you.*" I signal at him, top to bottom, his elegant looks and dress, the weight of my sadness and disappointment only crushing me further. "I've done you . . . a thousand times. And it's just not going to work." I turn to leave, but he catches me and spins me around again.

"Blondie, you've never done me," he counters.

I look at him again, tempted to just be taken home and made to feel good.

But this afternoon, I was at my best friend's place, where I caught her being kissed long and hard by her guy, a kiss so long and hot, he was murmuring sexy stuff to her the whole time, telling her he loved her, in a voice that was deep and tender, and I wanted to cry.

My insides are still warm and sensitive remembering, and not even dancing for a full night has successfully made me forget how truly loveless I feel. After seeing the way my best friend is kissed, really kissed, and after knowing she will have less time for me now that she has other priorities with her new and beautiful family, I'm starting to feel like I will never, ever find the kind of love that they have. She was always responsible, always a good girl, but I am . . . me.

The fun one.

The one-night stand.

"Come on, Blondie," he urges in my ear, sensing my indecision.

I sigh and turn. He pulls me close, and he looks at my mouth as if ready to convince me with a kiss. I'm a toucher. Brooke calls me her love bug. I love closeness, contact, crave it like I crave air. But I never really feel any man's touch reach past my skin. Yet I'm always tempted because I keep thinking that THE ONE is right around the corner and I can't help but try.

Leaning over and fighting the temptation to kiss one more frog, I search for the last of my conviction and say again, "No. Really. Thanks. I'm going home now." I'm tucking my bag under my arm, readying to leave, when a low rumble causes the tinted wall-to-wall windows to reverberate.

The doors burst open and a couple walks inside, soaking wet, the woman shaking her damp loose hair, laughing.

"Omigod!" I cry, my stomach plummeting when I realize it's fucking *raining*.

I run to the door when a man grabs the handle with a black-gloved hand and gallantly pulls it open for me. I almost stumble outside, and he grips my elbow to steady me. "Easy," he says in a rolling voice as he steadies me on my feet, and I blink desperately across the street at the light blue Mustang. All I have in my name. All I have to sell because I desperately need the money and who will want it now? It's a convertible and a little old, but it's as cute as it is unique, with white interior seats to match the tent top. But now it's outside in this rain, with its top down, becoming my very own *Titanic* with wheels.

My entire life is sinking right with it.

"I assume by that sad puppy-dog look on your face that that's your car," the rolling voice says.

I helplessly nod and lift my eyes to the stranger. A flash of lightning cuts through the distance, illuminating his features.

And I can't speak.

Or think.

Or *breathe.*

His eyes grab me and won't let go. I stare into their depths while also registering that his face is stunning. Hard jaw, high cheekbones, strong forehead. His nose is classic, sleek, and elegant, and the lips beneath are full and curved, firm and . . . god, he's edible. His dark hair flips playfully in the wind. He's tall and broad shouldered and dressed in dark slacks and a dark turtleneck that makes him look both elegant and dangerous.

But his *eyes.*

They're an indecipherable color, but it's not the color, it's the stare, the incredible shine. Framed with thick black lashes, his eyes shine as brilliant as the brightest lights I've ever seen. As they quietly assess my features in return, those narrowed eyes feel as powerful as X-rays, and they seem to be sparkling especially because I—*me*—have somehow done something to amuse this man, this . . . fuck, I have no name for him. Except Eros. Cupid himself. God of love. In the flesh.

I used to think Cupid used an arrow but I don't feel as if I've been pierced by an arrow. I feel like I've been hit. By a rocket.

As I keep standing here, floored by the over six feet of total *hotness* before me, he grabs my keys from me with one gloved hand and puts his other free one on my hip to hold me in place. And I feel it. I feel the touch race down my hips, knotting in my stomach, pulsing in my sex, straight down my thighs, curling my toes. "Stay here," he says into my ear, then he pulls up the collar of his turtleneck until it becomes a hood in the back, and he runs across the street.

I watch him head to where my car is getting soaked. The wind whips through the streets so hard, I have to use both hands to try to flatten my skirt so it doesn't fly up to my middle.

"Put the top on!" I force myself to yell through the pounding rain, suddenly as determined as he is to save my car.

"Princess, I got this!" He leaps into the front seat, turns on the car, and the top starts coming up until it . . . doesn't.

It gets stuck.

After a squeal of protest, the fucker starts coming back down.

"ARGH, SHIT!" I hurry into the street and suddenly the drops of rain bombard me like little cannon balls, soaking me in a second. I swear I want to yell *Fuck you!* at them. My car, the one thing in my life that hasn't been shit on, is being ruined and I want to scream.

"Are you kidding me? Get under the roof!" The guy leaps out and then pulls off his sweater in one quick jerk. He spreads the material over my head, using it to shield me from the rain while he herds me back to the small awning over the building entry.

"No! I'll help you. My precious car!" I cry and push at his chest, trying to get him to back off, but he's a head taller and built of steel.

"I've *got* your car," he promises. He hands me his soaked turtleneck and adds, "Hold this," before he runs back out.

He's wearing a white crewneck undershirt, and it clings to his sculpted torso as he tries to manually override and pull the top of my car back in place.

Raindrops sluice down his bare arms, the soaked cotton of his shirt plastered down on his chest, revealing every muscle in existence. *Fuck.* He's off-the-charts gorgeous; he just broke my Man Hotness Radar. I can't take my eyes off every inch of his body or the way it moves.

Thunder shakes the city again when he finally latches the top of my car on and signals for me to come over. He opens my car door from the inside, and I hurry into the passenger seat and shut it behind me.

My cold, slick clothes cling against my skin while he sits behind the wheel, looking big and manly, and suddenly we're ensconced in the small, almost cramped interior of my car. The seats are flooded with water, and when I shift to face him a little, I hear a *squish* that makes my cheeks burn in embarrassment.

"I can't believe this," I whisper. "My best friend tells me I'm the only idiot with a convertible in Seattle."

His eyes are openly amused. "I dig your car." He reaches out to the dashboard, and the hand he runs over it is covered in an elegant lambskin glove that makes my skin prick with goose bumps. He shifts his big torso in my direction with an irresistibly devastating grin. "Everything wet gets dry; don't worry, princess."

I can hardly take the way he says *wet*.

Or the way a raindrop clings to his dark eyelashes. Water sluices down his tanned, corded arms. His hair is slicked back, enhancing the beautiful face he has. I have seen works of art and beautiful men, beautiful buildings and beautiful rooms, but at this moment as he looks at me, I can't remember ever seeing anything besides him.

He's a ten. I've never, ever been with a ten. And the way that he looks at me . . . I've seen that look before. The look that Remington Tate gives Brooke. That look. He's giving it to me and I'm dying inside. Can I die from one look? And if one look can kill me, then what would one touch do?

"So," he says softly, his voice textured. He waits a little before speaking again, and it surprises me that he still only looks at my face, not my wet chest, not my bare legs—he's looking at nothing but my eyes while absently stroking the circle of my steering wheel.

"Want to go somewhere with me?" he asks, then reaches out with his free wet black glove to brush my hair back behind my ear.

What I feel is so far beyond lust, I can hardly answer him.

I tremble. "Yes," I say, dizzied with want.

He gives me a smile that sends my pulse racing, his hand lingering on my face for a second longer, then he shifts my car into gear and pulls us into the rainy streets. The air between us crackles in the silence.

The only audible sound outside is the rain and thunder. The inside of the car is dominated by his breathing. His breaths are deep and slow, but mine are fast and nervous.

He smells . . . like a wet forest. With a touch of leather. His eyes are on the road, but I'm only aware of him. The way his chest expands his wet T-shirt. His shadowed profile and how the city lights flicker across his face as we pass. His wet jeans clinging to his hard thighs. I think we both know we're going to do it.

We're going to have our hands all over each other in minutes, and the knowledge is causing havoc in my brain. I feel like some little sex gremlin in me has just emerged. I have a thing about man nipples and his man nipples are poking deliciously into his white T-shirt and his jeans are . . . god, his jeans are straining to the breaking point. He *wants* me. He wants to *do* me. This amazingly beautiful man who makes me cross-eyed with wanting.

"You always this quiet?" he asks me in a strangely thick voice, and I jerk my eyes to his face; that smile on his face really gets to me.

"I'm s-su-suppper-super c-ccold."

He signals to a tall hotel that I know is expensive even to dine at, but he doesn't seem to mind pulling into its driveway. "Seems the closest place where we can get dry."

"Yes, it's perfect," I say, too eagerly.

I'm into perfect things, beautiful things, things that are lively and fun. My parents as a couple? Perfect. I'm usually picture perfect myself. But tonight? I slide a hand down my hair as we cross the lobby and I can't imagine what I look like. Wet rat seems like a good bet. Why why why do I look like shit right now?

While he asks for room keys at the front desk, I examine his butt in his jeans, the fit of his clothes, and I can't seem to quell the flutters.

As I squish my way into the elevator along with a bunch of other people, I rub my arms and try to stop my teeth from chattering. He smiles at me across a couple, and his smile lights a spark of mischief in me and I smile back.

I follow him into the room and then into the huge marble bathroom. He takes his turtleneck from my cramped hand and hangs it aside, then, without warning, he reaches one hand to his T-shirt and pulls it off with one yank that makes all his muscles ripple. "Take off your shoes," he murmurs. I unclasp them and kick them aside.

When I straighten, my breath almost chokes me when I see his bare chest. Corded arms, every possible muscle in existence marked. There's a thin line of hair traveling down his navel into the waistband of his jeans. Ripped abs, thick throat, and those lips, kissable and beautiful lips. God. He has a scar—a big one on the left side of his ribs—and a wave of sympathy washes over me, then I notice he's *undressing* me.

My pulse jumps in excitement and my nipples peak. "What's a girl like you doing in a place like that?" he asks with his eyebrows drawn low over his eyes, and I start trembling as he peels off my shirt.

On impulse I reach out and touch the scar on his chest with one finger. "What happened to you?"

He unzips my skirt and as he pulls it down, he leans over and catches my earlobe between his teeth and tugs playfully. "You know curiosity killed the cat, don't you, little kitten?" he murmurs in my ear, urging my arms up so he can pull my shirt off.

I smile drunkenly and open my mouth to answer, and he kisses me. He takes me by surprise and I grab his shoulders to brace myself, shocked by my own responsiveness to his hot, silken, wild mouth. My own hunger unleashes in a torrent. His lips push mine open, hungry. I moan and bury my hands in his wet hair so he doesn't stop kissing me, and I rock my hips as his tongue pushes inside. Shivers of desire race through me as he leans over me, eating me with his mouth as my head falls back and a noise of pleasure purls out of my throat.

I shudder as I beg him to please touch my nipples.

"You're drunk," he whispers as he looks down at me in only my underwear, his eyes wild with heat as my nipples almost poke into the air.

"Only tipsy," I whisper, almost a moan. "Please don't stop, I ache all over."

With a notable clamp to his jaw, he reaches up and I feel his gloved hand sifting through my hair—then he looks at me, his eyes flashing as he seems to actually remember he's wearing gloves.

He peels them off, one by one. "Are you certain?" he says.

A frisson runs through me when I see his hands. Strong, big, tanned. *Oh god.* Suddenly I feel those hands on my waist and he lifts me up to set me down on the marble slab, easing his body between my legs. "You certain?" he insists.

He looks intently at me as he begins tweaking my nipples, and I can almost see the rigidness of his self-control there, that if I say no, he will stop, but I nod, then he groans and pinches my nipples in the most delicious way as he bends over, fitting his lips to mine, hard this time. Superhard. His tongue plunging, twisting, hard and hungry around mine, bolts of pleasure shooting from my nipples to my toes, my mouth to my sex. The marble slab beneath me, the room, the hotel, everything falls away until it's only hot, powerful, wet lips moving mine. Tasting me. Hands fondling my breasts, running down my sides. My thoughts spin, his kiss and touch rousing my passion like nothing ever has. My hands smooth up his damp chest and when I touch the metal of a piercing on his left nipple, I almost die.

"Oh god," I gasp, the intensity overwhelming as my bum aches from the cold of the marble. "Take me to bed."

He carries me to the room, throwing me to the bed like he means business. He flexes his hands at his sides as he jerks off his jeans and pulls out a condom packet. Oh god. His hands are huge, and tanned, with long fingers. A scar in his palm. I really want them on me. In me. He pulls down my panties.

"My name is Melanie," I breathe, edging back on the bed as he strips me.

Naked. He's moving with a predatory grace that sends my heart crashing into my rib cage and a flood of need between my legs. He whispers, "My name is Greyson, Melanie." He puts my hand on his and starts kissing me as we work a condom on him, and I can feel his heartbeat throbbing under my hand.

I love the way he keeps kissing me, our hands touching his hardness, huge, thick, pulsing, as we get the condom on him, a pool of need gathering between my thighs.

He slips a finger into my pussy and watches my eyes roll back. "I fucking want in you," he murmurs, kissing my throat. He turns his head to muffle my gasp and takes my mouth. "I'm going to give you the fucking of your life, princess." His wet tongue slowly drags along the shell of my ear. "I'll suck on you until my jaw hurts." His low voice drives me so crazy I can feel pebbles rise up on my nape as he cups the back of my head and starts kissing me again. "Make you come as hard as you can come."

He makes me so wet, my body starts bucking as he keeps sucking my breasts, making me pant.

I slide my arm up the coiled muscles of his chest. I rear upward and move my head to the source of his breath and whimper in the only way I know how to make him think about kissing me. He does. He gyrates his hips and presses against my hip bone as though he needs the contact, and makes a soft growling noise as he slips his hand between my legs.

I want him so much, I hurt.

I spread my legs wider apart and moan as he takes me. I squirm as my body begins tightening.

"I'm going to come," I moan softly. "I'm sorry . . . I can't . . . you feel too . . . good . . . I can't . . . "

"Come," he rasps, "it's all right, we'll do it again in a bit . . . *come* . . ."

Pure red-hot ecstasy radiates through my body, my knees falling open, my emotions whirling and skidding, my body clenching and clasping and unclasping his, his thrusts shooting currents through me until I do what his sinful body is making me do, and I come like a rocket.

I gasp from the force of my orgasm, twisting and arching beneath him. He pushes in as deep as he can go, and I shudder uncontrollably and whimper in gratitude every time he's seated fully inside me, making me feel . . . the opposite of lonely. The opposite of sad or empty. And when my climax subsides and he's still there—every thick, hot, hard inch of him snugly in my grip—my eyes flutter open, and I see him looking at me, with that look, wild, hungry, almost proprietary, but also strangely reverent and gentle as he starts to move in me again with expert precision, our eyes clinging, the way he fucks me gently now making little stars dance across my vision as another delicious climax builds and builds.

I don't expect to but I come again. Hard. If possible, even harder, because the walls of my sex are sore and sensitive, and my clit throbs every time his hips ram up against mine—and the pleasure grows exponentially until it's slicing me open in a pure burst of pleasure. My nails rake into his skin. I scream his name, almost scared from the intensity. He muffles my cries with his mouth, and this time he snakes his tongue around mine and cuts off his name to *Grey*. He groans as if he likes to taste his name in my mouth, his muscles are flexing against me as he goes off, his chest brushing against my breasts as he comes with me.

When his shudders subside after mine, he rolls to his back and, because he's still inside me and has both arms around me, I end up coming with him. We lie in breathless silence for a moment, tangled and not even caring about whose arm is where, or whose leg is hooked between the other's. I am so absolutely dazed, fucked, and blown the fuck away, I almost expect to see pieces of me scattered across the floor.

After a couple of minutes, I let out a noise of protest, wanting to get up. He releases me, allowing me to tiptoe to the bathroom to clean up. He follows, knotting up the condom, and as I wash my hands he comes up behind me to take the soap and wash his hands along with mine while our gazes meet in the mirror. I see my reflection and . . . no, I don't look like a wet rat. My cheeks are flushed pink, my hair is bed mussed, and when he smiles at me and cups my breast from behind, I'm done for. "Come back to bed so I can make you pant a little more," he whispers, into my skin.

"I don't pant," I say, taking his hand, the one on my breast, and pulling him out to the bedroom with me.

"You pant, moan, yelp, and now you'll do it all over again for me."

"I didn't do that!" I say as I drop back down, and when he crawls over me, I feel perfectly sober. I'm not even tipsy anymore. I know I will remember every inch of the way his face looks, intent and ravenous, and as he starts playing with my breasts I start panting as he trails his fingers along my rib cage, circling my bellybutton, watching me with a smile that tells me he knows exactly what he's doing. I smile back, because bad boys will always be the end of me, and I touch his nipple ring, feeling his erection thicken against my hips as I raise my head and start quietly sucking him.

I know how to play these games too, my sexy sex god, I think. "Now who pants," I murmur playfully.

"I think you're hot as fuck," he says as he rolls over and brings me with him, pressing my head to his nipple ring as though he wants me to suck harder. His big body shudders with pleasure, and desire pools between my thighs as I keep tugging with my teeth and using my tongue, feeling him swell hard and pulsing against me.

The entire night we play with each other, teasing, tasting, fondling, *fucking*.

Every touch, every whisper, everything I share of myself with him feels so right; like an electric wire plugged into the right socket, I feel a new life force flow in me, almost euphoria.

During our heated make-out sessions, I find him looking at me through thick dark lashes, a playful curiosity glimmering in his eyes.

He asks about me as if he truly wants to *know*, and I feel like we've known each other before . . . in some dark, forbidden place.

When he kisses me heatedly on the mouth during another make out, I come at him with the intensity of a natural disaster, and this may be what this is, but there is no stopping me, no stopping *him*, it seems, from having and *undoing* me.

Around five a.m. his phone rings for the third time. We're still kissing with lazy intensity and my lips feel raw and red and swollen and my breasts are deliciously sore but I'm still begging for more. Growing exasperated with the buzzing, he finally answers gruffly, "This better be good."

I flip over to my stomach to give him room to talk and quietly study his profile. His eyes and one of his hands stay on the curve of my ass as he speaks into the receiver.

As he discusses what I think is business in a low, gruff voice I can barely make out, I memorize the grooves of his abs, trailing my fingers along his stomach. I edge toward his lap and, as he keeps squeezing my ass in one big hand, I kiss his hard cock and lick up the wetness, which makes him squeeze his eyes shut for a moment and exhale roughly.

When he finally opens his eyes, they're hard and cold. He snaps a list of numbers into the receiver, then hangs up and remains thoughtful, and that's when I sense he's pulled back from me.

I sit up in bed with a sick sensation. This is it, and then my suspicion is confirmed when his glorious body rises from the bed where he was just mine. I watch him disappear into the bathroom, a sinking sense of despair burning in the pit of me. I know what's coming, don't I? I know. The look I thought I saw last night was a trick. A trick of the drink. A trick of the light. A motherfucking trick and I should've known it. Now I'm dying inside and it isn't of excitement. This little fantasy? This fleeting connection I thought I had with someone? It's over.

It wasn't a connection. Or even real. It was a little alcohol, some rain, some hormones, and a couple of sexy lines that made me believe he really was as turned on by me as he'd ever in his life been.

"I've got a flight early and need to take care of one last thing before I leave." He comes back with his clothes fisted in his hands and quickly jumps into his jeans. His jaw is a little too tight, as though he isn't enjoying this any more than I am.

"Sure," I say, and I hope to hell I sound nonchalant enough. All of these orgasms and the way I made those embarrassing noises for him are making this extremely awkward because I lost it. Omigod, I lost it, I lost myself in a complete stranger.

He looks at me, then opens his mouth for a moment before anything actually comes out. "It's fucking complicated—you don't want me in your life."

"Don't. Please don't. You don't have to do this. Let's leave it at this. I know how this goes. Goodbye, have a nice life. Adios, Pepe."

We stare, he whispers, "I shouldn't have touched you." He heads to the door. I look at his broad back while working on my brave face. I've done this a million times. I'm putting up walls around the parts where it hurts so that it doesn't hurt one whit. Not one whit.

"One of my guys vacuumed your car last night." He stops with his hand on the doorknob, then stalks back and presses the keys of my car into my hand, and strangely, he kisses my eyelids. "Your eyes," he whispers. Then he leaves.

My stomach literally aches when the door shuts behind him. I plop down on the bed after the most delicious sex of my life, completely . . . devastated. A crushing loneliness settles over me, magnified a thousand times from when I walked into that party just hours ago, hoping to make myself feel better. One more frog. No. God, he was not a frog. He was . . . something without a name. And now he's gone. And that fleeting connection I was so certain of is gone too.

And I am truly, inexplicably, *devastated.*

A ton of bricks sits right on my heart as I gather my stuff from the bathroom, and when I realize it's all still wet, I wince, struggling to pull the damp clothes over my body. I can't find my panties. I look around the entire suite. When I look under the bed, I swear I can still feel him in my swollen pussy as I bend. *Greyson.*

Fuuuuck, even his name is sexy.

"Did you actually take my panties?" Disbelieving, I go look on the other side of the bed, refusing to remember how sensual I felt when he took them off me.

While searching beneath the bed skirt, I hear a click followed by footsteps. I raise my head to face the door, and blink in confusion. He came back? He's standing right in front of me. An ache so deep its unfamiliarity overwhelms me.

My insides flutter as I stand. His dark brown hair is deliciously tousled and it goes beautifully with his eyes, eyes that are like all the glasses in a bar that reflect the light, shining almost unnaturally on me. He's tall and sculpted but he oozes some unnamable, almost unnatural power over me. When he looks at me with those eyes, when he stands even this far away, somehow aloof and untouchable, he only makes me want to touch him all the more.

"You forget something?" I say. I'm dying of embarrassment at being caught talking to myself like this. He makes me feel as girly and vulnerable as I've ever felt in my life.

"I didn't take your panties." He signals to a lamp and frowns slightly, as though he can't figure out why they ended up there. They're hanging right over the top of the shade.

My cheeks blaze bright red. "Thank you," I lamely mumble as I peel them off the shade. "I really like these panties."

He crosses his arms and quietly watches me slip them on. "I really like them too. They look especially gorgeous on that ass of yours."

I slide them on and pretend to be engrossed in my toenails when he comes over and drops on his haunches beside me, and tips my head around to his. The timbre of his voice drops to a level that is beyond intimate. "I want to take you home." My toes start curling, and he continues in that low, husky voice until my whole stomach feels like a knot. "And I want your phone number, and when I come back to town, I want to see you again."

"Why?" I counter.

"Why not?"

"You don't even know my last name," I accuse.

"I know the length of your legs." He reaches out to touch a strand of my hair with his long fingers, his eyes never once leaving mine. "I know that you're ticklish behind your knees. That you like to pant in my ear." He leans back against the wall and just watches me. "I know that I'd like to kiss you again. That knowing you were in that bed, I couldn't get on the damn elevator. I wanted to see these . . ." He leans over and rubs my eyes with the pads of his thumbs. "Again. So the risk analyst in me says no. This is a bad idea. But you look like a determined woman, and my guess is you'll be going to that bar, continuously, picking up men, until you find what it is you were looking for. And my risk analyst says that's far worse. Who will these men be? Who will you be picking up, Melanie?"

I feel embarrassed all over again, but I don't want him to know, so I shrug.

"Well, it may surprise you to know that I'm not okay with that. It may surprise you to know that if any man will be doing any number of things to that body of yours, it will be me."

The look. Oh god, the look. "So." A probing question comes into his eyes. "Am I taking you home?"

God. I'm defenseless against that look. That look I've wanted, I've memorized, I don't want him to break through my walls and make me cry, but I'm a little drunk and my walls are made of paper today. I bluff in self-defense.

"So chivalrous of you to come back. You'll make my eyes water."

"That's right. And when you orgasm your hardest, you shed a couple of tears too."

My cheeks flare bright red as I remember, and I roll my eyes at him. "If you say so."

"I *do* say so. That was the highlight of my night."

I strap on my shoes, beet red, and he pulls off his shirt. "This one's dry. Put this on."

I slip into his shirt and his scent and warmth engulf me as I watch him ease into his damp turtleneck, and it's with complete disbelief that I walk out of the room with him, with this beautiful god, feeling his gloved hand on the small of my back, guiding me to the elevator, his eyes studying my profile with an odd smile.

"Not exactly what you imagined when you woke up this morning, was I?"

My body is so well fucked I can barely walk, and my eyes, my eyes hurt, I can't tell him every day of my life I've tried to imagine him. "Not exactly what I imagined," I say. "Today was *nothing* like I imagined."

He tips my head and kisses me. Not with lust. Just a kiss.

An after-sex kiss that reaches to the deepest levels in me, pulls open my nerve endings and makes me feel exposed, and wanted, and raw, and I have to fight not to cry for real like you do when you made that last wish on your very last penny and it came true.

Men have mocked me, ruined me, used me, abused me. I like to get in verbal fights. I like to cuss, spit, scream, and be myself. Nobody has ever made me want to cry while just talking to me. Nobody has ever made me want to cry, but one lone memory and now this man, who's giving me the look, seems to manage it.

"What's your last name?" I whisper.

"King." He grins a panty-melting grin. "No majesty jokes, please."

I laugh, and then I stretch out my hand as if we've barely met. "Meyers."

He takes my hand in his, his grip warm, firm, and curling my toes all over again. He lets go and pulls out his phone, typing a password and handing it to me, watching me with eyes that seem the most intelligent eyes I've ever seen. "Meyers, type your phone number down for me?"

I add it under Hottest Piece of Ass I've Ever Had.

The barest hint of a smile pulls at the corners of his lips, enough to give me flutters. "Nice."

He writes something on his keypad and my phone vibrates with a new text.

And accurate.

I smile, and he looks at me, wearing that super-sexy *almost* smile.

And suddenly I cannot explain—and am not sure have ever felt—the kind of happiness I feel right now.

He drives me home in my own car, and when we reach my building, he rides the elevator up with me, walks me to my door, and brushes a kiss on my forehead as he rubs the pad of his thumbs over the corners of my eyes and whispers, "I'll be in touch soon."

When I slide my shaking, deliciously fucked body into my bed with about an hour to go to dawn, I can't sleep. I play with names for his profile on my phone. Sex fiend. Sex machine. Sex god. Playboy god. I settle on Greyson and whisper, "Greyson," the name rolling off my tongue like velvet.

I squeeze my eyes shut and feel like convulsing all over my bed. I text Brooke, Pandora, and Kyle, in a group.

Me: I just met someone. Guys I just met SOMEONE. Not a douche! He actually brought me home and all the way up to my door. AAAAA!!! Fuck you, guys, if anyone ruins my day tomorrow, I'm having your heads!

Kyle: You'll be too busy giving head to your new man to think about mine.

Pandora: Dude. Are you on ecstasy?

Brooke: WHAT? Tell me everything!!!

THREE

HER

Greyson

I flip my vibrating phone open as soon as I'm out of the building. "You might be wondering why you're tied to a bathroom stall with this particular number on your cell phone screen," I murmur into the receiver. "Well, you were about to do something that was going to cost you your dick. You were about to touch something you have no right touching, *get it?* You have a debt to pay. You have three days. Ticktock ticktock." I hang up and smash the phone to the ground. Then I grab my other phone and dial Derek.

"Come get me." I shoot off the address, then walk a couple of blocks and dispose of the phone before glancing up at the building I just left her in.

When Derek pulls over in a dark SUV, I jump in and open the glove compartment. I pull out my ticket, fake ID included. "Drive this to the warehouse. Stay put. Number twenty-four will be making a payment soon. How's your wife?"

"Good. You get some work done?"

"When don't I," I say.

Melanie. I'd seen her before. Been watching her from afar.

She's the sort of girl you want to fuck, but I never knew how badly until I saw she was going to pick up one of my clients at that bar. By god, I knocked that man unconscious without even getting the payment. I just wanted him down because he sure as fuck wasn't leaving with her. Nobody will.

I stroke my phone with my gloved hand and resist the urge to text her something. Anything. I've seen this woman go through men like I use phones. I've seen her leaving hotel rooms looking like a hot, blazing mess. I've seen her coming out looking perfect. I've seen her laugh, cry, I've seen her face in the women I've fucked, and I've even seen her in my dreams and when I wake up. What this woman wants is something I can't give. But I'm pulled, twisted, knotted, used, and useless when I look at her.

I like watching her twirl and toss her hair, flirt around, cross her legs, curl her lips, look at her nails.

I like the way she hunts for her next man; I liked watching because somewhere, deep down, I knew I'd have enough, and her hunt would be over the day I decided to let her know I intended to be that man.

FUCK HER PRINCE CHARMING.

She's getting *me*.

I'm halfway done. Twenty-four more names, and then Zero can be nothing. I shouldn't have touched her, but I did. I should stop touching her, but I won't. My guys, my boys, can never know there's a little Achilles heel somewhere in my body and it has her name on it.

The only reason the guys can believe I'm close to her is because her name just happens to be on my list.

FOUR

HIM

Melanie

I wasn't always an only daughter. I was born with an identical twin. She was born first at five and a quarter pounds, and I followed weighing a little more.

My mother says we were both precious, small and pink, but she can never seem to manage the rest. It was Dad who eventually told me the whole story. That I was not born perfect . . . that I was born with a malfunctioning kidney and my twin was born with a severe heart condition. We were both struggling to live and within the hour it became obvious she was struggling the hardest.

When her heart gave out, they gave me her kidney.

They named her Lauren and buried her next to my dad's mother. Every year my birthday is my saddest day of the year. But I go visit her grave with my favorite flowers—I figure, as my twin, they'd be her favorite too—and then I have the wildest party of the month because I sense she wants it to be worth it. "I want you to show me you are joyful and happy, always," my mother cheerfully tells me. So I do. Even when there's that ache of loss that never goes away, I am determined to be happy.

My parents told me they wanted me to be happy because they were so happy I survived. And so I try to live happy and I never, ever show them that I'm not.

My dad counts my smiles and says I have five smiles—total—and therefore I always make sure he gets to see one of them.

I'm living for two people. I'm trying to stuff into one lifetime what could fill two lives. So I get up every morning and put on my perfect face and promise myself to have the perfect day and to someday have the perfect family. But I'm failing.

And my parents know it.

"Your mother wishes, one day, when you marry, and settle down, maybe you'll have twins," my dad said wistfully to me once.

"That would be nice," I said with a heavy heart and a big bright smile on my face.

Sometimes I wonder if she'd be married already. Lauren.

Sometimes I have a bad day and am certain that maybe she'd have made my parents prouder or happier than me. All I know for sure is that if they'd picked her, she'd make the same hard efforts I do to live happy.

I won't even be picky about having twins, but I do dream of falling in love with the perfect guy, and having a baby girl and naming her Lauren.

I dream of my guy so much, he gives me an ache. I dream of that look, like the one Greyson looked at me with, a look that tells me that this guy—right here, this breathing human being—thinks I'm enough. Thinks, and is glad, that the one who'd survived was *me*. Because sometimes I really wish that if only one of us would make it, it would've been Lauren.

♥ ♥ ♥

The day after Greyson

WALKING OUT OF the corner Starbucks cafe is Pandora, one of my three closest friends. The man-eater. Well, not man-eater. She's just supremely independent, dark, gloomy, and secretive. But that's okay because I'm happy, chatty, and sunny, so we mesh. Well. We *try* to. Today she's going for her Angelina Jolie badass look and her usual dark lipstick and those boots she got on sale that reach her thighs. Even the way she walks intimidates men as she carries our usual coffees up to where I'm waiting at the corner—this was her day to get the coffee, after all—and without a word, we both sip and cross the street on our way to Susan Bowman Interiors.

You could say making things pretty is something Pandora does to make a living, but I do it as art. Because there's something about a room welcoming you that can brighten your crappy day, and I like making people happy, even in that small way.

"So," she prods me.

I smile secretly against my coffee lid.

"So, what?" I say. I want to make her beg because I'm a little evil like that. She just brings it out in me. The thing about Pandora and me is: we're different as hell. So it's always a push and pull with her, which we both secretly enjoy, I guess.

"So what the fuck. Tell me about the prince who charmed your pants off."

"Pandora, I can't even . . . I just can't EVEN." My grin hurts on my face and I shoot her a look that says *He fucked my brains off and I loved it.* "It was . . ." Out of this world. Perfect. Beyond *perfect.* "I never knew sex like that existed. I never knew I could feel a guy's touch in my BONES."

As we reach our floor and head to our L-shaped desks, situated right next to each other, I can't stop smiling.

Truly, I've never experienced anything like this before. I almost feel shy about sharing him with her. But at the same time, I feel like getting a loudspeaker and telling my work colleagues that I think I may, just may, have found the ONE!

"Well, don't stop there, coy virgin! Tell me the rest," Pandora insists, booting up her computer. "Dude, getting Starbucks today entitles me to some gory details."

"I got coffee yesterday and always get shit from you," I counter as I sit and absently rub the little mark behind my ear, almost a hickey. . . . "I'm not giving you gory details, those are for me to dwell on and fantasize over. But, Pan, the way we connected. The way he looked at me. And looked and looked and couldn't *stop* looking at me."

"Oh, boy, you really are on ecstasy." She sighs and puts her forehead on her palm as if she's in for a headache. I know that she hates it when I'm in my bestest mood, so I just grin, start humming, and wonder what my mother would say if she knew about this.

I was married and had you before I was twenty-five, she's told me all my life.

And I tell her that I'm twenty-five in three weeks and have great friends and a damn career.

But now, maybe, there's a boy . . .

As Pandora and I start mixing and matching fabrics for our current assignments, my mind drifts off to my phone.

I have this rule that the last one to text should be the one who is next texted.

Greyson texted "And accurate" last night and before I know it, I text him back.

Are you there?

To be honest, I don't know what to expect. This is uncharted territory for me. I hardly know what my name is today.

One moment I was at a party with so many people . . .

And then I was with him.

And he was with me.

Entirely focused on *me*.

And what frightens me—no, what haunts me—is not that he gave me the best orgasms of my life, though that rocked, but that I *felt something*. That his touch went farther than my skin, it went into me.

My skin prickles pleasurably remembering the way our eyes met as we made love, and I keep staring at my phone, waiting for him to text me.

Two days after Greyson

TODAY WE'RE DECORATING one of my client's new homes. At Susan Bowman Interiors, no matter who's in charge of the project, everyone pitches in on "the" day when the actual delivery and arrangement of furniture takes place. Basically it works like this:

I meet with a client and get the hang of their budget and taste.

I make a proposal detailing the approximate costs, room by room, and propose the decorating concepts.

I make the room plans, take room measurements, then deliver the PDF files with the prices of several options and images and fabric swatches, based on the concepts we discussed.

Once the client approves our choices, I show it all to Susan, get her stamp of approval, then I order the fabrics, the furniture, the window treatments, the rugs and carpets, and everything is shipped to the company warehouse, where it is checked and assembled and upholstered. And then, the fun begins. For we actually get to set a date, usually when our client is out of town, and we will get to make everything that we visualized mentally happen in real life.

I'm a visual person, and this is what I do. This is what I love. Since I was three years old, I visualized everything. From the way I would dress for the first day in school. To the way a certain boy would look at me. To the way the teacher would smile in delight at the apple my mother always had me take. She said if I put an apple in their hand, I would be putting their hearts in my pocket. I always felt ridiculous giving them the apple, but my mother is very big on being "generous" to everyone and is always giving out things, even hugs. Yes! She's done the FREE HUGS posters at charity events and just hugs everybody—and she's taken me with her. So I guess I'm big on hugs too. They just feel good. In any case, pleasing people and living a happy, relaxed, colorful life is what I love.

"Where's this going to go?" Pandora asks as she unwraps a pretty glass lamp.

"Oh, that little darling goes in the girl's room," I say, then I check all my files for the third time today. "It's over that old pink vanity and this little fellow." I toe a small striped ottoman that is so fun, it takes all my effort not to hug it. "Isn't it cute?"

"What's cute is how you keep pulling out your phone like it's a warm, live puppy."

"Oh, hush! I'm checking my signal."

And my signal looks . . . okay.

Hmm.

Interesting.

NO text. Still.

Sometimes guys need nudges. They're scared. It was too intense. He gave me "the" look. Right now, he could be sitting at home thinking—*What the fuck, Greyson man?*

I mean, it's very possible he could be having problems like I am. I cannot go to sleep without fingering myself. So there. He's made me think of only him, his skin, his touch, and I want it . . . I *crave* it . . . I freaking *need* it again. I've mentally checked myself into the Greyson Addicts Anonymous and only he can remedy my disease.

So for the sake of helping him, for the sake of easing the little sting of disappointment that's starting to grow on the left side of my chest, hell, for the sake of him *knowing* I am *definitely* still interested and please, dude, if you liked me at all, do as you said and call me, I consider breaking my cardinal rule of texting and maybe texting him again.

Should I?

Rules say I shouldn't. But I've never liked rules, and Greyson doesn't look like a rule man either.

What do I do?

I want to ask Pandora but I already loathe the smirk on her face.

I want him to know the truth, that I want him to call me. I don't want to play games. Not with him.

Even so, I force myself to tuck my phone back in my bag and remind myself Rome wasn't built in a day, and neither was any worthwhile relationship.

"Melanie," Pandora says, her lips flattening into a thin black line.

I blink innocently and smile. "What?"

"Face it. He was a douche."

"Not."

"Is."

"NOT!"

"Is . . ."

♥ ♥ ♥

Four days after Greyson

"NOTHING YET?" PANDORA asks.

I want to groan when she comes up to my desk, where I was hoping I could hide from her and her peering black eyes. But today, it happens that she's the one with a flat, angry little smile, and I'm the one with the scowl.

On Monday I didn't know my name; I was on cloud nine. On Tuesday I was still hopeful and upbeat, on about a cloud three. Today I'm not only back on earth, I fell a couple notches down to purgatory or maybe even all the way to hell. All I know is that today is Thursday, and I have heard zip, zero, nada from him in days.

Like a fool, I've been smiling, glancing at my phone and waiting for something, but to be honest, my phone has started to feel like a heavy, motionless boulder in my bag, and its silence is telling me things—things that GREYSON probably doesn't have the balls to tell me himself.

It was good. For a one-night stand. Thanks for the fuck. You won't be hearing from me again.

"Nothing *yet*," I defensively tell Pandora as I stand up and carry my phone to the ladies' restroom. I lock myself inside and go wash my face in the sink. I think of hazel eyes with flecks of green and the look Greyson King kept giving me . . . and I feel so beyond wretched and disappointed, I slowly type another text while a well of emotion keeps growing in my chest.

I keep thinking I imagined you. ☹

I wait for a couple of minutes. I wash my hands, dry them, check my phone, stare at my nails, check my phone. There's a knock on the door and one of my colleagues calls, "Anyone in there?"

Fuck.

I shout, "I'll be right out!" then I pace a little, reread the text I sent him, including that mopey sad face, and suddenly, I feel like the world's biggest fool.

This morning I Googled him and found, surprisingly, nothing at all.

No trace of Greyson King on the Internet. He could've been a ghost.

A ghost not answering my texts, not interested in me, not feeling the connection that has been eating and gnawing, haunting and consuming me.

A ghost that I, drunken Melanie, made up to stop feeling lonely.

FIVE

IT TAKES WORK BEING AN ASSHOLE

Greyson

I can't remember anyone fucking with my head more than my father has, so I'm not sure what's happening to me, except I'm distracted as fuck this week.

Melanie's deep in my fucking head and deep under my fucking skin.

I'm trying to shut her out of my conscious thoughts, but there she is. In my subconscious. Playing with my nipple ring like it's her own personal toy.

I'd wanted to taste her. Now I've tasted her, but I'm not satisfied.

I want to make her pant like she just won the New York Marathon—I want to make her moan like a fucking pro winning a fucking National Moaning contest. And I want to make her smile like she did when I took her home.

I've been forcing myself to focus, keep my head in the game, my eyes *open*.

But Christ.

She's not making it easy.

This week I've worked two more marks off my list. I've also

found out that my father's leukemia is real—at least the experts I brought in have confirmed it.

He's settled in a two-story gated home, close to where the Underground season will begin in a month. And it's strange. His voice has a different timbre even. His gaze isn't as hard. When I came in, he asked me how I was doing.

"I've got half the list . . ."

"Not the list. How are you doing?"

I stared, not with confusion, but with a slow, simmering rage. "You've done a great job at being an asshole for twenty-five years. Don't change it up on me now." I walked away.

"Why not?" he called, coughing from the effort it took to yell that out.

Quietly seething inside, I clenched my hands into fists, my knuckles biting into my leather gloves. "Because it won't change anything."

I'm now out of the house, working on my third mark, but she's still in my head. I keep seeing green eyes, green eyes turned an emerald dark as she comes like some fucking rocket, thrashing and twisting beneath me. She's that one precious diamond every robber wants to steal, that kitten every dog wants to chase, the mare you want to ride, bridle and tame—but not completely. Oh, no, not all the time because her wildness excites you. Her wildness makes you wilder. Her wildness makes you fucking ravenous.

Hell, these past days I feel like I haven't fucking eaten in a hundred thousand weeks.

Goddammit! Get out of my head, princess.

I'm settled down at the park table when my target finally appears.

I sit behind an open newspaper with my SIG semiautomatic hidden low and tightly underneath, my aviators shielding my eyes as he walks by.

I keep my voice low enough not to alarm anyone, but loud enough to be heard by the poor shit I'm here to fuck with. "Sit down," I say.

He jerks at the sound of my voice and reaches into his pocket for what I assume is some method of self-defense. "Guy like you, you can't see it, but there are several shooters trained on you from all angles. So you might as well sit."

He drops down like lead into the chair I kick out for him. "So," I say, folding the paper and leveling him with my attention, while my SIG semiautomatic is still, underneath the folded paper, trained right at his heart.

I slide my aviators to the top of my head and lean back as I study the man. Middle aged, probably he's realized he'll be stuck in a shit job for the rest of his life and thought he could bet his way to a better life, and instead it got worse.

"I stopped by your house yesterday to leave you a little present, but I was afraid your wife would see the contents, and considering the nature . . ."

With my free hand, I slide over a manila envelope. His hands tremble as he opens it. The blood drains from his face as images of him and his bare-ass naked lover tumble out. "Holy . . ." he gasps.

"She's got you by the nuts, huh?" I lean over so he can hear me well. My blood pumps hot as I think of my own nuts, and my own little sexy bare-naked problem, driving me more than a little crazy lately. "You thought you could fuck this chick once and walk away, but you couldn't. She was wild and you liked that. She looked at you like you were god's fucking gift to womankind; you must have liked that too."

I pause for three heartbeats while my mark keeps getting paler and paler. "I bet you're obsessed with the way she feels, the way her hair smells, how she smiles, how she walks, how she flirts with other fucking males . . . Well, Hendricks, I'm here to tell you that you owe the Underground $168,434 for your gambling losses, and we're ready to collect."

I lean back and slide my aviators back over my eyes. "You can't keep your pussy on my money. Are we clear?"

The guy is pale as a ghost, so it's safe to assume we're fucking clear here.

I fold the paper, SIG and all, into the pocket of my jacket. "One of my men will meet you here, tomorrow." As I rise, I lean over and say, "I've got copies of these images. You'll get them when you pay up what you owe, but don't test me. I have a motivation as strong as yours." My mother. My freedom. And my own fucking nuts, in a twist over a girl with golden hair and green eyes and a smile that guts me. Yeah, I'm in even deeper shit than this poor guy is.

When the target leaves, C.C. and I go check up with the team in silence. All of them are at the "yacht," like some sick Big Brother sea home, including the surveillance cameras.

My father sits there, glad to be out of the house and getting the gist of the planning. As for the team . . .

I've got tabs on Derek to make sure he's not betraying what he knows, but the rest, I'm always watching, monitoring calls, replaying surveillance tapes. Blood oath is fine—except I don't trust my own shadow.

The first I had to test was C.C.—because he's the closest to a brother I've got and I had to know if his loyalties are to my father, who's fed him all these years, or to his blood brother, who's been me.

"If I told you this glass held a very deadly substance, and asked you to take it to my father, what would you say?"

"I'd say yes, asshole, what do you think I'd say?" C.C. replies, sticking a toothpick into his teeth and letting it dangle there. We're outside my dad's bedroom, where he's monitored by his medical team 24/7. The door is opened partway, and we can see my father talking to Eric, oblivious to us watching.

"Good. Since you're the only one I trust, I say you better go. So go." I hand him the glass. "Take it, *discreetly*."

He looks at me. "I know how to be discreet. Just tell me. Will it be painful for the dude?"

"Not as much as he deserves, but yes." I edge back and watch C.C. maneuver the liquid into my father's medications. The motherfucker carries it over, murmurs to my dad, "Are you thirsty, Slater?" and makes sure my father slowly drinks it. He comes back and sits. "It's done," he says calmly.

C.C. is about as coldhearted as I am. Ice under all circumstances.

We sit in silence. "It wasn't poisoned, was it, you dick?" he asks, spitting out the toothpick in anger and betrayal.

"No." I stand. "I just needed to be sure."

I could so easily end my father. Slip something into the IV bags and he'd be gone. But even a criminal has to have a code, and I have mine. I don't kill for pleasure or even for myself. I don't kill family.

That doesn't mean I don't think about it. Constantly, I do. I've dreamed I've killed my father many times and I wake up relieved. Until I remember I didn't kill him—he's alive.

Rage pulses through me that I have to even look at him, let alone do his fucking dirty work.

C.C. follows me down the hall of the yacht, where we're parked a couple of miles away from Los Angeles. One of the rooms is set up with phones and charts—the gambling bookkeeping, tracking all the bets of every fight of the Underground. "We're your guys, Z, you can trust us. I know it's not in your nature to, but you can."

"I'm working on a couple of other names; in the meantime

call Tina Glass. Tell her I need number ten in a compromising position with her. She's not to deliver the evidence to anyone but me, personally. I have another target to work on this weekend. I'll be leaving town—use the code if there's an emergency."

"Eric wants the rest of the team to support."

"I don't need their support. But I need you to help me nail number ten. He's squeaky clean and he's pissing me off."

"I know what else is pissing you off!" C.C. laughs.

I growl and tell him where he can shove it. He knows there's "a skirt"—he suspects, at least, and trips me when he catches me staring at my phone unawares. I am *never* caught unawares. I trip him back then pin him up by the collar to the wall. "Stop fucking with me, C.C."

"I'm not the one who's fucking with you." He taps my temple, then hisses, "Get her out of there, dude, before your father finds out."

I feel so messed up I'm getting pissed that I ever thought it was a good idea to touch her in the first place.

But there's that one phone I haven't disarmed, and it's only because I get these little texts from her.

Are you there?

Fuck, I wish I wasn't. I wish I wasn't sitting here, staring at this screen, poleaxed in the goddamned chest every time I read it.

I keep thinking I imagined you.☹

I haven't answered her, but I feel like typing:

Princess, you have no idea how close you're dancing to the flame.

It's a day since this last text. I keep pulling it out to look at it, tempted to tell her to fucking forget about me, princess; I'm going to use you, abuse you, and throw you the fuck away when I'm done cause that's what I do.

Sometimes I tell myself if I'd stayed one night longer, maybe even one fuck longer, I wouldn't be so obsessed. But she has a mouth made for oral, thick, full lips and a crazy hungry tongue. Fuck me, I've been jerking off like crazy because the mere thought of her going down on me gets me hard.

But no. Even if she'd sucked me all night long, I'm sure I'd still be hungry to push her head down and feed her more of me, make her eat me, every last drop.

The fact that I got pissed because our night together ended too soon, and I actually wanted to lie there, in that bed, for a couple more hours and see what it felt like to hold her for a while, only confuses me further.

I call Tina myself on my other phone. Tina Glass, aka Miss Kitty. She's exactly who you need to frame a man. She's clean, good looking, and lethal. "My men call you?"

"Absolutely," she purrs.

I slip on my gloves as I talk to her. "I want the evidence delivered personally to me."

"With my absolute pleasure. I'll make contact when it's done."

I hang up and stare at Melanie's text again.

Just trash it, you fucking pussy.

She's a hot button, but this is *me*.

Do I really need a hot button? Do I need to wake up in the middle of the night with a hard dick? A twenty-five-year-old with a bunch of whores asleep so near, I can probably stumble over a couple just by opening my bedroom door. But those green eyes like forests, that pussy tight around my cock. And those sounds she makes. Do I really have to torture myself, remembering how good it felt, how fucking clean and sweet she smelled?

"This can't happen," I whisper down at my own phone, my

blood roiling in my veins when I think of how stupid I was to think I could have one night, just one night, of what a normal man does. "It can't happen again," I say.

I have a job to do. I AM the job.

My mother's life could be at risk, and so could anyone's who has contact with me. My father could take anything I'm interested in, just like that. Just to prove that he can. Just to try to own me. Doesn't matter if I want to layer my princess in fucking jewels when she's lying all sated and sweaty right next to me. Doesn't matter if I want to go back and watch those eyes go dark when I fill her, over, and over, and over. Doesn't fucking matter what I want. Only what I have to do.

Swiftly I pull the back off the phone. "Can't happen to you." I start pulling the phone apart. "It can happen to anyone but not to you. Whoever she ends up with, there's a ninety-nine point nine percent guarantee he'll be better than you."

I pull off the battery of my permanent cell phone, remove the SIM card, the wire cage, until I've got dozens of little pieces in my hand that will ensure I will never get another text from her and will ensure she never again hears from me.

Until I come to collect on behalf of the Underground.

SIX

FIVE GOING ON SIX

Melanie

Five days after Greyson . . .

"So, he's out of the picture?" Pandora asks today as I organize the pricing PDF file for one of my clients.

I bury my face in my hands. For a second, I want to pretend Pandora isn't here, breathing over the top of my head, her angry concern like a little cloud with thunderbolts over us both.

Five days.

Five long, awful days where all my hopes have dwindled to nothing, all my fantasies have gone black, all my expectations have become nil.

And here's Pandora, worried and angry on my behalf, probably happy she gets to have a good excuse to be a bitch today.

"Yes," I finally grit out. "He's fucking out of the picture. I hope you're thrilled."

I pull my phone out just to show her how textless it is.

She looks at the barren screen, grunts, and shakes her head and drops down on her chair. "Scumbag," she says.

"Dick."

"Asshole."

"Scumbag!"

"I already used that," she points out.

"And as quickly as the bastard used *me*," I mumble. Literally, the disappointment piles up by the hour, and a fresh wave hits me as I tuck my phone away. Never have I felt like I've misjudged a situation as much as I did ours—his and mine. It's officially Friday. If the guy wanted a date, you bet your ass he'd have called before today.

I'm so hurt I can't even understand why I'm so hurt. Maybe because I thought he was different, and he turned out to be just what Pandora said. I *hate* it when she's right and I'm wrong.

I especially hated her being right this time, when I really wanted her to be *wrong*.

Thank god she's sitting down quietly at her desk and I'm not hearing any *I told you sos*. If she even starts, I will hit her as hard as I want to hit myself right now for being such a *fool*.

"I'm so done with men," I burst out when I find Pandora's silence equally as annoying as the stuff I know she wants to say. "I don't need them to be happy. I'm going to get a dog. God! I just remembered I probably can't even afford the luxury of a little dog anymore."

"Stop buying shoes," she chides.

Sighing because I'm not going to explain to her I owe more than a pair of shoes, I click on my search engine and navigate to the online advertisement of my car. A picture of my Mustang stares back at me—with a bright red number on the top and a big FOR SALE sign. It's all I have, and still not enough to cover what I owe. Like me. We're both not enough.

For the first time in a week, my reality crashes down on me. Hard.

I have no more hazel eyes with adorable green flecks to make me feel hopeful and expectant. I have no more texts to look forward to. I have a car to sell, a debt to settle, and a whole lot of misery to deal with.

My grandma, before she passed, always said the best way to feel better was to focus on someone else and do something nice for them because you weren't the only one with a problem.

I look at Pandora, thinking of all the times she's been called a bitch in this very office, and I reach out and tug a strand of her onyx-colored hair, saying, "All that black hair is so drab. You should make a change too, add a pink strand to all this soot?"

"Fuck you, I hate pink."

I roll my eyes and tell the heavens—okay, Nana, I tried!—then get back to my computer to stare at my car. Whoever dried it while Greyson dried *me* did a great job—*Brain, please focus on my Mustang.*

It took me a full day to get the perfect images when the sun hit my car at just the right angle. It's so pretty I can't believe it's been several days and no callers.

What if I get no callers?

The stress starts creeping up me like a big ole whale choking my windpipe when Pandora rolls around in her chair to face me. "Come on, bitch, talk to me!" she cries. "What made you think he would even be more than what you always get? He gives you a ride when your car won't start; you go to a hotel. What do you even know about him except that he apparently fucks you stupid and now you're not the Melanie I know? Where's the smile, where's the spark? You're acting like me and I don't like it."

I fling my arms up high. "He said he'd be in touch . . . he came back to give me a ride home and I read more into it, which was a mistake, all right—*my* mistake. Believing him. Believing he was different or that we had some special . . . connection. God, I'm so lame, but I bet that's no news to you."

"Fuck him, Melanie."

"I already did. Now let's stop talking about him. Let's order me a T-shirt online that says I RULE, MEN SUCK. I need to raise my bar higher. I need to really make them prove themselves before I give them a chance. Let's go see Brooke today."

Brooke's baby was born premature in New York over a month ago, but since her fighter husband is currently off-season, they're living in Seattle while they plan a small church wedding.

Pandora grabs her backpack as we get ready to leave for the day. "Have you noticed the way daddy holds the baby? It's like the baby's head is half the size of Remy's biceps," she says.

God. I hope I can take seeing the way Remington Tate looks and smiles with his dimples and his loving blue eyes at Brooke.

"By the way, I asked Kyle to go with me to the wedding. I just want to put those lesbian rumors to rest, you know?" she tells me on the elevator.

"Really?" I ask, suddenly feeling abysmal. "Great. I'll be a third wheel then."

SEVEN

MARKED FOR A LIFETIME

Greyson

I t's always the same dream.

Never varies.

Always the same number of men.

It's always 4:12 p.m.

I've been dropped off by the bus.

A line of cars is in our driveway.

My mother's words ring clear as a bell in my head: One day he will find us, Greyson. He will want to take you from me.

I won't let him, I'd promised.

But right then I know, he'd found us. The father I didn't know. The one my mother didn't want me to end up like.

I pull the strap of my backpack from my shoulder and hold it with my fist, ready to knock someone out with a hundred pounds of homework and textbooks.

Ten men stand in my living room. Only one is seated, and I know it's him when the blood in my body starts rushing faster. It's just blood, but my entire being recognizes him even though I've never seen him before. He doesn't have my eyes, but I have his eyebrows, sleek and long and almost in a perennial frown. I have his lean nose, his dark looks. He sees me, and a parade of mixed emotions marches across his face, more emotion than I allow him to see in my own expression. He gasps, "God."

I see my mother then. She's also seated in one of the single chairs, her honeyed hair in a tangle, her ankles bound, her arms pulled tight behind her. She's trembling, gagged with a red bandanna, and trying to talk to me, words that get muffled by the cloth.

"What are you doing to her? Let her go!"

"Lana," my father says, ignoring me, his attention now slowly turned on my mother. "Lana, Lana, how *could you*?" He looks at her, his eyes filled with tears. But for every tear my father sheds, my mother sheds a dozen, trails of them.

"Let her *go*," I say again, lifting my backpack, preparing to launch it at him.

"Set that down . . . we will." My first mistake was listening to him. I lower my backpack. My father kneels before me and holds out a black weapon, then lowers his voice so that only I can hear. "See this? This is an SSG with a suppressor, so nobody will hear it. It's got no safety—ready for use. Shoot one of these men, any man, and I will spare your mother."

She's crying hard, shaking her head, but a slimy, bald man behind her forces her neck still. I step away from my backpack. It's close to me, close enough to kick like a soccer ball. I play, and I can send it flying across the room. But to who? What if I hit my mother?

I inspect the weapon and wonder how many bullets it has, not enough for all these men but for the one holding her, yes. I take it, confused that my hand doesn't shake. It's heavy and there's no fear, only the need to free my mother.

I look at the one holding her neck still.

Her eyes crying.

One day he'll find us Greyson . . .

I aim farthest away from her to the largest body part of the man that I can.

I fire.

A clean dark hole appears in his forehead. The man drops.

My mother screams inside her gag, and cries more hysterically, kicking both her tied legs in the air.

My father takes the gun from my hand with a look of wonder and he pats my head.

More men pull my mother up to her feet and drag her down to the garage staircase.

"What are you doing? Where are you taking her?" I grab my pack and swing it at one man. Another comes and grabs me, squeezes my arms as he talks and spits in my ear, "Son, son, listen to me, they made a deal, she lost you. She lost you!"

"She'd never lose me. *Mother!*" I grab a knife from his belt and stick it into his eye, twisting. He releases me with a howl and a spurt of red blood, and I go running down the stairs as I hear a car start.

My father catches me. Slaps me. Then cocks the gun at me. He smiles when I go still.

"Greyson, my son, even your instincts made you stop. You know this just killed a man. You're not going to die. If you die, you can't save her. Can you?"

My whole body is paralyzed. He smiles sweetly at me and hugs me, keeping the gun against my temple.

"I knew you were my son. I told your mother, it wasn't nice to keep you from me. Thirteen years, Greyson. Thirteen years looking for you. She insisted you weren't my son. I told her if you proved to have my blood in you, you were coming with your father, where you belong." He eases back and studies me with pride. "I gave you a choice to shoot a man."

He looks up the staircase, where I know there is a motionless body. A body that won't move again because of me.

"You killed him. Bullet straight to the head. You're my son, every inch of my son; you will be powerful and feared."

His voice chills me. I don't feel anything when we go upstairs and I see the dead man, no remorse, nothing. I want to kill more, kill everyone who hurt my mother. "Where is she?" I ask, my voice odd. I killed something else with that man. Me.

"She will be taken somewhere else. Because real men are not raised by women, you hear me? My son will not be raised by a woman. Not without his father. No, you will be like me."

I look at the car pulling out of the garage, driving my mother away. The look in her eyes when I shot that man. A cold panic like I've never felt spikes and spreads through me. I want my mother to explain to me what I did, why it was wrong, why it was wrong when it was all for her. Why she's being taken away. My face is suddenly wet, and I get another slap, this one shooting me across the room and against the wall.

"None of that, boy! *None of it.* Now see that man?" My father points at the man covering his eye where I stabbed him, blood staining his shirt, his jeans. "He's your uncle, Greyson. Uncle Eric. He's my brother, he's our family. *We* are your family. Apologize for what you did. If you're good and I'm happy with you, I will let you see your mother. She will be kept alive only for you. She was family too, and I take care of my family—but she shouldn't have betrayed me. She should never, ever, have taken you."

It took me very little time to realize how this family worked. Very little time to realize that my father used only his newest men for these antics. The guy I killed, standing like some mannequin behind my mother, had been working for him for three days when my father whispered the dare in my ear, all the time expecting and hoping I'd prove myself Slater enough to make my first kill.

Many nightmares later, I supposed my mother had been try-ing to tell me not to shoot. If I hadn't been so determined to de-fend her, if I'd proved to be weak, she'd be with me. I'd be left in school, thought unfit to be a part of this family. But I played my father's game and instead of saving her, I doomed us both for the rest of our lives. I showed him I was thirteen and yes . . . I would kill, even him, for my mother.

I was good. I trained. I sucked back every emotion in me. I became nothing. Zero. And left when the promises and promises that I could see her turned out to be nothing but empty words . . . I followed every lead, and found nothing. A whole big world, and all these skills, and I still don't know where she is.

A noise in my bedroom filters into my dreamlike state. I awaken instantly, and move by instinct, reaching under my pil-low for my knife. Lightning fast, I flip around and send it flying, slamming it within a grazing hair from my intruder's face, against the door.

"Zero?" a stunned voice says in the dark.

I've got my gun cocked and aimed before Harley finishes my name. Then I sigh. "Never do that again." I shove up to my feet and flick on the lamp.

I turn back to my list. I'm anxious to get this over with. So many names. So many. I can't even stand looking at her name, there, next to number five. "Your father wants to see you. He wants to know how the situation is going."

My father has the oddest hours. We're still off-season. Ev-eryone is sleeping. The meds and the morphine they give him make him sleep all day, and wake only for small periods during the night. I grab the list and shove my legs into my slacks while Harley waits for me.

He grins. "You'll enjoy that one."

"Excuse me?"

"Number five?" he presses. "Your finger . . . it's on number five."

I drag my finger away and my heart starts pounding with the sudden urge to choke him as I fold the page into a tight little roll.

He didn't attack her, but the fact that her name is on my list bugs me. The fact that all the guys know she owes us money. Wyatt, Harley, Thomas, Leon, C.C., Zedd, Eric, my father . . .

I think of her, feminine and vulnerable, exposed to these assholes, and things uncoil from inside me, like cobras out of a basket. Only she can make me feel this. Like I'm the home of a deadly hurricane, and it has no outlet. I told myself last night before going to bed that I would use what little honor I had left to protect this girl from me. I told myself *She doesn't want you. Not the real you. She wants a prince, and you're the villain. You're the one she's working extra hours for. You, your father.* I don't want to remember how she smells like summer and the way she slides into bed. Warm. Hot. Real. Melanie. Number five on my list.

"This chick. She came to ask for more time to make her payment," Harley says, "which got her name almost to the end of the list now. She asked for an extension. Leon told her she could become an extension of his fucking cock and they could forget about it. If she can't pay, we'll all pitch in for a chance to fuck her."

I breathe hard.

Nope.

Doesn't calm me.

There's just no fucking way anyone will touch her. No FUCK-ING way.

"Go. I'll go talk to my father in a bit," I snap out darkly, holding his gaze pinned.

I slip into a shirt and then wait for him to leave. I'm so fucked up by what he said that I grab my knife and fling it at my target across the wall. I do it several times . . . I won't leave this room until

I've hit my bull's-eye twelve times, straight up, which means I'm calm again. I could probably blame this possessiveness on my cock. I never did like sharing for shit. Or I can blame it on some false sense of justice—I never believed it fair when someone stronger took advantage of anyone weaker. Pure cowardice. But that's not it either.

I wonder who's taking her home.

Jaw clamped, I swing my knife and hit dead center.

❤ ❤ ❤

"SON," JULIAN SAYS, his eyes lighting up when he sees me. I hear the beep of his heart monitor, and notice, to his right, Eric is rolling up his shirt sleeves.

"Update?" I direct myself to Eric, crossing my arms as I assess the trio of nurses around them. I not only owe Eric his eye, I have owed him my life, here, in this fucked-up, strange family.

"He needs platelets," Eric explains.

I hate myself for being unable to stand there and just watch. I hate that some sense of duty, of loyalty to my own blood, makes me hold my shirt up and expose my veins. "I'll do it."

My father lifts a hand as I take a seat next to him. "No. You get nicked out there, you'll bleed to death. Not you." He looks at Eric and makes a hand gesture for him to proceed.

Eric waits for my approval, and I give it with a nod. I've always taken his words—I'd say to heart, except I don't have one. But I've taken him seriously all these years. Whereas my father refuses to engage in anything that might hint at weakness, Eric has, once or twice, patted my back and called me "son." But loving uncle or not, karma is a bitch, and I owe Eric an eye. For my father's side of the family, an eye for an eye is not only sworn by, it's stamped on each of our birth certificates.

"This list," I tell my father, unrolling it from my hand, looking at Eric first, then my father, a threat—smooth and cold as steel—in my tone, "I want your word, and therefore the word of any man under you, that nobody is to touch any of my targets. Any name here is exclusively mine to deal with as I see fit. I guarantee the amount owed. I want a guarantee to my methods."

Eric looks at the list and his one eye focuses on number five. Melanie. He wants a chance to fuck her? They all want her. I want her. I want to grab him and tell him this little piece of heaven? This is *mine*. But I cannot do that or I'll look weak. I can't outright buy her name off this list without endangering her, and not only to my father. She could become my every enemy's target, known or unknown.

"This list and every name on it is mine to enforce," I repeat, my voice level. "Only I make contact, only I retrieve and direct payment—as I see fit."

"On the condition that Eric be filled in on a daily basis of progress as he keeps me company here, yes," my father agrees.

"Your word," I insist.

"So stubborn, Zero." He slaps me, hard enough to make a sound, but not enough to make me move a muscle, and laughs. "I give you my word."

His word alone should be enough, but words, blood, I will *never* live a day when I believe in something without reservation. He could be lying. So I bend over and pat his shoulder, giving the impression of a loving son to the nurses nearby as I whisper, "Any of them step out of line, I'll wipe them out. Even my brother."

Once again, I see the respect in his eyes as I ease back and he nods at me, betraying no expression as I straighten. I glance at Eric. "I'll be gone for a few days. I'm taking one or two of the team, no more. I'll summon backup if needed." I glance at the nurse injecting the needle into his veins, then back at Eric. "Thank you."

When I head back to my room, I feel a buzz, the kind you get when you're hunting. Or killing. Or want to.

I wouldn't want to mess with me tonight. This talk of Melanie begging the Underground for an extension? *"Please, can I have some more time to pay?"*

It's got me charged.

I'm charged with a fierce protectiveness I've never felt before and it's spiking my adrenaline in ways nothing else ever has.

I grab a couple of new phones, change a couple of chips, then I book my ticket online and pack a few things. The buzz in me changes to something dangerous . . . not deadly, but dangerous, not only to me, but to her.

While watching her these past months, something's happened to me. *I want you too much, sweet princess.*

She's gotten to me, under my skin, into my head, it's like she's flowing in my damn *blood*.

I shouldn't have her.

She deserves more.

More than any guy I know, and definitely more than me.

But to let her run around loose, single and available? When I can make sure the damn bed she's sleeping in is mine? When I can hold that face in one hand and look into those eyes and fucking know—certain as I breathe—that she wants me too?

I've been working my way up the list, instead of the usual way, from top to bottom. But I'm stalling because I don't want to collect from her. I'm stalling because she's a little burst of life and I don't feel like charging in there like the apocalypse, shrouding her with my darkness.

I don't want to remember a month ago, when I watched her spill her coffee as she walked to the office, how devastated she looked because she'd messed up her scarf, her whole outfit ruined. From all the way across the street, where I ducked behind my newspaper, I heard her rant that she'd rather be fired than head to work wearing only two colors! Looking drab! That was no way to meet a client!

God, I laughed. I laughed, and I was still grinning over what a passionate little thing she was on my flight back to where my team was stationed, hiding my grin under my palm as I stared out the window.

From the moment I found her on my list and then laid eyes on her, I've followed her.

I've followed her in the pretense of finding out her social habits, her weaknesses, so I can sweep in for the kill, but the truth is, I follow her because I'm a sick fucking asshole, obsessed as a dog with the way she walks, all the colors she wears, all the ways she smiles, the bubbly, lovely little package that she makes.

I had two emotions in my life before I met her, anger and detachment.

Now she's given me ten more. Lust, frustration, concern . . . even joy. I have never, ever wanted anything the way I want those green eyes to memorize me the way I've made it a *religion* to memorize *her.*

I grab my duffel, the ziplock bag with all the phone pieces, and the card. I build it back up as I ask Derek to drive me to the airport.

The phone comes alive in my hand and my gut starts to heat when I start texting her back, finally, at last:

Be home tonight.

EIGHT

MESSAGE

Melanie

Saturday morning, as dictates our comfortable little routine, I find my parents having breakfast, bathed, perfect, and smiling. Maria, their cook, has the best breakfast in town, and having breakfast at Mom and Dad's makes me happy because the table is always set with linens, silver, and the food is placed in such a perfect way that you feast with your eyes first before reaching into the offerings and serving yourself.

"Lanie!" Mom says as I walk in. "Your father and I were just talking about Brooke's wedding. When did you say it was?"

"Less than a month." I kiss her cheek and then hug my tall, handsome dad. "Hey, Dad, you look cute."

"See? She noticed I cut my hair, unlike you," he tells my mom, pointing an empty fork in her direction.

"You hardly have any hair, how am I supposed to notice? So tell us about the wedding. I still can't believe she's getting married before you. You were always prettier and so much more lively," my mom says, squeezing my hand as I sit down.

"I'm sure her fiancé would disagree," I counter. I hate when my mom always puts Brooke down merely to make me feel better.

I don't feel better—*she* feels better, making excuses as to why a good guy won't want me. Sometimes I think her own desperation to see me happily married makes little ole Murphy poke his head out and lay down the law—the more she wants it, the less it'll happen. Woe is me.

"Still doesn't excuse why no decent man out there can see that my baby girl is about as good as they come. You're fit, you have a beautiful smile, and you're sweet just like your momma."

"Thank you, Daddy. I'm sure my unmarried state has everything to do with the fact that all men are assholes except you."

"Lanie!" Mother chides, but she doesn't really chide, she laughs softly.

"Well, Ulysess's son is running for senator and he always asks about you. He's not the brightest nut out there, but he's good looking and—"

"He's gay. He wants a beard, Dad. A sham marriage to fool his constituents. I can do better than that on my own."

"When I was twenty-five . . ." my mom begins.

"You were married and already had me, yeah yeah yeah. But I have a career. And I have a . . . very busy dating life. In fact, I've been dating so much I wouldn't know who to pick to take to Brooke's wedding," I exaggerate.

My mom and my dad, what can I say? I love them. I like pleasing them. They've loved me my whole life. I have been showered with love. They not only love me, they want me to find the kind of love they share. I don't ever want them to suspect what I already suspect myself—that for some reason, it's just not happening for me.

"Just remember what I told you, Flea," my mother says. "Choose the man who treats you best. The one who will not break your heart, who can be your friend, who you can talk to."

I poke at my French toast. "You say that because Dad was your best friend. I, however, have a female best friend, and I would never marry my closest guy friend, Kyle. *Ever*." I shudder when I think of my sexy Justin Timberlake-look-alike-BFF and me having so much as a kiss. Continuing to poke my food and softening my voice, I add, "I don't think you can plan these things, Mom. I think they just happen and suddenly you're standing on the side of the ring, meeting the man you're going to marry when he winks at you. Or you find yourself standing in the rain, and all you pray for is that whatever feeling just struck you struck the man in front of you too . . ."

I look at my phone wistfully.

God, I'm such a fool fool FOOL!

The only thing that struck that man was lust, and now he's been stricken with the Run-Away-From-Melanie syndrome.

A syndrome that's much more common than you'd think.

"True, you cannot plan who you fall for," my mother agrees. "But if you can step back so you can hear yourself think, you'd realize you don't want to be out in the rain, hit by thunder. Always choose the path with sunlight, is what my momma used to say."

"Naturally. Nobody picks an awful life out of wanting, Momma," I groan. "Some people are just luckier."

"It's all about choosing wisely," she insists.

I fall quiet as I wonder why I couldn't have been wiser a couple of months ago, when I bet my life away on a single night, a single moment, one single outcome. I glance at my parents—so sweet and perfect, in our little bubble of happiness—I couldn't bear to ask them for the money, could I? Disappoint them this way? How can I take their money and all their pride in me knowing how hard they fought to keep me alive?

❤ ❤ ❤

BY THE TIME I go home, I'm sad. I'm sad about my debt and about my man. I brush my teeth and look at my blank white wall and scowl.

"Bastard," I mumble. "You ruined my whole week, you fucking bastard. I bet you're fucking some triple-D blonde right now and her triplets all at the same time, aren't you? You're not even a two-timer, you're like a three-timer, liar, feeding me an I'll-take-you-to-the-movies fucking line. I swear I was fine until you came back like you 'got' me, like you 'got' me even if I looked like a hungover mess. God, I can't believe myself!"

I kick the tub as if it's the tub's fault, then yell, "OUCH!"

Scowling, I walk into the bedroom, grab my sleep clothes, pad outside to my living room/kitchen combo to grab some ice cream, slide on my *The Princess Bride* DVD, and turn on the TV. A couple of pounds of fat, here we go. I plop down and a vibration buzzes across the couch. I scowl and feel around for my phone. I find it way in between the two couch cushions, pull it out, and set it aside so I can scoop out some ice cream. I almost choke on a mouthful when I see a text I hadn't noticed before.

Be home tonight.

What? My stomach vaults. I read who the text is from and suddenly I want to throw my phone into a WALL. *Greyson.* I scowl at it and throw it down to the couch and start pacing. I'm not going to answer him. Why would I? He seemed in no hurry to talk to me before, and now he orders me? Like an almighty *king*? No thanks. I'll pass on our second date, thank you.

But I check and notice the text was sent hours ago. I tell myself I am not going to respond, I will wait a gazillion days like he did. I set the phone aside and put a big spoonful of ice cream in my mouth, letting it melt on my tongue, but my stomach is squirming and now I can't watch the TV, I can only stare at my phone and suck on the spoon. Then I bury the spoon in the tub and grab my phone, squeeze my eyes shut, and type.

I'm home but that doesn't mean I'm staying home. Just depends . . .

On? comes the reply, and quickly.

Whoa, was he waiting, with phone in hand, to answer? It seems like he was.

I wait one full minute. Trembling. Type: On who's visiting

I don't mean that as an invite. I mean it as in: I'll hightail it out of here if he sets foot in my building. But his answer is lightning fast and my heart starts pounding as it keeps staring back at me.

Me.

Crap! I have to leave. I have to leave; I can't see him! I can't be this easy! A line must be drawn. He's already shown what our night together meant to him, and I won't let myself be devalued by him or any other moron again.

I should leave before he arrives, or when he does, yell through the door, without opening it even an inch, and tell him that I'm NOT INTERESTED! *You stood me up, you didn't get in touch soon enough, I am not your booty call, have a good life!*

Yeah. That sounds right.

Determined, I head over to close the living room blinds. When I glance out the window and reach for the string I see a dark sports car pull over and a man in black step out of the driver's seat. He looks up toward my window and all my systems stop when our eyes lock, hold, *recognize.* My insides go into chaos mode. A strange excitement makes my knees knock.

Fuck me, it's really him.

What is he doing here? What does he want?

He heads into the building and I turn to face my closed door, panicking because I haven't changed, I didn't *change*. I'm in my pj's, if hardly that.

Noticing the pint of ice cream still grasped in my hand, I run to shove it back into the freezer, spoon and all. I start pacing around in circles, trying to come up with a new plan, but unable to think for shit. I consider telling my building guard not to let him in, but I hear the ring of the elevator and realize the guard must have recognized the motherfucker from when he brought me home last week.

Deciding not to delay the inevitable, I swing the door open as he steps out of the elevator. He looks straight at me and his gaze drills into me, making a hole straight in my thoughts. One of my neighbors and her husband pass along the hall toward their door.

"Well, hello there, Melanie. A little chilly out." She gestures to the white silk shorts and near-transparent camisole I'm wearing in complete disapproval and continues on.

Greyson follows behind her and fills up the space one foot away from my threshold with muscle and beauty and testosterone and, I swear, god, I swear, he's as lethal as a nuclear bomb. My knees, oh, my knees. My heart. My eyes. My body feels both light as a feather and heavy as a tank. How can this be? He's so stunning I can't even *move*. Or blink, or hardly stand; I'm leaning on the door frame.

I'm fully sober. Something I might regret. He's no longer blurred by the rain, by vodka, or by my stupid illusions of Prince Charming.

The man standing at my door is very real, very big, very tan, and his smile is very, very charming. There is no word for the way he stands there, his eyes dark and glimmering, his cheekbones hard and his jaw smoothly shaven, his mouth so beautiful, tipped up mischievously at the corners. His suit is perfect, playboy perfect, and his tousled hair run with wayward streaks of copper that makes me want to rake my fingers straight through. And he's here, looking at me as if waiting for me to let him in. A memory of the night he brought me home flashes through me. Where I felt sore because of the way he'd loved me all night. The little mark behind my ear that I found the next morning.

Hanging on to my every instinct of self-preservation, I hold the door only halfway open when he catches it in one big, powerful hand.

"Invite me in," he says softly, holding the door in his firm grip.

"My car doesn't need a tune-up, it's fine, but thanks for checking in on it," I say, pushing it closed with more effort.

He shoves the door open and strides inside, and I'm frustrated over my inability to keep him out. Now he's on the wrong side of the door, shutting it behind him like he owns my place. "This building has a laundry chute?"

"*That's* your line?"

He crosses the room and pulls all the blinds shut, then he sweeps his gaze across my space with such thorough intensity my insides quiver.

It's almost like he's making sure there is no other man here.

He can't possibly be jealous, can he?

And now . . . now that he seems assured no one is here but me, he starts walking over to me and looking at my mouth, and I'm walking away because every instinct of self-preservation in me tells me to walk away.

"You're here. Why are you here all of a sudden? Some other date canceled on you last minute?" I demand.

"I have a date I'd like to schedule with you." His eyebrows pull low over those brilliant, hawklike eyes. "You're not nearly as excited to see me as I'd hoped."

"Maybe I thought you were a drunken hallucination. Maybe I *hoped* you were."

I back into my kitchen island and he locks me in with his arms, his eyes hungry and almost desperate. Then he cups my face and sets his mouth to mine like he thinks—mistakenly—I belong to him.

"I'm not," he says softly, then he kisses me again, so deeply I lose my train of thought until he speaks against my mouth again. "A hallucination. And if you need me to, I'll spend all night reminding you of what it feels like to have my tongue and my cock buried deep in you and how much you liked it."

He leans over as if to kiss me again. My voice trembles as I turn my head. "Don't, Greyson."

"I don't like that word, 'don't,'" he rasps against my cheek. "But I do like you saying 'Greyson.'"

He tilts my head around with the tip of one finger and stares at me like he loves the look of me. I lift one of his arms and he lets me, and I start easing away again, free of him, but not free of his stare. The first night he just kept staring at my eyes like he couldn't tear his gaze free, but now, now he's seeing all of me. I'm wearing shorts and a camisole yet my body starts heating as his eyes rake me up and down.

"I gave you a chance and you blew it," I breathe.

"I want another one."

I shake my head, but I can't stop the stupid wings of some huge living thing batting around in my stomach. Suddenly my place smells like leather, like *forest*, and Greyson freaking King stands there looking like he does, confident, self-contained, his presence somehow demanding all my attention.

"Why are you here?"

He signals to the TV as I watch my dear, perfect Westley whisper to Buttercup, *"As you wish,"* then he looks at me, smiles as if at himself. "Are you watching a movie?"

"Not now, right now I'm watching you."

He just smiles that rather sexy, rather annoying almost grin of his and sits on a side chair like some mighty king. I can feel myself frown because he just managed to shrink my place with his presence. Feeling little pinches in my stomach, I sit down on the couch, Westley forgotten, Buttercup forgotten, everything but HIM forgotten. I wait.

"How are you?" he asks softly, signaling at me.

"How do you think?" I sullenly ask.

"Looking pretty damn good from where I sit."

"Do you always make yourself at home in places you're not wanted?"

His soft laugh runs across my skin like a feather, pricking the little hairs on my arms. He leans back and crosses his arms behind his head, watching me with cool, knowing eyes. "I'm here to prove to you that, no, Melanie, you didn't imagine me."

The way his sensual tone combines with that brilliant narrowed gaze tells me *we both know that I am definitely wanted here*—and makes my toes curl. Fuck, he turns me on.

"I was about to eat a thousand pounds of chocolate because of you," I accuse.

He stands and then comes to drop his body right next to me on the couch. "Well now, two hundred twenty pounds of me are right here. With you."

"We're not sleeping together again."

"Considering I've been inside you, you should at least let me put my arms around you while we watch . . . what are we watching?"

"*The Princess Bride.* My favorite movie of all time."

"Ah."

He stretches his arm along the back of the couch, and my heart thumps like mad.

"Buttercup is engaged to Prince Humperdinck but her true love, Westley . . ."

His lips curl, and I shut up when I notice how amused he looks. Secretly amused by . . . me. It's hot. And frankly, it bothers me. I whisper, "You're a playboy. I know you are."

"You know nothing about me."

I roll my eyes. "I know your name. *Greyson*."

"You mock my name with that evil glint in your eye like you love it, all it does is make me want to fuck you until you moan it." He pulls my face to his. "I know every time you lie because I've been taught to detect liars since I was very, very young. You learn it when your father lies all the time," he breathes, his hot breath on my lips causing a fire to stir inside my stomach. "I think of you, Melanie. I see your face in every woman. I flew here just to see you. Communication. Relationships. Those aren't things I'm good at. There are other attributes I have that are far better. Like I see I'm good at making you pant. I see your pupils are dilated, you keep looking at my mouth instead of your favorite movie, and it's taking all of my self-control not to give us exactly what it is we both need right now. It's been a week, but as far as I'm concerned"—he cups the back of my head and nibbles on my lower lip—"I've been waiting a lifetime to sink myself in you."

He presses me close, and I ache so much, I'm scared. By him, by this, this need to claw into his skin, press my lips to the hard line of his jaw, touch his thick, silky hair.

"Let me watch my movie, let go," I protest feebly.

When he chuckles, his breath moves a couple of tendrils of loose hair at my temple. "If you want me to let you go, you need to stop pressing your pretty nipples against my chest as you say so, stop getting closer when you ask me to let you go," he murmurs, rubbing his nose against mine, and his closeness, his scent of forest, his warm breath, his lips so close I can almost taste them, trigger a flood of need between my thighs and a hot, aching ripple in my sex.

I gasp as we almost kiss, and he groans and gives me space to breathe. He lifts his head, and I see him appraise me like a connoisseur would appraise a jewel or some antiquity. Why does he look at me like this? Why like THIS? Like he wants inside me as much as I want him. Like he wants more than my body, like he wants to suck the blood out of me, eat my soul up, and then pray to me.

Quietly, I close my eyes, trying to pretend we're just dating, have never had sex, are just watching a movie. I force my muscles to relax and watch the TV, and I sense him relax gradually too. He stretches his big body suddenly down the length of the couch and pulls me up against him. Oh my. I hate how he assumes control of things that pertain to me, but I love it too.

I feel his gaze on the top of my head. Pretending to watch the movie, I weave my fingers in his hair and bring his arm around me, complaining, "Your elbow's digging into my rib cage."

His chuckle—I can't even explain how much I love the sound of his chuckle—tells me he knows I just want to get more comfortable. And I do.

"Better?" he asks, shifting that lean, hard, long body of his underneath me.

"Shh. I like it when he fights with the Spaniard."

I'm pretending to watch, but really, I'm struggling with how much I want to give him a second chance. But what if I fall? What if it gets out of control, and not only do I fall, but plunge into him?

That night with him?

It was incredible. *He* was incredible. He still feels, smells, sounds *incredible*.

His muscles flex and I fear he will pull away, but he doesn't. He tucks me closer, cocooning me in his arms. I breathe softly in a nearly overwhelming sense of contentment, engulfed by the feeling of security he gives me, and I finally succumb to the urge to set my cheek on his chest. "This feels good," I murmur. Beyond good.

Suddenly nothing feels righter than this. On my couch. With

this man. His spicy, comforting scent is like a drug, and I can't help but take deeper, more conscious breaths of him.

"Princess," he says in my ear, conspiratorially.

A shiver runs through me as I close my eyes. "What?"

"I wasn't going to call."

"I know, douche bag. Why did you?"

Westley and my Spaniard are at it with swords but it feels like the real action is in my ear, in his whisper: "You need me."

I scoff and sit up to glare at him. "I don't need you."

He sits up too and his eyes flash in challenge. "Maybe *I* need you."

When I only stare, he shoots me an adorable grin that's cocky but also sad. "Do you know what it feels like to carry the weight of a dead heart with you your whole life, like you're just looking for your grave?" He waits for me to answer, but I'm speechless. "I *live* the moments I'm with you. I live a lie, but this isn't a lie, watching this stupid movie with you."

"Stupid!" I gasp.

He laughs and stands, and says, "When I go out, lock up. I'll be back with food."

"If I fall asleep, I'll be too tired to come open it again," I warn, but the truth is, I just don't want him to leave!

"I can open your lock without you so much as waking," he says easily, then he comes back and slides his gloved hand under my camisole. "But lock up anyway."

"You're bossy."

"And you're fucking sexy in what you're wearing right now." His thumb traces the underside of my breast and my breath snags when our eyes meet, and there's no shutter in his eyes, no filter. What I see galvanizes me, the roiling tumult in the very depths of his gaze taking me for a spin.

"I've been told I have a photographic memory. That some images just stick with me with extreme clarity . . . but that night, Melanie, I remember everything about that night more clearly than any other moment in my life." He grasps the back of my neck in a big, square hand and gives a little squeeze. "Your red thong. Your perky little nipples. The way you looked at me like a princess and told me your name was Melanie. I remember it too well."

I'm transported there for a moment. It's all a haze of passion and desire and teeth, tongues, hands. I ache, but I don't want to be his toy. I don't want to be his booty call. My throat hurts when I take his hand, pry it off my neck, and start guiding him to the front door.

"I think . . . Greyson, I think you should leave. I can't think when you're around. I don't know what you want from me but I can't play these games with you . . . not with you . . ."

He looks at me when we reach the door, almost as if he wants me to kick him out. Almost as if he wants ME to be the one to tell him I never want to see him again. Will he feel relieved? Well, he won't be! I can't even begin to explain what that touch of gold tan does for his looks. How I can't stop admiring the intriguing angles and planes of his face. How long I've waited in my life to feel something, a sparkle, a tingle, like *this*.

"My best friend gets married in two weeks," I whisper, then I tell him the church as I start pushing him out, all the while holding his gaze. It's hot, hungry. THE LOOK. "If you want one more chance, if you're serious about this, you can come to church," I tell him, then I lean over and kiss his lips, very softly, hearing his low, rumbling groan, then I step back and close the door.

I lean on it, squeezing my eyes shut as I struggle to breathe. God that kiss was nothing and yet it made every inch of my body shudder.

After a minute, I hear him growl *"Fuck"* on the other side of the door. Did it take him that long to recover from that kiss too? Then I swear I can *feel* him lean on the door. I close my eyes and breathe slowly. When he whispers, "Melanie," it's right where I have my cheek pressed against the door. I tremble down to my toes, struggling to get my voice level.

"Yes?" I say.

"I'll be there."

I hear the elevator a good while later. I lift my fingers and touch the door, and for the first time in my life, I'm terribly afraid about meeting him, the one man I've been waiting for.

Suddenly every fiber in my body, my sober body, tells me he is the one.

He is the one.

The one who's going to wreck me. Hurt me. Demolish me. The one who is going to remove every inch of the girl in me. He will be the memory I will never forget, and good or bad, he will be THE one I dream of.

Except he's all wrong.

There's something exciting and alarming about him.

The dark in his hazel eyes, the brilliant gleam that makes him so attractive to me, the way he smells of leather and metal and forest and *danger to me.*

I think of my mother and I always thought I'd do her proud. I remember my best friend, concerned that a Riptide would sweep her away. Greyson won't be a riptide. I don't know what he'll be, but I'm thinking tsunami, hurricane, something natural and unstoppable.

I wonder if he will show up at the wedding. If he is as helpless to this pull as I am.

I plop back down with my movie and curl into a couch pillow, my thoughts no longer with the most beautiful fairy tale ever written. I whisper into the emptiness of the room, "Please, if you're just going to hurt me, please, please, don't come to Brooke's wedding."

NINE

RESTLESS

Greyson

What in the fuck am I doing?

The surveillance camera screens flare bright when I get home after days of nonstop working, of chasing my marks, city to city, home to home. The house is asleep. Father, the guys, everyone in the rental. I bite off one glove, then do the same with the other while I bring a loaf of bread, a jar of PB, and a steak knife over.

We've set up the surveillance cameras that watch the entries, exits, windows of the home. Pounds of computers weigh down several tables, lights flickering among tangles of wire. I spread the PB onto a slice of bread, slap another one on it, and gobble it down as I search the boxes of recordings and pull out a card from last year, labeled with the date of the fight. I've been thinking about her. Every second of the day, I remember her.

Wet and vulnerable, in the rain.

Wet and warm, in my arms.

Telling me her name is *Melanie.*

Inviting me to her best friend's wedding.

She triggers every synapse in my brain until she's alive in my mind, laughing a laugh I've only ever heard her laugh . . .

cuddling with me as she watches her movie . . . pushing me out the door like she can't stand the sight of me, then pulling me back and kissing the bejezus out of me.

I stood there like a moron leaning on her door, my heart slamming in my chest as I waited for her to open it. Hell, I was ready to kick it open.

Instead, I left and went to rent a tuxedo and then I started looking at apartments nearby.

I'm dangerous to her; hell, *she's* dangerous to *me*. I can't let myself get distracted for this shit.

So what the fuck am I doing?

I slide the recording into a card reader and play it, my eyes straining for the glimpse of her, my daily dose of Melanie I need to see.

"And nooow, ladies and gentlemen . . ." the announcer begins with his usual flair, "Remington Tate, your one and only, RIP-TIDE!! RIPTIDE!! Say hello to RIPTIDEEEEE!" he yells.

One of our fighters trots toward the ring, into the screen. It's Riptide.

He's not good; he's the best I've ever seen. The most lucrative fighter my father has ever sponsored in the Underground—and one we all hope to continue to sponsor, thanks to his reckless streak.

"Riptide, Riptide . . ." I hear the crowd through the speakers.

I drink my soda as I keep watching the screen, waiting to spot the blonde on the sidelines. *Melanie.* She's about to appear, jumping up and down as usual, and I'm tensing with anticipation when the image freezes, blacks out, then cuts to the next fight.

I smash a fist down to get the computer going. Nothing. I scowl, rewind, play. Same shit happens. Draining the last of my soda, I toss the can in the trash can and roughly scrub a frustrated palm over my face, then I stalk to Wyatt's room and flick the light on. "Who the fuck messed with the tapes?"

"What?"

"You tampered with them, Wyatt?"

"They're from fucking last year. What's so important about it? What do you see nobody else does, huh? What does my father think you can do nobody else can't?"

"He wants to break me. That's all there is. You're fucking lucky he didn't try the same with you. Tomorrow I want the full footage, I don't care what you need to do."

I flip the switch back off and go to my room and stare at my phone.

What the *fuck* am I doing? I grab a knife and feel its weight, somehow satisfying me. I set my SIG aside, pull out several knives, slide them into my slacks' back pockets, six inside each, then I start sending them flying, over and over, rapidly twirling them a dozen times in the air, so fast you don't realize the blade is turning until it slams into the wall. I pull them out of each pocket, one every second. *One. Two. Three. Four . . . five, six, seven, eight, nine, teneleventwelve.*

I've got a rental tux. I've got a place in Seattle, a ticket to Seattle. I've got an itch in me and her name's Melanie.

My phone rings. "Yeah?"

"She's home now. Safe and sound."

My eyes flick to the clock. 11:34 p.m. So late? "C.C.'s coming to relieve you tomorrow. I'm working a mark and then flying in. Why's she out so late?"

"'Kay, boss."

"She alone?"

I wait for Derek's answer. "Alone. She had dinner with the friend and the blond guy who hangs out with them. And no, he didn't sit close to her."

"What's—"

"She's fucking wearing some sort of dress. Floral."

"And what—"

"It's pink, boss. With yellow tennis shoes and her hair loose and lots of bracelets."

I see her in my mind and breathe out through my nostrils while a strange sensation of peace and longing flow through my muscles, tensing then relaxing me.

"Keep an eye out." I click the line off and stare at her name in my phone. I'm not a fucking teenager to be texting a girl. I don't like leaving traces. I need to change this fucking phone.

I rub a hand roughly across my face. If my father knows I'm chasing after her, I don't know what he'll do. What Eric will do. Anybody I've ever come after could come after me through her.

So leave her alone. . . .

I pull out the knives, stick them back in my pockets, and swing again. "Can't," I say. *Can't leave her alone. Don't fucking want to.*

She makes me feel like I'm not a robot, like I'm flesh and blood, a man, not a number, not a job . . . not a monster, not a bastard, not a zero.

TEN

ANTICIPATING

Melanie

The worst part isn't wondering for the next two weeks if I'll have a date for the wedding. It's not even my compulsive checking of my texts. Or hearing mean ole Becka snicker at the office about how quiet I've been and speculate on whether or not I'm broken-hearted. None of that is the worst part.

It always amazes me how one day you can think you're at the highest point of your misery, but it's not even the beginning. Okay, so I want to look good, right? I want to look spectacular. If—not *if*, Melanie, *when*—Greyson King shows up, I want him to lose control because of me. I want that man to want me like I'm his next breakfast, lunch, and dinner. Hell, I want him to crave me like a feast. And take me like a beast.

So I get a Brazilian. I get a massage. I get pedicures and manicures and my nails are now a pretty, shiny red. I smell the best I've ever smelled and am so ready to be taken to bed by a man with hazel eyes, I can't even think what I'll do if he doesn't show up.

He said he'd be there and the eerily soft and low determination in his words didn't frighten me; it's the fact that I hope he will be there because he wants the same thing I do.

But that's not the bad part . . . the bad part is that I'm so very ready, and yet the evening before the wedding, my bridesmaid dress isn't ready from the dry cleaners.

I'm waiting inside the small shop as they scramble to find it in their carousel, and I'm getting so nervous, I'm drumming my nails on the counter as they keep pulling out dress after dress. I shake my head. "That's not it. That's not the bridesmaid dress, sir, and I'm really starting to panic here. The last thing I want is to call my friend and tell her I lost my bridesmaid dress, please! It's red. Strapless. Look for it again, please?"

"Ma'am, ma'am!" Another guy appears from the back of the carousel with my ticket in his hand. "I'm sorry but we checked and we delivered it to the wrong address."

"Urgh. To which fucking address?!" I pull out my phone and write down the address, then track it on my phone and see it's only a few blocks away. "Do you have the correct delivery for them so I can make an exchange?"

The man nods. "But I can get in trouble."

"My dear sir, you're already in trouble and I'll make a shitload of trouble for you if you don't just give me what's theirs so I can go get my dress. Call them and tell them I'm on my way. Please!"

Reluctantly, he hands over a suit and a floral dress, and I grab the clothes on their plastic hangers and hurry down the street, and up several flights of stairs, where I knock on the door and say to the man who opens it, "Excuse me, there was a mistake over at Green Dry Cleaners, and I believe this belongs to you, and you have something that belongs to me, which I need desperately for tomorrow."

He stands there holding a beer and looks me up and down like I'm some escort sent to pleasure him.

I repeat exactly what I just told him and use his damn clothes to shove between us so he stops looking at my legs.

"I don't check this shit, my wife does, and she's not in."

"Please just take this in and verify if it's yours, and check your closet or somewhere for a recently cleaned red dress. This here must look familiar to you, does it not?"

After a huge hassle with the suspicious man, I finally get my dress and breathe when I realize it's still hung up and in plastic. Thank god.

I head back to where I had to park my car two blocks away. These little alleyways have zero parking spots and I'm skipping around puddles, taking care of my shoes, when I hear a whistle from across the alley. I stop and look up, and a man stands there, right in the middle, his stance menacing, wide. One of my eyebrows flies up, and then the other.

What the?

My heart picks up speed as a flicker of alarm flutters through me. I turn around when I hear footsteps behind me, and I see two men. A ball of anxiety knots within me as I scan the area. A dark car is parked near the end of the alley where I'm headed. I think I see one man behind the wheel, and the passenger door is slightly ajar, as though the single man before me just got out of the vehicle.

Some sixth sense in me flares awake and keeps ratcheting up my heartbeat. My dress, my shoes . . . all of a sudden nothing matters but getting out of here. I duck my head in caution and continue walking straight ahead, not even caring about the puddles anymore, only intent on gripping the hanger, which may be the only thing I can use to . . . to *what?* Wild animals will chase prey if they run the other way, and everything about these men screams *Predators, Melanie!*

Fear pulses like a live thing in me. Every step that takes me closer to the one lone man at the edge of the deserted alley gnaws away at my confidence.

I'm about to pass him when he takes a step forward and I meekly whisper, "Excuse me."

One hand grabs my upper arm, clenching like a manacle. "You're not excused," he growls.

I flinch and retreat a step when I see his frightening expression, but he yanks me tighter against him, the scent of sweat and cigarettes mingling in his breath as he repeats, looking down at me with red-rimmed eyes, "I said you're not excused, bitch."

Panic like I've never known wells in my throat as I swing my dress in an effort to jam the tip of the hanger into some part of his face, but before I can make the hit, another pair of strong hands grabs hold of my arms and jerks my elbows back by force.

"No!" I cry, my dress falling to the ground with a clatter, and suddenly I'm kicking in the air as a third man grabs my thighs and the second keeps his hold hooked on my elbows as they start carrying me toward the car. Icy fear wraps around my heart as I twist my body even harder, gasping and panting in terror when I can't get free, their fingers digging into the flesh of my wrists and calves now.

There's a man behind the wheel of the car telling them, "Quiet the bitch down," as I keep struggling. One seems to try to cover my mouth and I use my free leg to kick his knee. "NO!" I keep saying. "No! NO!" A rag is pressed to my nose and for some reason I hold my breath because I know it's meant to knock me out; I'm fighting my own urge to breathe. I land a kick in the nuts and hear him yelp, then they both shove me into the back of car. "HEEEEEELP!" I yell when they pull a black hood over my head and pitch black darkness descends.

My breath leaves me from the shock as they shut the doors. I feel one of the men tighten the bag lightly around my throat, securing it. My panting breaths echo in my ears, blackness engulfing me as the reality of my situation begins to sink in and my eyes begin to sting. Hands start cupping my breasts and kneading while another jams a hand to feel me up under my lovely summer dress, and I start fighting with renewed vigor, screaming and hearing the lonely, muffled sounds of my own screams dying inside the hood covering my face. I can't hear things they're saying, whispering, as I start to flail with my arms and legs, gritting my teeth as I try hitting them, hitting anything I can.

". . . little feisty one . . . let's have our fun with her before we deliver . . ."

My dress is pulled high and I kick and squirm as they start the car, whimpering when a pair of hands grabs my thighs and forces them open.

"Just drive, we'll stop on the way there and take turns with her."

The car seems to jerk forward and, just as immediately, it stops.

"SHIT."

I hear this word clearly.

"What?"

I also hear the alarm in that question very, very clearly.

"FUCK, MAN."

The hands stop touching me, and for some reason I fall still, sensing that something is happening.

"Who the fuck is he? One of Slaughter's men?"

"There's two."

Before anyone can answer that, there's the sound of a tire popping, then another tire wheezing out air. I hear three clean shots, then another to my right, which seems to pop open the door handle. Hinges creak as the door seems to be wrenched off. The only hand that remained on my breast, frozen from the shock, is yanked away and I hear a scared yelp and a crunching sound, like bone breaking.

"Hoooooly shit, it's really you!"

I hear a crack, a howl, then the sound of a body hitting the ground.

"I'll take him somewhere nice and cozy so we can have a little chat," a Texan voice drawls from farther away.

Panicked, I'm feeling around with my hands and just as I find something hard and metallic in the jeans of the dead weight next to me, a pair of hands reaches out for me. As I feel new hands start curling around me, a bolt of adrenaline kicks through me. The hilt of a knife—I seize it and swing, and, miracle of miracles, I manage to plunge it into hard male flesh with a sickening jerk on my end. He growls over the top of my head and as he lets go of me to remove it, I push and stumble out of the car, finding my footing on the ground. The knife clatters to the ground the second I start running, trying to pull off the ties on my hood, hoping I'm running in the opposite direction from the new arrivals.

"You got a live one all right, Z," the Texan drawls.

I squeak when I realize I'm heading straight for him and swing around when I'm swept up in a pair of strong male arms. My fight starts instantly but this guy won't have it. He grunts when I kick his nuts, then starts to secure my hands and my legs with some sort of rope material, swiftly, so that I can't escape. I kick in the air but he's strong and fast, and what several men couldn't do to subdue me, this one does in less than a minute.

Binding my ankles and wrists, then binding my knees together and my elbows together, he holds me against a chest that feels muscular and broad as he carries me somewhere. Adrenaline rushes through my body with nowhere to go and I'm seized with tremors when I realize I'm so fucked and I have no way to get free.

I think I cut the man, and his blood is dripping on me. I squirm in my last futile effort to get free but I'm crying too, the sound of my own sniffles echoing inside the hood.

And suddenly I know what this is. It's that *debt*.

It's so real now, these men are so real. They wanted their money. But supposedly I have a month and a half left. Did they grow impatient? Did they plan to kill me or just use me? Were they delivering me to that one-eyed guy and the skinny one who offered to give me an "extension" of their dicks when I asked for more time to pay?

"I'm . . . I'm getting the money," I say, catching a sob in my throat.

I must be going into shock because I can't seem to fight him, to fight for my life, am trembling uncontrollably. I feel a new soreness in my thighs and calves when I feel a leather glove against the bare skin of my back. I whimper and I am so shocked when I remember Greyson and my Brazilian wax and my spa day, now I smell like pig, and like blood, and other men, and I start choking back sobs that all this could really be happening to me.

"M-my car is . . ."

He keeps walking, and I can't talk well, am panting for air and sniveling.

"My-my dress . . ."

He stops, then I hear plastic shuffling and I realize he picked it up in lord-knows-what condition from wherever it fell.

"Thank you," I snivel. Then I realize, he's not a good guy, he doesn't want to help me! If he did, he'd have let me go.

An uncontrollable shaking takes over my body, making my teeth chatter. He straps me into the backseat of a car that smells remarkably like the lavender sachet I put in my car after it almost became a boat and the tires screech as we leave.

We end up parking somewhere, and once again, we're in movement, pauses, movement, stealthy, as though he moves and stops, not to be seen. We climb some stairs, and I hear a crack of a window. We keep walking. Then I hear running water.

He sets me down somewhere soft, which I think is my bed, and unfastens the binding on my wrists, his gloves rubbing against my pulse points. I close my eyes and pretend it's another glove, from another man, comforting me, but the fact that he's not really that other man makes my misery all the more intense.

He mechanically starts freeing my legs, then rubs the wounds again around my ankles.

"P-please don't hurt me . . . !" I cry, kicking then calming down when he eases back. "Is it because of the money . . . ? I'll get the money, I'm getting the money," I start rambling. "My car is up for sale, I just haven't had takers and owe half of it anyway, so I need just a little more . . . !"

He does something unexpected. He reaches for my hand and gives me a squeeze. Not an angry squeeze, a reassuring squeeze. I fall quiet. My heart skids as he keeps his hand on mine for a moment too long, until he seems to be sure I'm breathing right. He lets go. I feel his footsteps and the creak of my window, and suddenly I reach up and scramble to remove the hood.

I'm in my apartment. The shower water is running. He left . . . through the balcony and emergency stairs?

There's blood on me. There's blood all over me as I slide into the tub, fully dressed, and take a bath, scrubbing myself clean. Quietly crying. I went to beg those awful men for more time, and they gave me some, but I'm running out of time again. Why on earth did I ever think I could make a stupid bet and not get involved with these kinds of people? I think about asking someone for help, but I'm too proud to. I'm too proud to tell my best friend, my friends, I'm too proud to tell my parents who think I'm perfect and can do no wrong. And Greyson. For some reason thinking about him makes me most sentimental of all. He makes me feel so safe, like he could protect me from the world. Even from men like these.

But I'm too proud to let the only guy I've had a connection with know about this. He probably doesn't like me that much anyway. *No.* It's never like that for me. I cry quietly in the tub, feeling so dirty I never, ever want to get out.

ELEVEN

KILL

Greyson

"FUUUUCK!"

These bastards want to play around? Touch what's mine? Then they better all. Be fucking ready. *To die.* Whoever sent these four to retrieve her, whoever made the call, they're dead. And as for the asshole C.C. brought back with us to the warehouse? I'm going to motherfucking kill him, tear him apart, limb by limb.

Hissing in pain, I stick my bleeding upper arm into running water, my eyes burning from the rage, the impotence, the pain of knowing what they were about to do to Melanie tonight.

I couldn't even fucking talk to her. I couldn't even tell her it was going to be all right. Because of the list, because of Zero, because he can't be known out of the Underground; so I had to hold her in my arms and hear her sobs. I had never, ever held a crying woman before. Hear her beg me to please not hurt her, only adding fire to my already roiling gut. They were going to . . .

Goddammit, I can't even think.

I stare at the mirror in the dingy warehouse restroom, nostrils flaring, my face pale from blood loss, my eyes brilliant with that cold gleam of death. I look deranged. I feel deranged. I pull the mirrored cabinet open and search for bandages, things clattering to the ground when I find nothing.

I press a towel tighter to the wound and try to knot it, all while unable to tame the urge to kill rushing in my blood.

I haven't had a drop of real humanity in me since my mother left. But despite my upbringing, I wanted to tear that dirty hood off Melanie's head, wipe her tears, look into her eyes, and command her to stop crying because it does something to destabilize me. And command her to stop shaking because it makes me shake in rage. And promise her that it's going to be all right and the next time she's touched, it will be by a man who wants to please her more than himself. Most ridiculous of all is that somewhere in my twisted mind, that man is me.

C.C. stalks into the bathroom of the small warehouse where he brought the sole survivor of our encounter.

"Where the fuck is he?" I yell.

"Hell, you've looked better. We need to stitch you up, man."

I follow him outside to where the group of girls who usually trail after C.C. is gathered around. "Get a needle," I tell the one I see first, then I kick a chair out from a plastic table and lean over to talk to C.C., just me and him. "Tell me he at least fucking spilled something?"

C.C.'s eyebrows furrow low. "He doesn't seem to know who hired him."

"What about the others?"

"I stashed the bodies. Just the lucky survivor will be getting a visit from you."

"I wouldn't call him lucky." I scan our surroundings, wondering who could be after her, and why.

My father, Eric, any of the guys. Is there a hit on her? Is this my father dabbling in his own affairs after he gave me his word? Was this a warning from one of my own "loyal" brothers-in-arms?

My arm is so numb, I can't feel it, but my skin is sticky and warm with blood and I'm so frustrated I want to kick something.

By all that's holy in the world, if my father's behind this, I will kill him.

I'm battling with my emotions as the brunette comes back with the needle to stitch me, and she brings a bottle of alcohol.

"Well, well, now, looks like I'll have my hands on you after all," she purrs. "What have we got there?"

I extend my arm as she opens the bottle of alcohol.

"It's a nick from my girl," I growl. "She doesn't like it when I don't call." I don't want to remember how she was sobbing and I wanted to rip off that hood . . . and do what? Reveal myself to her? Can't do that.

The girl pours the alcohol over the wound and I bite back my reaction, gritting out, "Make it nice and tight. Small." I tear a piece of my T-shirt and bite down on it and don't make a sound, watching as she sews me up.

"She did good. For a princess," C.C. tells me.

I'm in pain, and I'm still fucking fuming. I clench my teeth around the cloth.

A redhead comes and sits on my lap as her friend bandages me. "Oh, Z, we were so worried." She licks her lips. "What do you need?"

"Mindy," I say, spitting out the cloth. "That's your name, right?"

She nods eagerly.

"Mindy, I've been teaching my girlfriend how to shoot her new gun. I don't think she'd appreciate you sitting here."

"Oh." She eases off me.

"Come here, darling, I'll give you a long, slow petting now." C.C. edges his legs open and makes room for Mindy, eyeing me. "Girlfriend, huh? She know about it yet?"

"I'm informing her tomorrow." I turn my attention to my best friend now. "C.C.—this could be coming from the Underground. This could have something to do with that fucking debt." I tighten the bandage just a little more. "I need her name scratched off ASAP and I think I know how."

"Well, you can't let Slaughter know you so much as thought to buy her a paper or he'll fuck with you, man. He'll make her disappear just like he did Lana."

"Don't you think I fucking know that? No. I need her to have the means to pay without her ever sensing it."

Stalking to the small bar, I pour myself two fingers of whiskey and drink, gazing at the path of my own blood on the floor. She's too good for this, but now she's involved. Now she's more than a name on my list. She's on somebody's blacklist and I am one pissed-off motherfucker here.

"Whoever it is, they fucked with the wrong girl." I toss back the whiskey and pop some Vicodin back with it.

"Ah, god, I'm vastly entertained by the look on your face. I'm almost sorry for our guest."

"Take me to him." As I follow C.C., I ask him to get me a plane ticket to my apartment in D.C. for early morning. "Make sure I'm back by six so I can make the wedding."

❤ ❤ ❤

THERE ARE THREE types of knives for throwing. Blade heavy. Handle heavy. Or balanced. Grip and angle are most important. Long range, you keep your wrist unbent when you throw so the knife won't turn too much in air. Mine hardly turns, it shoots straight ahead. I used to practice on cardboard cereal boxes, then willow, birch, pine slab, hanging in the wind. Now there's a man before me and I know exactly how to shift my weight from my dominant leg to the other to create momentum, how to swing my fore-arm, elbow straight out on my release. It's not about strength, but about finesse. Little force is needed. The knife gathers strength on its own.

If you hit with the butt, you don't change the force, only allow more or less rotation by standing back or forward. I have all this science behind my technique and I've never been more ready to apply it.

He's tied to a chair, at a small corner room in the warehouse. One light flares bright over his head. He's bleeding and swelling, but the sight of his blood isn't enough to give me satisfaction.

He looks at me, I look at him.

His trembling increases, and it pleases me. Immensely.

I start approaching, keeping my voice low. "Who hired you?"

"I'm n-not talking, like I told your ff-friend."

I pull open my knife roll and shoot, grazing his temple. He yelps, and I keep throwing until knives are stuck into the wall all around him, outlining his asshole face. Then I aim for the center of his thigh. It hits.

"*Fuck!* Another crazy fuck? I thought you were the good one!"

"I'm sorry to break it to you, but you already met the good one." I don't even fake a smile, I feel nothing for this mother-fucker. Not even pity. I pull out another knife and test its tip. "I'm the guy whose girl you just fucked with, so I'm making this extra painful. I'll be taking a little piece of your skin, one throw at a time. One ball at a time, a piece of your dick at a time. I'll draw it out, make it slow and painful, until you tell me who hired you."

I hit him in the tip of one finger, pinning him there. He cries out. I smile and pull out my next knife.

"Was she a surveillance?" I ask.

A lot of contracts begin as surveillance and end up as some-thing else. I hit his next finger. He cries out and stains his pants.

"Was this ransom, kidnapping?"

He's choking on sobs. I hear the faint sounds of traffic outside. I hear her, my big dreamy green eyes, sobbing under a fucking black hood and I clamp my jaw and send one knife that lands straight in the center of his palm. "WHO'S YOUR BOSS?" I demand.

The blood's pouring now; but I won't stop until the words start pouring too. Just when he's falling asleep, numb from the pain, I quietly command C.C., "Music please. We won't be sleeping tonight."

❤ ❤ ❤

Four hours later

I DON'T HAVE a name.

I have a shitload of anger, a ton of fucking frustration, no sleep, some pain. But *no fucking name.*

We don't know if she has a mark on her, whose target she is. I need her off that list, and fast.

How will your pride take it if I give you the money, princess?

Will you throw it back at my face?

You will, won't you?

Hell, I know you will . . .

Stepping into my apartment, I'm still hung up on the glimpse I got of her in bed, sleeping with a mountain of pillows on both her sides as I left her dress on the knob of her bedroom door.

She looked exquisite. Fuckable. Vulnerable. And I stood there, the blood rushing faster in my body, my cock throbbing as much as my patched-up biceps and the left side of my chest.

Now I open up the safety deposit box and nearly yank the handle off its center. Some of our debtors are in so far they have to pay in barter. Watches, gold, jewels. Sometimes we keep "scraps" for bribing officials, anyone who gives us any trouble in any undertaking. Sometimes my father won't take the scraps and I'm forced to provide the cash while I pawn, sell, or otherwise.

I grab a brilliant diamond necklace from one of the extras I've collected. Once, I thought my mother would enjoy wearing it. Now I hope, instead, that Melanie will enjoy selling it.

I've got that sweet little girl pegged, even if she's a complicated little thing. In her fun little brain, it probably never occurred to her that she would lose her bet. She must've pictured new shoes and wardrobes in her future, and maybe, to finalize the payment for her car. Instead, now she owes her life to the Underground. To my father. To *me*. We have a highly elaborate team for bookkeeping and collecting all debts, organizing the fights, selling the tickets. The tamer "Underground Committee" handles the tickets and the fight organization. But it is the Slaters who handle the gambling and the funding—the collecting, and the things nobody else should ever know about.

If Melanie is like any woman I know, she'll accept a gift from her new pursuer then say someone stole the necklace rather than tell me the truth. That she sold it to pay a debt. And that's all right, she can lie about this. I'm lying to her too. We'll be even. She'll have paid her debt, learned her lesson, and won't ever have to know I'm part of her nightmare.

And I won't ever have to see those green eyes of hers stare at me in horror like my mother's did.

TWELVE

WEDDING

Melanie

I wake up to find my red dress hanging on the knob of my bedroom door, facing me. I blink and terror spins through me as I realize he was here. In my bedroom.

"Is anyone here?" I cry, pulling my sheets to my neck.

Silence. I leap out of bed and race to slam open all my doors, hard—in case there's someone hiding behind them. I'm exhausted by the time I've gone around my apartment like some deranged person. Sagging against the wall, I let my eyes scan my dress. It's perfect. No mark on it. It even has the dry cleaner's stamp. My arm trembles as I touch the silk, snippets from last night flashing across my mind. *Hands. Blood. Tears.*

Seems like we both survived, my dress and I—but I'll die before I sleep at home tonight. I'll make Pandora invite me over for a couple of days, or I will spend the night at a hotel, alone.

God, but I don't want to be alone.

I want another night with Greyson. I have lain in my bed for two weeks remembering that night we were together, and what I feel for him is so far beyond wanting, it feels like a needing. A hungering. I want his arms and his mouth. I want his heat and the look in his eyes to make me forget that I have bruises on my thighs, in my pride, and in my heart.

Exhaling, I hurry into my bathroom, lock the door, fill up my tub, and remind myself my best friend is getting married today.

After my bath, I rub myself with coconut-almond oil, slide on my sleekest thong, my red dress, some turquoise heels, a thick yellow wristband—at least three colors on me, which always makes me feel good—and I hurry over to Brooke's place, telling myself to *stop* wondering if I'll really have a date, if I'll ever pay the debt, if I'll ever have a good night's rest again. Today it's all about my best friend's wedding and I am *going* to enjoy this day.

I've dreamed and dreamed of this for Brooke even before she knew she wanted it herself, and the moment Remington Tate leapt out of the Underground ring and asked for her number, I felt butterflies on her behalf and immediately gave him the number myself. Brooke would have never given it to him otherwise.

Now she's as in love as I never imagined she'd be. She's covered in white and I've just shooed the men to the church—because there's no way in hell I'm letting Remy and Brooke start with any bad luck on their side. The groom just cannot see the bride in her dress until the wedding.

Grudgingly, they left, though Remington did not look pleased about it. Now big ole Josephine, the bodyguard turned nanny-bodyguard, and I are helping add the last crystal flowers to Brooke's hair as we wait for Brooke's mother and sister to arrive.

"Whose turn to hold Racer? He just drooled on my dress and I don't want him puking on it too," Nora says, nodding in the direction of a little dark spot on the bodice of Brooke's dress.

Dropping her gaze, Brooke studies the stain and rubs it with her thumb, a weary disappointment showing on her face.

"Brooke, your guy won't even notice the spot, I guarantee! Hand Racer over to me!" I demand as I grab little Racer and set him on my lap, rubbing my lips over the top of his round little head. He smells like talc and slaps his arms all over the place.

Brooke is busy texting the groom and glancing ahead. "I swear, this traffic," she groans.

"It's not like he won't wait for you," I squeak excitedly before handing Racer to his grandmother, who goos and ahs all over him, and I go and switch seats and try to hug Brooke even through all the tulle of her skirt. "Brookey, Remy was waiting for you all his life! He'll wait ten more minutes, trust me."

Brooke points a finger at me. "Don't you say anything to make me cry," she warns, discreetly patting the corners of her eyes.

I nod with a grin, but my windpipe tightens when I take her hand and squeeze it.

She's my best friend. I'm an only child.

I have Pandora, my goth friend who's my opposite—negative, sarcastic, and dark, and who I love. But Brooke is Brooke, and there's only one for me. Brooke won't be staying in Seattle because the nature of her husband's work demands he goes on tour with the fighting league, and this moment is a very emotional one for me. Nobody ever thinks about the best friend when the bride is getting married. But right now, I'm so happy I could burst, and, at the same time, as miserable as I could be. First because I will miss her, and second because since I was a little girl, I've always wanted to be draped in white and to have the kind of groom she has waiting for her at the altar, madly in love with me, ready to protect me, spend the rest of his life with me.

Instead, I've never gotten through a month of dating anyone.

Instead, last night I was almost . . . *God, don't think about it now.*

Brooke steps out of the car and I'm glad for the distraction of getting her ready to enter. I told her that since Pete, Remy's PA, is the best man and also Nora's boyfriend, she should just ask her sister to be maid of honor. Who wants Nora scowling at her for the rest of her life anyway? Not me.

So I'm the proud bridesmaid along with Pandora, who's also in red for probably the first time in her life. Not that she seems happy about it, but that's nothing new.

As I walk behind Brooke into the church, I see *him.* By the door. And my legs turn mushy under my dress.

Greyson. He wears this really nice black suit as easily as he wears his self-confidence. God. It's almost as if those nearby sway toward him.

I almost can't handle the tug of his magnetic presence. He doesn't know that just standing there, dark and powerful by the wide church entrance, he's rescuing me from my thoughts and my fears and my loneliness, which yesterday felt as absolute as night. After twenty-five years of not being good enough, in the eyes of this man, I am. I am desirable. I am worth being here. What I feel is odd and exciting. Raw and gritty, precious and fragile. He doesn't know the sight of him curls like warmth inside me, warming me in secret places, taking my fears away. My mind is on a one-track speed all of a sudden.

He came.

And by the way he levels those fierce hazel eyes on me, he's not going anywhere. Not without . . . me.

During the ceremony, I start crying. I don't expect to, but the fear of last night mingles with the much-wanted fact that the guy I want is *here* for me, all of that mingled with the low, rough words of my best friend's boyfriend pledging his life to her.

I hate that I'm ruining my makeup but as I stand by and hear my best friend pledge her vows to one of the most protective, sexy, and kind men I know, I remember how it was me who told her, DO IT! Go after him! I remember it was me who said, have an adventure, live your life, come on, Brooke, it's REMINGTON FUCKING TATE, nobody says no to the guy!

Now I feel a pair of narrowed hazel eyes on my profile, and when I steal a look his way, that possessive look he wears couldn't be improved on by the devil himself. My heart squeezes as I try to stop crying, telling myself that at least for tonight, I'm going to be safe. I will *feel* safe. Because he doesn't look like he's letting me go anywhere without him.

God, I could've died yesterday.

I could die tomorrow.

I've always lived my life in the moment, but always planning and waiting for my perfect future. What if there is none? I don't care what he's here for and suddenly nothing matters but that I know what I want tonight.

I sniffle and wipe my tears, then meet his gaze almost imploringly, my tummy aching when he returns my stare with one that tells me so much more than simply *I'm going to do you*. There's concern in his gaze, but there's fire, simmering in there, promising to burn me in the most delicious way. He's here because he wants me. He craves me and I crave him back. I crave the man I met that night in the rain, the one who wouldn't let me get wet and quietly asked about me as he kissed me all night. The one who came back to see me and asked for another chance. His magnetism just pulls at me, the pull irresistible. *Unprecedented.*

And as the vows are exchanged in the chapel, I make a vow to myself. I vow that whatever this thing is between him and me—a fling, a catastrophe, the worst call of my life—tonight I'm going with it. I'm diving in, and I'm following my gut, my heart, and every single tingle in my wanting body or my fucking name is not fucking Melanie.

THIRTEEN

TONIGHT

Greyson

The ceremony takes a million fucking years.

I stand here armed with my SIG semiautomatic, just over two pounds of steel, but my cock feels twice as heavy and my chest ten times as much. I'm like week-old roadkill. Seeing her crying yesterday wrung me out. Now her gaze is stripped naked of emotion as she seeks me out in the crowd, and I can't even process how I feel.

From the moment she stepped out of the limousine with the bride, I groaned at the sight of her. I'm still raging with the impulses to get close to her, touch her, smell her.

Melanie's a bundle of contradictions in a bridesmaid's dress. All smiles, but snapping out orders like a general. I watched her pull the train of the bride's dress behind her so it "looked pretty" while a dark-haired girl with a frown passed a set of flowers to the bride. Melanie avoided looking at me. Maybe on purpose, maybe not.

Now that the vows are done, I'm on the sidewalk outside the church, impatient. There's a chorus of people around, but above their noise, I can hear her laugh. I turn my head and see the priest saying something that delights her. God, I want to kiss that fucking laugh to silence. Then I want to do something to wake it up again so it trails into my mouth, where I can trap it. Taste it. Play with it.

When a group starts to gather around the limousine, I don't waste another minute. I close the distance between us, stopping a mere two inches behind her, taking a moment to enjoy the fetching picture she makes: loose hair tumbling over her shoulders, tight red silken dress down to her ankles, the open back dipping in a V that ends almost at the start of her round, perky ass.

"Are you deliberately ignoring me?" I murmur, sliding my hand around her waist.

"No." She smiles down at the sidewalk as she tucks her hair behind her ear.

I drop my head until my lips are almost grazing that ear. "Good, because I'm not someone you ignore." Using my grip on her waist, I pull her back against my front. I'm testing the limits, glad that instead of making any sort of protest, she leans against me.

Good fucking sign, King.

Fuck, now I'm itching for more. Taking her by the elbow, I ease her away from the crowd and tuck her into an alcove near the entrance to the church.

Her breathing's heavy, and that's an even better sign. *She wants you too, she wants you just like you want her.*

I push her up against the stone wall using my body. Her breasts press against my chest, her thighs against mine. A low groan gets trapped in my throat as I slide my lips over the lids of her eyes. To say I'm starved is an understatement. I wish I had ten hands—two are just not enough as I run my palms up her sides, fingers cupping her butt and then pinning her to my hips so I can feel her, alive and perfect, safe and untouched.

She nuzzles my throat and takes a deep breath as if she craves my scent. I squeeze her against me, feeling her shiver in my arms.

I'm highly trained.

I can sense fear, arousal, excitement.

But the mixture I seem to produce in her intoxicates me more than anything ever has. I bring her tighter to me. A gasp leaves her lips, and it takes everything in me not to bend my head and take it. *No.* When I take those red-painted lips, I'm not stopping until she's naked beneath me and I'm as deep as a curse inside her.

Tonight, I vow to myself.

I reach into my suit coat and pull the necklace I brought her out of a velvet bag.

"What is this?" She peers down at my fist.

I let her open my hand, and she looks down at the diamond necklace in my palm. It's a high-quality tennis diamond necklace, simple yet extraordinary. Like her. "Something for my girl," I murmur.

"Your girl?"

I lift the necklace and hook it around her neck.

"It's too much, Greyson, I can't take it," she protests.

"I can't take it back and it's not my size." I run my knuckles up her throat, and it's warm and silky. "Besides, it's meant for a queen, a princess."

I adjust the sparkling strand so it rests against her collarbone, just beneath the flutter of her pulse point. I'm tempted to bend my head and slide my tongue in there. Hell, I'm tempted to do more. I dip my finger into the little crook instead, touching her pulse and lifting my eyes to hers. "Melanie, when you're waiting for me to call," I stroke the pad of my thumb over the diamonds one more time, "look at these stones and know for certain that that phone *will* ring."

"Who are you?" she asks me, breathless and amazed.

My lips curl in a sardonic smile. "I'm the twisted version of your . . . Westley," I say, holding her gaze.

We hear shouts outside and realize the bride has thrown the bouquet in the air. Melanie rushes out while I'm left behind, struggling to get a grip of my Neanderthal. She's five feet and three inches of fun and she fills my entire being with shit I never intended to feel, let alone want.

I'm so fucking fucked.

I follow her into the crowd and stop right behind her, my front pressing against her back as I look down at her profile. Her nostrils flare. She's smelling me again. I remain in my place, letting her get accustomed to me. My size, my scent, my height, me. I reach out with my glove to touch her hair, and she trembles. I shift to stand right beside her, dragging the back of my fingers along her bare arm. She starts breathing faster, and I hear her stop breathing when I lace my fingers through hers in a way that tells her—*you're with me tonight.*

We watch the bride and groom ride away in their limousine, and Melanie waves them off without letting go of my hand. As the car disappears in the distance, she tips her pretty face up to me.

The diamonds look so stunning on her that for a moment I forget they serve a purpose other than to adorn her throat. They seem to mark her. Scream at me, *yours yours yours.*

"Looks like I don't have a ride anymore," she tells me.

Damned if I don't like that pout. "No worries, you'll be coming with me," I say.

"Mel! We have your car keys!" a man calls in our direction, keys jangling in the air. He walks them over and I can see he's the shit-faced blond dude who's been eye-fucking her since I got here. He glares at me in silence. I level him an even blacker look. *Keep glaring, asshole, I'm gonna be the one fucking her tonight.*

Melanie's dark-haired friend taps his elbow. "Riley, why don't you guys take Mel's car? She and her date can come with Kyle and me," she interjects. She gives me a warning look as though I should be concerned about this for some reason. Not intimidated, I nod my agreement.

As soon as we're in the backseat of the car, the girl speaks. "That's some bling you got there, Melanie."

"I know." Grinning happily, Melanie pokes her thumb in my direction.

"He *gave* that necklace to you?" The friend sounds shocked.

"Yes! And his name is Greyson, Pandora."

"Well! Greyson, will you be paying for the prescription glasses I'll need after the retinal damage I'll receive from all that bling?" she asks.

"Send me the bill," I easily respond.

"What's next? Are you going to tie her up and pick out safe words or what?"

I smile. "No. There's no word on earth that will make anyone safe from me."

"Haha. I'm glad your *boyfriend* is enjoying himself," Pandora tells Melanie, pronouncing the word "boyfriend" like one would pronounce the word "excrement." She returns her attention to me. "We're very protective of our Mel. She believed in Santa much, much longer than the rest of us. So tell us about yourself. You're like some Gatsby guy, with lots of money, but a very mysterious past. Kyle and I Googled you but couldn't find much. What are your intentions with our girl?"

"Pandora!" Melanie kicks the back of Pandora's seat. "Ignore my friend, Greyson," she tells me.

But the friend doesn't feel like ignoring me. She keeps peering past her shoulder at me. "Are you glad Melanie didn't catch the bouquet?"

"Why would he be?" Mel counters.

"Dude, judging by that bling, the man has no intention of marrying. Just fucking."

"Pandora!"

I laugh; I find it highly entertaining how protective this girl is. There's no doubt in my mind some fucking loser made her like this.

She shifts in the front passenger seat so she can fully face me. "Do you have a wife?" she persists.

"What?"

"Are you married? Are you gay? What's wrong with you?"

Well, let's see now. Currently, she's what's wrong here. I could stare her down easy, but why stare at this Bitter Betty when I have princess beside me?

"Pandora, you're totally ruining my evening!" Melanie kicks the back of her seat again then shifts over to face me. She looks delicious, all in red. I feel like the Big Bad Wolf, staring hungrily at those kiss-me lips and those highly dangerous, innocent green eyes. "Is she right? Are you playing with me?" she asks me curiously.

I don't know what it is about her, but the way she looks at me makes my cock start thickening. It's my natural response to her. I can probably help it as much as I could help killing for her last night, which is not at all. No matter how much in control, you can't command your instincts. Sometimes they command you.

I've only ever killed for one other person in my life.

The difference is, I felt no remorse last night. I wouldn't change what I did for Melanie last night. I'd do it all over again, kill the first three just as fast, torture the fourth one just as slow. Hell, even slower if I could've prolonged it. In fact now, the reminder of her soft, helpless cries under the hood twist a knife of fury in my chest.

One hand curling around her waist, I drag her closer to me and whisper in her ear, "I'm not playing with you."

Christ.

I'm being serious here.

As serious as I've been about anything in my life.

"Be honest," she whispers back.

"I'm not playing with you," I repeat.

We're being watched from the front of the car, so fuck that. In one move, I pull her over to sit on my thigh and lower my head to her. She smells so fucking sweet and juicy I want to bury my nose and find the source of her scent. I rub my nose along the back of her ear, turned on by her nearness, her shape, her smell, her.

She trembles, and my muscles pull taut in response.

What are you doing to me, my sweet, lovely number five?

I reach out with my thumbs and force her eyelids to close so she won't see me. So she won't stare right at me with those fucking green eyes that scream *save* and *keep* and *do* me, and I whisper in a voice roughened with lust, "When I'm not with you, I think about the next time every inch of you will belong to me. I play games and I play them hard and I play them dirty, but if you're a game, princess, then you're the first fucking game that's ever played back with me."

She opens her eyes. Those fucking DO me, LOVE me eyes.

Her friend Pandora is quiet now, and the car crackles with Melanie's pull to me, and mine to her.

Hell, I've played nice with the friends for a while now, but I don't do nice for long. It's just not in me.

I rap the roof of the car. "Drop us off here."

"Here? It's the middle of nowhere."

"I insist."

With a dramatic sigh, he pulls over at the curb next to an empty lot across from a dark apartment building complex. I help Melanie out, then I grab the roof of the car with my good arm and lean in to tell Pandora, "Happy her friends are genuinely concerned for her. I'm not perfect, but on my word, no one will hurt her when she's with me."

She shoots me a quiet glare and her friends drive off.

"She hates men, don't worry about her." Apparently trying to soothe me, Melanie grins up at me and brushes a hand over the flat of my shirt.

I take her wrist in my hand, the move instinctive, to keep people at a distance. "Cheerful is the last of my worries. You hungry?"

I squeeze her wrist and notice how sleek and small it is in the circle of my fingers, then I realize she's the only thing I allow myself to touch without a glove. And she feels good. Real. Warm. How can something so fucking vulnerable have a pull so strong on me? I want to run my hand beneath the jacket and touch all of her, her collar, up her throat and upward, so I can cup that sweet, vibrant face in my hand and squeeze it and kiss the shit out of it. My voice roughens when I whisper, "Don't eat that lip, I'll take you somewhere."

She lets go of that lip as I slowly release her wrist, then we stay there, staring at each other with hardly any city lights around. The diamonds glitter on her neck like her eyes shine in her face. She wraps her arms around herself and I keep my eyes on her as I text Derek, and we walk down the block toward the corner, my gaze glued to her profile. I'm not good at conversation with women—I fuck them, pay them, get rid of them. I want to talk to her and at the same time, I know I should be running from her.

I laugh softly because I never knew I could be so awkward in any situation, and I cover her in my suit jacket. It's not cold, but that dress makes me want to devour her. Derek picks us up in a silver SUV then drops us off at one of those twenty-four-hour restaurants that have bad breakfasts, bad lunches, and bad dinners, but it seems to be the only choice to hit up nearby.

I lead Melanie to a booth in the back, one where our backs are covered and I can see the door and every entry. She eases out of my coat and sets it aside, opposite where I sit.

We sit close.

But not close enough.

While we view our menus, I can't resist myself. I lower my hand under the table, to her thigh. She stares at her menu, but I can see her breath quicken when I start to rub my finger higher into her thigh.

"What do you like to eat?" I ask her, watching her bite her lip again.

"I like what's bad for me. Doesn't everyone? A little alcohol. A lot of chocolate and nuts. But I force-feed myself a ton of vegetables to counteract the bad stuff with good. One positive and a negative . . . kind of thing." Her eyes meet mine, and they're dancing playfully. "And you?"

I want to feast on nothing but your mouth, your tits, your pussy, and that fucking lip you're torturing with your teeth, teeth I want to feel rasping along my cock.

"I'm a fan of international foods. Anything. Thai, Chinese, Mexican, Japanese, I like different tastes. I enjoy being . . . surprised when it comes to my palate. I like spices."

"Do you come into the city for work?"

"Sometimes."

"What do you do for work?" The genuine interest in her eyes makes me feel like a fucking douche bag.

"Security." I slap my menu shut. "In my father's company."

"Really now? How interesting! I wouldn't peg you for a man who worked with his father. With anyone, actually."

My lips curl in amusement as I signal for the waiter, then raise one eyebrow in question at her. "You mean to say you don't believe I can play well with others?"

"You just give off the impression of separateness."

"Do I?"

There she goes again, biting that damn lip. "It's intriguing."

"You give the impression of playfulness and comfort. I find that intriguing too."

She grins, a sheepish grin that can't quite conceal the way her emerald green eyes flood with feminine delight. Maybe I don't grin like she does, but trust me, I'm just as delighted with her. Once we order, she looks at me and plays with a yellow cuff bracelet on her arm.

"My work is my passion. I'm absolutely obsessed with colors. I can't leave the house without wearing at least three different colors. Two is too simple. One is absolutely drab and I don't want to be drab."

I find myself laughing again, something which seems to come naturally around her. "No way you're fucking drab. In fact, right here, sitting with you, I feel gray."

Her smile flashes the instant mine does, and we laugh until our drinks are set before us, and she sips from her straw.

"I like this," she says with a long sigh of intense pleasure as she sits back in relaxation. She takes an even longer look at me. "It feels like a date. And it feels like forever since I've had one of those."

In my peripherals, I just noticed that Derek sat at a table nearby, across from C.C.

"It *is* a date. You invited me to your friend's wedding. That's a date in my book."

"I did *not* invite you. I said you could *come* . . ."

"And we both know how much we love me *coming*."

She smiles wickedly, and it does nothing to calm my raging libido. I can tell she likes it when I'm bad. She likes bad boys.

Fuck, princess, you don't know I'm the baddest of the bad, I think and then, another thought, *Hell, I'm not a bad boy, I'm a bad man!*

It brings me down a little to realize I'm no good for her.

"Come on, admit it," I press her, reviving myself with the playful glint in her eye. "I came, I conquered—at least getting you out to dinner makes me feel like a conqueror—and I even survived your angry black-haired friend."

"Pandora." She laughs. "But she's right asking about these, these are too much, more than I'm worth."

She absently strokes the necklace on her throat, and I whisper, a warning, "Melanie."

"Greyson . . ."

Hell, I can see the seeds of doubt her friend planted almost spinning in her little head. I keep my voice level, low even, but stern.

"Do whatever you want with the necklace. Just don't return it to me."

Swear to god, if I could only telepathically send this woman the damn message to do what any smart girl bent on survival would.

She may wait, but when the time dwindles, she'll do it. I *expect* her to. Hell, when she's spent enough time with me, she'll be sick of me and anything of mine and she'll dump it faster than she can say Greyson.

The thought makes my gut heat up in anger.

My hand edges higher up her thigh. This urge to touch her eats at me. I'm always gloved, but tonight my gloves are in one of my suit pockets and my hands are bare—and I can't stop devouring the sensation of having her smooth skin under my fingers and palm.

She twirls her straw as if she wants something to do, but most important of all, she knows exactly where my hand is and makes no move to remove it. "My best friend, whose wedding you just saw . . . When we were young, I used to be Barbie and she was Skipper whenever we played. I always used to get Ken. It just seemed that she wasn't interested in Ken, so I used to make sure he was all *mine*. She didn't even want to fall in love. I wanted to be happy, carefree, and fall in love one day, and she wanted the Olympics. But she was the one who ended up falling in love, hard, you know? The real thing. The real man. I could not be happier, she could not deserve it more. But now you look at me like her husband looks at her . . ." She lifts her eyes to me and absently rubs a pink fingernail up her glass. "But you're not my husband, you're not in love with me. What do you want?" She holds my stare with hers. "Pandora's right, you don't give something like this to just anyone. Men give diamonds to women they need to buy, or hide."

"And yet we're in plain view. I'd never hide something as beautiful as you."

She touches the rim of her glass with one fingertip, and I let my eyes drag up her lean, toned arm, down her body, my craving to have her growing fiercer and fiercer every second. "You look stunning in this dress, princess."

Her cheeks flare. "Thank you. I almost thought I couldn't wear it."

"You look lovely. The way your hair curls at the tips. I can't take my eyes off you and I can't wait to take that dress off you."

She drops her gaze to the table, biting on her smile.

I lean forward, testing my limits; pushing them. "We've been intimate. You're wearing my necklace. I have my hand on your thigh. Your friends have drilled the crap out of me. Why so shy?" When she just lets go of that delicious smile, I curl my index finger under her chin and tip her head back. "You been thinking about me?"

"You mean dwelling on and pining over the guy who didn't call?"

I cock a brow. "The man standing at the church, waiting for you to throw him a bone? That was me."

"Oh wow, thanks for clearing that up!" The delicate sound of her laugh makes me stone hard.

I slide my hand higher on her thigh, pulling up the silk of her dress so I can touch more bare skin. I am about to kiss her when a familiar face enters the diner. My eyes slide over to him and I ease back when C.C. makes a brief hand gesture to let me know he's on it.

Fuck me, I have no energy for any criminal bullshit tonight. I haven't slept in almost forty-eight hours. The knife cut on my biceps aches like a bitch, and I'm running on pure adrenaline here. As I wait for C.C. to make a sign that it's clear, Melanie picks at her salad, and the old familiar pattern of staying apart from the world settles over me.

"Thanks for coming to the wedding," she says, softly.

"My pleasure," I reply, low.

I can suddenly sense the distance between us like a ten-foot abyss, keeping me from making a connection.

"Why did you?"

My eyebrows fly up. "Why did I come?"

She nods, and I don't know anything else except that I still crave a connection with her. *Any* sort of connection. I'm stroking my longest finger up the creamy inside of her thigh, all the while watching the newcomer leave in my peripherals. "I came for you, Melanie."

"I have had a thousand one-night stands in my life, Greyson."

"I've had a thousand and *one*."

"Counting me?"

"No, princess. When we do this again . . . you're on a whole other list."

We stare, neither of us smiling, my eyes greedily taking in the quiet curiosity on her face, her long golden hair, the pretty small breasts jutting against the fabric of her silk dress, the tender curve of her shoulder, and Jesus, I want all of that more than she will ever know.

She sets her hand on my thigh. "What list?" She tilts her head and studies me. "What will this even be?"

The unexpected feel of her hand on my thigh sends a primal heat across my veins. One second we're talking, the next I catch her face and hold it still as I look into those green eyes, suddenly fierce as I study her small nose, her generous mouth. "For me, this is a fantasy. You're the fantasy. For you, this will be a mistake. A long, pleasurable mistake." I watch her eyes darken, and I've never been a man to mince words. "I'm going to be everything you never wanted," I warn on a gruff breath, "nothing that you need." I slide my other hand farther up her thigh. "Sometimes my work will take me away, and I won't call, and I'll piss you off." I graze my longest finger over the silky V covering her sex. "I'll be selfish. I'll take everything I want, whenever I want it. I'm not the man of your dreams, Melanie, I'm your worst nightmare."

Her eyes glaze, and she stops my hand from caressing her and presses her lips into my ear. "I'm not your fucking toy."

I catch her by the shoulders and pull her back to me. "But you'll let me play with you."

"If I wanted just sex, I could get that from anyone."

"Not the kind of sex you'll get with me." I push my thumb into her mouth, making her taste me. My whole body feels that lick. "I'll make you want it. I'll text you when I'm flying into town so you're twitching and soaked by the time you see me at your door."

She bites my thumb and drives me so wild with lust, I'm about to slam my mouth down on hers.

Fuck me.

Maybe I will never make a worthwhile connection to anyone in my life.

But I can have this—I can have her, her body, her wild, hot pleasure.

I can have *this*.

Oh, yes, I'm having this tonight.

I lean over, ready to take a long, juicy bite out of the lip that's been driving me crazy, when she stands. "You're an asshole," she whispers, panting. "Take me somewhere. Just for the night. Take me somewhere."

I peel a hundred-dollar bill from the stack in my pocket and set it on the table, slip my jacket over her shoulders, and usher her out.

FOURTEEN

WEEKEND

Melanie

We drive to an apartment in a high-end neighborhood so pricey and coveted that everyone where I work would whore themselves out for a decorating gig in this zip code. It's got a gated entry and high-level security on every entrance and exit. The apartment itself is covered in wall-to-wall windows, with limestone floors and stone fireplaces.

I take in the spacious, mostly empty space with one wide-eyed sweep, jaw hanging. "Did you just get a place in the city?" I hand him his coat, his gaze a delicious, palpable thing on me as I walk inside.

"You like it?" His voice holds no inflection, but something in his eyes tells me he *wants* me to like it.

I notice that the only furniture is one massive king mattress in the middle of the room, and the sight of those paperwhite sheets and plump pillows gives me tingles. Both of us. In that bed. Touching, kissing, *groping*.

The windows closest to the bed face toward my building and for a moment I wonder if he's noticed that, even if somewhat distant, my apartment faces this way.

"It's such a stunning space but so very empty!" I spread out my arms. "I can already visualize exactly what could go where. Dare I say you came to the right woman?"

"Dare I admit I'm not hiring your design services? I don't like clutter." And yet he looks amused by my offer—that *almost* grin I've come to really, really dig hovering on that full, dirty-talking mouth of his.

Oh god, I'm still so turned on by what a sexy asshole he is. He makes me want to slap him and fuck him; no man has ever pushed my buttons like this!

"How'd you know I was a designer?"

Arms crossed, plus that almost grin equals to me almost panting. "You're not the only one who can work Google."

"Pandora Googled you, not me."

"Right," he agrees.

I laugh because he's clearly on to me, then admit, "There was nothing on you. *Nothing.*"

"And there's quite a bit on you."

"Well, I can make this place come to life with a flick of my fingers! I'm like a Mary Poppins of decorating!"

"Princess, it's already alive with you in it."

Surprised by the compliment, I slide my eyes back to him, and the very way he stands there screams at me that he's someone, someone strong, someone you don't mess with, someone you want on your side. His dark clothes can't hide the muscles beneath, or the grace and virility with which he moves.

I can hardly stand looking at him without launching myself at him like a rocket—a haywire rocket on a permanent, pretty worrisome detour. I restlessly walk around the place, wondering if he's watching my ass as I move.

I let my hips sway even harder on purpose and head down the hall; he whistles to call me back.

"That room is off-limits."

"What? What do you mean?" He comes over and sets a hand on the small of my back, the very rough touch filling me with a sense of safety. "Do you realize that telling me that was an invitation to just try to pick this lock and find out?" I ask him.

"You won't be able to open it. I've got a mess of stuff there, nothing for a girl."

My interest piqued by this, I steer away from his hand and turn back to jiggle the doorknob. The door is steel, almost like a bank vault.

"Melanie," Greyson warns.

I laugh and back off. "Okay. That's your man cave, I won't go in. Don't look so worried."

"I'm not worried. You couldn't open that door with a chainsaw. What concerns me is your determination to do exactly what I told you not to."

"I'm curious!" I say, laughing again. My laugh, I can't explain it, but it seems to get to him. He looks hungry to quiet me with his mouth. When he licks his lips and scowls down at my mouth, the sudden memory of his mouth on mine zips through me, of my nipples against his tongue, and a shiver of anticipation bolts down my spine.

"Do you mind if I freshen up?" I blurt out.

"Babe, you're spring incarnate, but go ahead."

I shut the bathroom door behind me and lean against the sink. I can hardly breathe, the flutters are everywhere in me, from my head to my toes. He's a fucking asshole who openly admitted to probably just wanting to use me and I should've slapped him but instead, I'm going to fuck him because he makes me mad. Because he's responsible for an awful, insistent throbbing between my legs. All these weeks wondering what he wants from me, if he was coming tonight.

No matter what he says, he still *looks* at me the way he does—and the way he looks at me says other things. That he wants me. That he desperately wants, craves, maybe even needs me, like he said in my apartment that day.

I have *never* worn anything a man has given me. Now my throat is adorned with a line of sparkly white diamonds and I'd never imagined a gesture like this could stimulate my mind, my heart, and my body so much.

He wants to use me for sex tonight? Then I will use him back because it's killing me. The way he looks at me kills me. The way he smells, walks, the sound of his voice.

Tonight I'm not sleeping home alone no matter what happens.

Quickly, I wash my hands, under my armpits, and then I lift my dress and glance sadly at the bruises on my thighs. I pull out my makeup kit from my clutch bag and start covering the purple stains with my concealer, one by one.

When I'm done, I notice a towel with streaks of red and wonder if he cut himself. Shaving perhaps? A wave of protectiveness takes me over. Is he all right? *Of course he is, Melanie. That man is about as penetrable as his steel door.*

As I grip the doorknob, the steady pulse between my legs continues to throb. By the time I pull the door open and quietly cross the room toward the bed, my heart races at full speed.

I've never been to such a luxurious or empty apartment. He's like some Spartan, with no belongings. I glimpsed his closet and he has the same three shirts, the same three jackets, same three style of shoes. Like some sort of methodical superhero—and as if he doesn't plan to stay long?

A pang hits me at the thought, but it's quickly replaced with the bolt of lust I feel at the sight of him. He's leaning back in bed, one lean arm folded behind his head as he stares out the window.

Oh god, *why* do I like that so much? *Because he's staring at your building.*

The fact that he can see me from here might make me feel protected even when he never calls. Even if he will never look me up again. I need that little feeling of safety and I cling to it.

"Can you see my apartment from here?" I ask. I start pulling down the side zipper of my dress. He turns to me, and a twinkle of moonlight catches in his eyes as he watches me approach. My heart thuds. He has a massive, self-confident presence, and an air of authority that makes my knees wobbly. He's strong. Magnetizing. *Vital.* And he fills my whole being with crazy, wild wanting.

"Yeah, that's why I got this place."

I know he's joking, but the words are sober—he's looking straight into my eyes. "You'd think a player like you would have something better to do than stare out the window trying to get a glimpse of me," I tease.

"I do more than stare out the window, princess. It involves me taking off my gloves."

Bastard.

Fucking delicious bastard.

He's like riding a motorcycle at full speed. He feels like the engine, the ride . . . the wind . . .

I stop by the foot of the bed and I feel a ripple of excitement when I notice the way he watches me, his eyes shimmering like lightning.

"Strip me, or strip for me. Lady's pick." He speaks calmly and succinctly, making no move to yank me down on him.

Really now? So confident of this magnetic, electric pull, tugging me to him?

My gaze greedily runs up and down his thick legs, the bulge I'm mad over, up to his chest, which stretches the material of his snowy white shirt in the best possible way. Feeling heavy and warm, my pulse thundering in my veins, I crawl over him, his gaze boring into me with silent expectation.

"I think you're a bastard. But you're so sexy in this suit . . ." I whisper as I start working his belt off his slacks, straddling him so that if I wanted to, I could drop my hips and rub the most painful spot in my body against that big, delicious bulge on his lap. "And I want to fuck you hard because you made me think you were better, you made me think you wanted me for more than this," I add. "Asshole."

He grabs his belt when I pull it free, tosses it aside with a clatter, and then moves like lightning, rolling me to my back, and whipping out my arms to pin them over my head. I gasp, and he smiles. "Caught you," he rasps, sliding a hand down the inside of my arm. Starting to pant from the delicious weight of his body pressing down on mine, I wiggle my hand free, pull his shirt out of the waistband of his slacks, and start unbuttoning his shirt from the very bottom, hurrying to the top.

He releases my wrist and slowly pushes my dress up to my hips. "You have a filthy mouth, Melanie. Did you know that I can fill it with come, just like that, so the next sound you make is that of you swallowing?"

"Maybe the next sound is you yelling when I bite the head of your thick pink cock," I breathe and my thoughts scatter when he growls, "Shut up now," and kisses me. Hard and deliciously.

The actual next sound in the room is nothing but wet, slippery tongues meshing, rasping of fabric as he pulls my dress higher. I melt beneath his mouth, hot and powerful and more ravenous than any mouth that's ever fitted itself to mine . . . and it truly feels like all we've said means nothing, that this means everything.

His scent fills me like a warmth curling in my tummy as he hikes my skirt up to my waist to expose my lacy black thong. The air caresses my bare ass cheeks, and the next second, he's palming them in his warm hands.

"Are you happy to see me now, Melanie?" he murmurs, his voice low and textured as he uses my ass to draw me flat up against him.

I whimper, I'm so turned on. "Not yet," I lie.

He brushes his lips across mine, teasing me. "You sure?"

Once again, his lips make a pass over mine, warm, velvety.

My blood feels thick and hot in my veins. Suddenly I can't think of anything that I want more than this one, one kiss. But I can never let a man like him know it or he'll break me.

"I'm sure," I lie again, holding on to the back of his strong neck as I flick my tongue out to run it along the seam of his lips.

That lick proves to be our undoing.

He groans and comes out to play with my tongue with his, his lips closing over mine at the most perfect angle. A shudder runs through us both. It even feels like we groan at the same time, our kiss degrading from slow and sensual to fast and raw. I unbutton the rest of his shirt, my hands trembling from the rush. He grabs the top of my strapless dress and yanks it down to my waist, exposing every part of my body except for where the silk of my dress circles my hips.

When he edges back to look at my not-so-large breasts, but my rather outspoken nipples, I'm almost drowning with a sudden shyness.

It doesn't last long, for he cups the mounds, as if he were holding diamonds in his hands, paying extra attention to the beaded, hard little points at the tip. His thumbs pay extra attention to them, rubbing, stroking.

"You might not be happy yet," he rasps in my ear, "but these little beauties are thrilled to see me. Thrilled . . . to see me." When he sucks one into his mouth, an exquisite pleasure curls my toes.

My head falls back into his pillow as I moan, low in my throat. He rocks his hips to tease me with his erection. I'm teased, tortured, consumed, throbbing. I shudder and start rocking up to him too. God, he's going to torture me and I know it.

He tugs my dress over my head, then his hands explore my thighs and move onto my taut stomach, then up to tweak my nipples. My pussy burns and clutches as I slide my fingers through the parting of his shirt, running my hands up his warm, sculpted chest.

I stroke his scar, then use my thumb and forefinger to tug on his nipple ring. His body contracts with pleasure and I see it. I see how he responds to my touch, so I greedily run my hands up and down his chest, every possible muscle in existence bulging under my fingers.

"You like that?" I whisper.

I don't even let him answer because my mouth blends into his again as I push him around and straddle him. Lowering my body, I can feel his erection settled perfectly between my legs, straining hot and large against his zipper. God. Edging his shirt aside, I bend over and start licking his piercing, shivering when he slides the tips of his fingers into the elastic of my G string . . . dipping into the lace V.

"Come here, you hot little thing you," he murmurs as he holds the back of my head and forces my lips to come over his again. The moment his mouth is on mine, his finger is in me. My sex clenches as a moan escapes me and I rock my hips, needing the friction of his hardness against my clit as he rubs his finger in me.

He thrusts back like he needs the contact too while the scar on the center of his palm rasps over my nipples as he cups one. "Juicy cunt, juicy tits, juicy blonde princess."

When he licks one nipple, I arch and throw my head back,

gasping in sweet agony. I grind my hips instinctively, wanting more, craving more as we both strain to get closer. He bites and sucks me, then shoves his tongue against the tip of my nipple, making it poke back. I run my hands over his hair, then try to shove his shirt off his massively muscular shoulders.

He pulls his finger out of me and stops me with both hands. "Leave it on," he murmurs, then he rolls me onto my back and yanks my arms up over my head.

"But I want to touch you," I breathe, undulating my body against the weight of his.

He pins my arms up in one hand and pulls off his tie with the other, then he wraps it tightly around my wrists. "Tonight, only I touch."

"Why?"

"Because I say so."

I can't suppress my shudder of excitement as he peels off my panties. He ducks his head and flames lick across my body with each open kiss he places on me, and I tilt my hips upward as he dips his tongue inside my belly button. I gasp, my body craving him like sugar, like chocolate, like *sex*. "Please, oh . . ."

He murmurs *shhh* and opens my pussy with his fingers, eating me with his mouth. My head falls back and a noise of pleasure purls out of my throat as he starts thrusting his tongue into my channel, rubbing in a way that has me thrashing in absolute pleasure. "God, you make me lose it," he breathes, tasting me again.

I quiver under him, spine arched, thighs spread open, aching for his touch, his tongue, his closeness. "Greyson," I say, breathing in deep, soul-drenching drafts. He's like every boy I made out with under the bleachers, every boy I've ever wanted who didn't want me, everything that was forbidden to me. I groan as he licks a circle around my clit. "Oh god! Grey . . . Greyson . . . *please* . . . You're—"

My breaths rasp in my throat when he lifts his head and I see the unmistakable possessiveness in his eyes. He kisses my taut nipples, then studies me, bound for him, in his bed. Using my legs, I curl my thighs around his hips, urging him closer. "I've never begged before, but I'm begging you to *touch me*."

"What is it that you beg for, Melanie? I should be the one begging to touch you."

His hands start dragging up my sides. Sensations so intense, every touch of his fingers crackles over me like burning fingertips. My muscles tense and knot as my body once again heads to that place where only he takes me, where he's not only fulfilling a physical ache, but he gets access to a place where he can rip my soul open.

Closing my eyes as I feel some moisture burn inside them, I keep my arms over my head, bound by his tie, as he uses his thumb to play with my clit.

He does it harder, deeper, *expertly*. Our eyes meet, he crushes my mouth and whispers, "I'm the one who doesn't fucking beg, but I'll beg for this pussy," he rasps as his fingers prepare me, because he's so big I need to be wet and ready and oh god, I'm so ready.

"Yes . . ." I say, the nearness of my orgasm audible in my voice, then his mouth is on mine again, our tongues making out, slick as he keeps rubbing me, his palm burning hot as he cups me and slides one finger in so deep. I tilt my pelvis, desperate for every inch. When he's got me lathered up to explosion, he eases back to unzip his slacks.

My vision is blurry from wanting this. He doesn't even kick his pants off. He shoves them down to his knees, baring his erection, his thick, powerful thighs.

Our mouths roam over each other as he aligns our bodies. "Hard!" I plead as I hook my bound wrists around his neck to keep him close, my lips raining kisses on his jaw. Last night, afraid and dirty and vulnerable, he was all I wanted. All I wanted. *"I want you so much. HARD,"* I gasp, suddenly vulnerable, shaking, needing.

Hungrily, I nibble on his nipple ring, and he responds with a growling noise and forces me down on my back. "Impatient, hungry little girl." He grabs his cock and rolls on the rubber, and he looks as desperate as I am as he starts feeding the head to me. "Is this what you want?"

My eyes roll back from the pleasure and I cry, "Yes, all of it." He groans when he sees my first tear fall, and when he cups his hands on my face as though to catch them and starts fucking me for real, my body melts into his as the world becomes full of him. Just him. Only him.

He impales himself deeper, and I soar higher and higher. I can feel my nipples brushing his shirt, his hot breath on my face, his body in mine—and that's all I know as my world careens on its axis. His hands won't let go of my face, holding me for his every hard, fast, expert thrust. "That's right, that's exactly right, let go for me, let go for me, Melanie, I got you," he murmurs, kissing my throat.

My breasts are budded pink at the tips from the scrape of his shirt; I love it. I love his smell, his hands, his voice. "Yes," I gasp as he thrusts harder, my rhythm completely clumsy now. All I want is more of him, more of him, ALL OF HIM. "Yes, yes."

He roars, head falling back, veins popping out in pleasure as he starts jetting off and I spread my legs wider apart as he grabs my hips and thrusts in harder, watching me lose it.

I moan and start to thrash, somehow aware that his eyes are devouring me as I shatter into a million glowing stars.

Moments later, I stir from my dazed stupor to notice he's caressing one hand across my wet face, the other on my thighs where I was bruised. The touch melts me deep where it hurts me to remember, but right now, in his arms, a contentment and peace wash between us. I can feel it in his body too. As if he likes wiping my tears.

Sighing in relaxation when he kisses my temple and dries the rest of my face, I hook my bound hands around his neck and press myself into his chest.

"Nobody pushes me as far as you do," I explain, my voice cottony.

"That's because I'm bad," he says. He slides one hand up my arm, to where my hands are linked at his nape.

"I'm fucking"—he kisses one eyelid—"bad for you." He kisses another eyelid, then he kisses my mouth, and his fingers begin playing with my pussy again. My body surprises me, responding even when I didn't think it possible.

"Ready for more?"

I nod.

I can't put a name to what I feel when he's inside me, so maybe I won't try to. Does it even have a name? This connection between human beings. Between a woman, and a man; a *fucking asshole*.

I look at him, and he doesn't scare me.

He lures me.

He tempts me, exhilarates me. He makes me want to claim him as if I'm claiming back a part of me that was once lost.

Makes me want to tame him. Let him tame *me*.

He rolls another condom on his thick cock and comes up to his knees, and I feel vulnerable and open but I don't feel like hiding right now. I openly show him my hunger and lick and kiss his thick throat as he grabs my waist and pushes into me. I shudder uncontrollably when he's all the way in, biting a tendon that juts out on his throat, close to my mouth.

The rumble of the sound he makes tells me he likes it. *You like it when I'm feisty?* My eyes flutter open, and he looks down at me with a look of wild, hungry, proprietary lust, but also strangely reverent and gentle. We fuck lazily this time, without the initial rush, our bodies moving in synchronicity until I see stars as another climax builds and builds.

"Go on, bite me all you want, little kitten." He prods into my mouth, his eyes on mine as I comply, licking him, tasting him. "Do you want that to be my cock in your mouth?" his husky murmur taunts in my ear, breath hot. "Do you want to be sucking on this cock? Biting on it?"

I gasp with renewed hunger. "When I bite it I'm going to bite hard." With my arms hooked around his neck, I rake my nails into a part of his scalp, my hips tilting faster to keep up with his increasing rhythm.

His laugh, once again dark, sensual, intimate as he brushes his wet thumb along my lips, the bed squeaking beneath us. "If you think I'm afraid of a little bit of teeth, you need to get to know me better, princess." Just like that, he bites my lower lip and sucks it into his mouth, thrusting harder so I moan.

I bite back, and he groans such sexy sounds it only makes the sex that much more intense. My wet, snug body grips him greedily because I want him in me for as long as I can have him, but the pleasure is too absolute to last as long as I want to, even though we both seem to be trying to last.

The mattress squeaks beneath us, harder and harder with his thrusts. I'm being just as noisy, and Greyson? He's releasing low, male noises of pleasure too. "Get ready, princess, I'm coming so hard," he rasps.

"*Come,*" I beg. He has no idea how much I'm aching to feel him go off inside me, go off with me.

He waits to feel me clench around him. Then, the moment it starts for me, he lets go. He comes full force, his body tightening like a bow, and when I feel him jerk in me, his hands clenching on my hips, my pleasure explodes inside me until I'm convulsing so totally I can't keep my eyes open.

Oh.

My.

God.

I lay in breathless silence for a moment, realizing Greyson is untying me. He rubs my wrists with the pads of his thumbs, then plops onto his back and stares up at the ceiling, his chest heaving, his nipple ring glinting with the little rays of sunlight peeking through the window.

The sun is rising already. I really didn't want it to rise yet because I don't want to leave yet.

In silence, I go to the bathroom and when I come back to bed, he's staring out at the city looking satisfied and exhausted, his shirt all wrinkled, his hair all mussed, his beautiful mouth swollen from me. I should get going. Probably, I should. Instead I stare at him and that mouth and I wonder how many women kissed those lips.

Many, Melanie.

He's warned me off, but I don't feel like being warned off. I feel as though somewhere, deep down, he's bullshitting me. Why would he give me this necklace otherwise? Why would he give me, over and over, THE LOOK?

Even so, I've gotta go, so I walk back to that big bed, my eyes scanning the floor for my dress even though the thought of going home alone to my apartment makes my stomach churn. I could call Pandora, but I'll have to be prepared for her drilling the shit out of me, I guess.

"Do you see my dress?" I whisper to him.

His voice is gruff with tiredness, his eyes hooded as he pulls open the bedsheet for me.

"Yeah, I set it aside to avoid the clutter. Come here and get some sleep."

Oh, god, I really didn't want to leave, but I don't want him to know how much I want to sleep here tonight either.

So I stand there, naked and unsure for a moment.

"I don't have to stay," I say, but there's this way he has of looking at you—as if he's commanding you. It's very odd. I've never encountered anyone who could have such control with a single look.

Caving in to it, I find myself quietly heading over. His lips curl as he lifts the sheet higher and I see his naked body under the cover.

I feel strangely awkward as I slide into bed with him, first sitting on the corner of the bed and quickly braiding my hair; I wouldn't fall asleep otherwise, I simply can't stand waking up and feeling it on my face.

I sense his curious gaze watching my every move, and when I sigh and lie down on my side, facing a stone fireplace on the far side of the room, he laughs behind me. "You really plan to sleep way over there?"

"I don't want to intrude!" I laugh nervously. "I don't stay over usually."

"You just like to fuck and get away, that's fine, princess. Except for the fact that I'm not done with you."

He reaches out and guides me toward him by my braid, and when I don't protest the maneuver and actually feel like tucking myself closer to his warmth, he exhales softly. "You're something, aren't you," he murmurs, taking my braid in his fist and forcing me to roll over and face him. Then he pins my head against his, forehead to forehead. "Maybe I'll sleep tonight; you wear a man out."

"What do you mean?" I peer up at him, notice the hard set of his jaw. "You don't sleep?"

"Not well, but I'll go for it if you will," he softly teases me.

"Then let's go for it," I say, grinning.

It feels like, for several minutes, we stay as we are, him with the merest curve of his lips while I'm smiling completely, both of us looking into each other's eyes. I have no idea what he sees in my eyes that holds him so intently engrossed, but I can't look away from his gaze either. It's so closed and mysterious while, at the same time, I can see a fiery rawness in his gaze, as if he desperately wants something from me.

Not something: *all* of me.

"Come here," he rasps. He makes the first move, easing one of his arms around me, pulling me against his side. I cuddle into his large body, a little tense at first, but at the same time, achingly aware of every spot where our naked bodies are touching. Where my breasts press into his ribs, my cheek on his chest, one of my legs hooking in between his.

God, this is as intimate as it gets with a man and I cannot relax, I cannot oxygenate, I cannot formulate a thought.

His breathing begins to deepen and . . . oh, wow. He's asleep.

He fell asleep holding me, with his arm locked around my shoulders, and I don't understand why I get butterflies over this.

There's a little blood on his shirt, on the sleeve of the arm curved around me. I touch the red stain, wondering if I scratched him. Then I stare up into his beautiful, masculine face, wondering about him. For the first time in my life, I want to lie in bed next to a guy and listen to him breathe, slow and deep, like he's breathing. I don't understand my visceral reactions to him.

This hot man with a secret room. Who in the world has a secret room?

This man does. And I'm so curious about him, I study his features and tell myself I can sleep when I'm alone . . . so I touch his nipple ring and watch him lie in his big lonely apartment, deep asleep with one arm around me, wondering what other secrets he keeps from me.

❤ ❤ ❤

A PHONE IS beeping, and beeping, and beeping. I moan and twist around, feeling something against my body that's so hot and so hard it's definitely not a pillow. "What is that sound?"

Sleepy hazel eyes open and meet mine, and my lungs tighten in the most delicious way. *Did I really sleep in this man's arms? This man who told me he was going to be my worst nightmare?* He sits up in bed and works the kinks out of his neck, stretching out his arms until every muscle is tight and flexed, then he curses as the beeping continues, grabs the offending machine and stalks out of bed and steps, buck naked, out onto the balcony of his apartment. I survey his butt with a tingly feeling in the pit of my stomach. What day is today? Saturday? Sunday?

Brooke. Remy. Wedding, I remind myself. You and Greyson. *Melting.*

I shake off my sleep and realize I've been here over thirty-six hours. All of Saturday early morning and now, today, is it already Sunday?

I stretch and my body is sore all over. I remember yesterday. Eating with him on the floor, picnic style. Lounging in bed. Teasing him. Watching *Blow*. God. I haven't had a weekend this amazing in my dreams.

He asked about my fantasies last night.

I laughed. "Well . . . I might have one, but I'm not going to tell you," I whispered in mischief as I peered up into his face. "What's one of yours?"

"Fantasies are for people who don't do what they want."

"So you've done everything then?"

"Everything that I've wanted to do."

"Including me?"

He laughed, a delicious sound. "Including you. Now a handful of times."

"Including a threesome?" I teased.

"Of course."

"Really?" Perking up with curiosity, I propped my chin on his chest. "Is it fun?"

He ran his thumb down the dents of my spine, glancing at my smile with a smile of his own. "For the guy, yes. The girls don't seem to be able to forget it's not a competition."

"You only do threesomes with two girls?" I prodded. "That's very asshole of you."

"Baby, I don't share my girls with other men, that's not how I roll."

"Well, I couldn't share with another girl either. I'd kick the bitch out of bed right now. I'd want both your hands on me, not just one. Pfft!"

He laughed and threw his head back a bit, his voice rumbly and rough, his Adam's apple bobbing. "You're enough for any guy, trust me."

Sensuality oozed off him so bad I want to lick him. The way he's been fucking me is so . . . I can't even explain it. I've never felt such a strong connection, such a primal awareness of him as a man, and me as a . . . woman. "What about anal?"

Lord, his next laugh was so dark and sexy. "Of course. That's always fun." He looked at me, then understanding dawned in his eyes, and they started shining brightly, almost too brightly as he cupped my ass in one warm, long-fingered hand. "Come here, Melanie."

My heart sped up at the lust thickening his voice. I love sex. Sex is the only way I've ever connected with the opposite gender, but never like this. Never with anything risky. Anything where I had to trust the man being with me not to hurt me.

"Do you want to get ass-fingered, princess?" he whispered in my ear, and my blood rushed hot in my veins as he dipped his thumb along the fissure between the curves of my buttocks. All my body squeezed in reaction as he headed for that spot.

"Grey!" I said, my cheeks burning a vivid scarlet when his thumb grazed me, like the brush of a feather.

"Does that feel good, princess?" He watched me with liquid whiskey eyes, his eyelashes seeming heavy as I caught my lip between my teeth to keep from making an embarrassingly wanton sound. I became so wet I heard the slick sound of his thumb brushing over my folds before he started dragging his hand backward again, passing over every nerve on my backside, soft and languorous.

"I'd like to be taken that way," I confessed, looking deep into his eyes. "But only with someone I trusted. Who'd care for me and my safety."

"Come up here," he said, spreading me over him. "I'm only going to use my finger. You're already quivering so much."

"I do like it, it feels exciting, but I don't know . . . Greyson . . ."

"Shh." He brushed his lips over mine to quiet me. He was hard under me. He liked touching me, whispering at me as he kissed me and slowly I relaxed as he dipped his thumb into my ass, and when I moaned, he tipped my head back and slowly kissed me some more. "Just relax, let me in." He teased me with his thumb moving, ever so slowly, in and out, and I began shivering more, moving over him until I felt the wetness seeping from the tip of his cock against my abdomen.

He rolled me to my stomach. In silence, he bent over and bit one ass cheek, cupping the other in his hand as he slid his thumb up my ass again.

"Fold to your knees, Melanie." He ran his hand down my spine as I did what he said, whimpering softly.

"Greyson, it feels intense . . ."

"Let it take you, princess. Give me this. Fuck, let me watch you come apart like this."

He stroked his hand up my back while the other kept fingering me. Sensations took over. I whimpered, closing my eyes as his intoxicating touch did new and profound things to me. He nibbled my other ass cheek and fucked his thumb in three more times, and when he slipped his middle finger into my pussy, I started coming. And coming. And coming.

He pressed his cock against me as I came, so I could feel it close, tempting me, hard, pulsing, his voice gruff with arousal close to my nape, exposed as he shoved my braid aside.

"Thatta girl," he purred, pinching my nipples, rubbing the outer rim of my little ass as the contractions eased.

"It was . . . incredible."

I turned, and he rolled to his back and folded his arms behind his head as I tried to catch my breath. But it was hard to breathe when the air was thick with it—with lust, with want, with this animal, chemical attraction I have never, ever felt. I wanted his cock in me, I wanted to do it all with him, but would he be careful with me?

His body oozed tension, muscles tight with it, cock up at full mast again.

"You've had a lot of lovers?" I whispered, gripping him in my hand, strangely jealous.

"Lovers, not really. Fucks, yeah." He grabbed my face in one hand and gave a firm squeeze to my cheeks. "But I've never fucked a little mouth like yours. Now open up, princess."

I was wet again as he came up on his knees, pulling me up by the braid. When he filled me, I made eye contact, he didn't take his eyes off me, watching every swipe of my tongue, every inch I licked, every breath I let caress the length of him. "Fuck," he rasped, pumping and drawing out his pleasure. I ran my tongue over him, our eyes connected like magnets. "You like that, don't you?" he cooed. The way he talked to me excited me. If he'd touched me again, I'd have come. I almost slipped my hand between my legs and touched myself. Instead I grabbed the base of him because I wanted him to fantasize about this one blow job whenever it is he plans to leave. . . .

He jetted off and, usually, I pull away when men do, but when I felt him tense up and I was about to pull back, he cooed, "Every last drop of come is yours, Melanie." He fisted my braid, his eyes demanding and commanding, and suddenly I wanted to please him, taste him, and I did.

I close my eyes briefly and exhale out the memories of yesterday. When I open my eyes, he's out on the balcony, still on his phone. His legs, thick like tree trunks, are braced apart, long, muscular, and just dusted with hair. His calves are shapely and powerful, his tan golden, his ass perfection, as perfectly molded as the muscled, upside-down triangle of his broad shoulders and narrow hips. And he's just out there for anyone with binoculars to see, buck naked. Standing right there.

A fucking sex god.

When Greyson rolls the glass door open, he's still on the phone. As he comes back into the room and hangs up, I notice he's got a thick bandage wrapped around his upper arm.

As he approaches, I lift the sheets because I crave his heat, his nearness, the smell of him on my skin.

"Work?" I ask.

"You could say that," he says as he gets under the covers with me. I hold my breath because his hard cock tells me he craves me too. I kiss his throat and curl my fingers around most of his girth, loving how hard he got, so fast. His cock had turned semihard by the time he took the call, but it's fully swelled again. Oh, fuck, I really dig this guy. What he whispers when we fuck?

My skin tingles everywhere, remembering.

He looks down at me with sleepy eyes and my toes are curling full force. When he smiles that sensual smile, I die.

Unexpectedly, he slowly pulls the sheet off my body. Full sunlight streams through the window, and when he tosses the covers aside to look at me, I squirm on the bed.

"Don't," I protest, attempting to pull up the sheets, squeaking in embarrassment.

"Yes," he sternly counters. He grabs the sheets in a fist and tosses them aside again, pressing me down on my back.

Immediately I think of my kidney scars. "I'm not used to being seen like this."

"Get used to being seen like this by me," he says gently.

Though I've turned bright red, he's got me mesmerized enough that I've fallen utterly still, on the bed, my breasts heaving up and down as he looks at me. THE LOOK he gives me feels like a live, physical touch. It travels every inch of my body, from the top of my head down to my toes, like a tremor.

I never thought a look could be this powerful.

It makes me forget my scars, my every hurt.

You'd think that because I had the kidney transplant when I was a baby, the scar would be tiny. It's not. It's a slash on the lower right of my abdomen, and it's grown with the rest of my body. It's faded a very light pink and makeup does wonders for it, but the makeup is gone by now.

And Greyson sees it.

He traces the scar with one finger and sets my hand on his own scar. The gesture only endears him to me. Because he's scarred too, but he's not embarrassed about it.

As he bends over and presses his lips to my scar, my eyes well up.

"What happened here?" he murmurs.

I don't know why he makes me emotional, but I blink back the tears and slide my hand down his chest over his own scar. "What happened here?" I counter, my voice thick with emotion.

"Ladies first," he says gently, easing back and watching me with eyes that are no longer sleepy, but dark and patient.

I'm not sure I want him to know that one of my kidneys is not mine. That I'm a transplant patient. That I need to take pills to make sure my body doesn't reject my donor's organ. That maybe in a couple of years, I'll need to exchange this one for a new one yet again, if it starts giving up.

These are not things you tell a man when you're starting to date, or just fuck, or whatever we're doing. There's this show called the *Millionaire Matchmaker,* and I will never forget how the expert Patti went all over a girl who'd dumped some serious issues on a poor bachelor's lap.

You do not do that!

Guys do not care about it unless they genuinely care about you first!

Quietly, I touch Greyson's nipple ring instead, and hearing him hold his breath when I tug it playfully, I grin into his suddenly very dark, hungry eyes and say, "I should get a nipple ring."

He laughs, then sobers up and shakes his head. "Yeah, that's not happening."

"Why not?"

He rubs my butt. "That's not fucking happening. No one's getting anywhere near my business."

I realize the thick bandage on his right arm is stained with blood, so I sit up with a start. "What happened here? Did I scratch you?"

He merely smiles to himself as he tightens the bandage. "It takes a little more than a kitten's claw to make me bleed."

"Let me help."

Shifting closer, I take the bandage and carefully wrap it around his bulging arm. "Are you okay?" I ask.

"I'm good," he says dismissively.

When I finish wrapping it up, I impulsively set a kiss on it, slowly setting my lips on him and closing my eyes as a tenderness sweeps through me. A man making me feel this tenderness is so alien to me. Usually men are just . . . guys to me. Not even human. More like enemies that must be handled with care. Used, on occasion. But what I feel for this one is the most powerful *thing* I've ever in my life felt. Almost as if I know him from before. In some past life . . . in my dreams . . .

Before I can lift my head, his nose finds my ear, making me smile against his bandage and squirm when his breath tickles me.

He trails his hand lightly down my spine and settles it at the small of my back. This man gets my lower body on overdrive, but my upper body is getting the same workout, just ask my heart, which hasn't beaten right for over thiry-six hours. And is he giving me the look too? I raise my head, and I'm tingling from my fingers to my toes. His smile is lazy, sleepy, and it melts me.

"That's nice," he says in a rumbly voice.

"What?"

"Nurse Melanie," he whispers.

Something inside me buzzes and zings and I groan at my body's stupid, instant reaction, then I tip my head up to kiss him while holding his head and pulling him down to mine. He brushes my lips, teasing me with a smile.

I groan in protest when my phone alarm starts screaming like mad, and I realize it's Sunday—for a fact.

"Ufff, I've got brunch with my parents." When he doesn't

seem too willing to let go of my waist, I push at his thick wrists. "Mister, I have to go."

"I propose you cancel," he says lazily.

"I can't. I'm the only one who comes to brunch, and we always do brunch on Sunday." I start gathering my undergarments and hunting down my dress. "You can come if you want to," I blurt out, and when I notice his closed expression, I add, "No strings. I mean, it's just breakfast. Not even that, brunch."

"Nah, don't think so."

He's still sleepy and in bed, stretching as he checks his phone, first one, then he pulls out another. "Can I use your shower, real quick?" I nervously ask.

"Use anything you like."

Once again I feel strangely shy . . . I don't know why he does that to me. Normally in a fling I'm uninhibited and can boss a poor boy around, if I want to. But clearly there's no bossing this one around. Aware of his eyes on my ass as I retreat, I walk to the bathroom and turn on the warm water, easing inside the stall. I slowly exhale as the water runs over my head.

Greyson stalks into the bathroom just as I'm coming out of the shower stall, and while I wrap my hair in one towel and my body in the other, he flips on the water and showers in about a minute flat.

This is completely alien, being with a man in the bathroom. Brooke has mentioned that after Remy works out, they take a shower together, and fuck like mad. I'm finding it terribly distracting. In a mind-fuck sort of way. Hell, in a let's-fuck sort of way too.

In fact, I end up losing my brains and just stand there, ogling him as he towel-dries his hair in the nude, shoulders working, abs clenching, the V dipping to his beautiful cock which I swear is so big that even in its normal state . . .

"Just gave you some of that. But it seems like the lady still craves a little more?"

His voice jerks my eyes up to his and to that heart-tugging smile he wears as he pulls off a plastic wrap that he put around his bandage to keep it dry.

"Like you're not tempting me on purpose," I say with a smirk, drooling as I watch his muscled ass walk into his closet.

"Sure you don't want to come?" I ask.

"Yeah, I'm sure." He comes back with some clothes wadded in one arm and stops before me with a smile. "I've done enough coming for a while."

"Asshole. But we knew that about you, didn't we?"

I lean over the counter and start applying my morning makeup.

"You didn't mean it. Inviting me over? Did you, princess?" he asks, looking seriously perturbed.

I scowl. "We just talk and have breakfast. It's not like we plot a world takeover or anything top secret you couldn't listen in on. It's not a 'meet the parents' thing. Urgh, but forget it, you're look-ing at me all weird."

I've start brushing my fingers through my hair when he comes and hugs me from behind, holding my gaze in the mirror. He cups my face and turns it around, then his mouth is near my ear, his voice as thick as the feel of his cock against my tummy. "All I want lately is to drag you to bed and fuck you from behind, side-ways, then several angles from up front, so every muscle in your body will remember me when you move today. Every breath will hurt, every step you take. I want to feed you, and spread my next meal all over you. I want to lick up my meal, head to toe, clean you up in the shower next, then I want to soap you up and fondle every inch of your sleek little body as I feed you my dick. When I take you out of the shower, I want to towel you dry, massage your sweet tits, flip you around, and give you that long, sweet fuck in the ass you've been waiting for."

The blood has left my other organs only to concentrate fiercely on my sexual ones. I try to push him away and not get excited over his attentions. "Please not now."

"Do you want me there, Melanie?" He nips my earlobe and sends a rush of desire down my watery thighs as he cups my ass like it belongs to him, his longest finger grazing me there. *There. Again.* "Here, baby. Do you want me big and hard, thicker than ever, right here? I want to be the man you let loose with."

"You're going to make me late for brunch, and I'm going to be mad!" I cry, slapping his hand away and quickly whirling back to the mirror to add some lip gloss.

"You'll be mad?" His laughing whisper shivers down my skin as he holds me by the hips and looks into my eyes over the top of my head. "You know, I have a thing for mad princesses. It turns me on."

"Move to Europe then."

He massages my buttocks in his hands. "*You* getting angry, showing me that little fire, really turns me on," he continues in that gruff morning voice.

"Oh, you haven't seen angry," I assure him, pivoting around. "It takes a lot to make me angry but when it happens, it's a sight to behold. Not many nearby articles survive me."

"Oh?"

"Any shoes around or . . . lamps . . . could find themselves flying . . . crashing . . . and dying."

"Is that right?" he asks, a mocking light in his eyes.

"So right. I'm a slow boil but when I boil, I BOIL!"

As I force myself to slip into my clothes, he's still in the nude, and before I can zip up my dress, he's cornered me against a mirrored wall, my breasts squished against him.

My nerves crackle at the brush of his lips. I set my hand on his chest to push away again, but my fingers just seem to lie there instead, absorbing him, spreading over thick, hard, delicious muscled pec.

"I have to go," I whisper, rubbing his nipple ring with my thumb.

Mischief glitters all across his eyes as he brushes his mouth against mine. "You know where the door is."

He licks into the seam of my lips. "I really, really have to go." I loop my arms around his neck, intending a quick kiss, but he seems to have a different, slower, headier kiss in mind.

He makes it happen.

His hand eases into my wet hair and cups me by the scalp as he angles his head and kisses me, deeply, our mouths tasting of toothpaste and heat, my body arching to get closer to him while he seems to stand there, hot and hard, supporting us both as I melt under his mouth.

"Greyson . . ." I protest.

He runs his fingers through my hair and takes a kiss from another angle. "Nobody's stopping you, Melanie."

I turn my head to get more access into his mouth too, rubbing my tongue against his, my nipples to his chest. "God, you're danger, Grey."

"You have no idea, princess." He tongues me hard and unapologetically. More kissing, deep and slow, the kind of kiss that makes me hear our breathing, our slow, slick sounds.

"I think you do plan to tie me up and make me pick out safe words," I breathe in between lazy, hungry sucks of his tongue.

"Just pick one."

A soft moan leaves me when his lips trail my throat as I think of my word. "Dickhead."

His chuckle vibrates right between my legs, where my clit feels extra sensitive this morning, and suddenly very, very achy.

"That filthy fucking mouth just begging to be quieted," he rasps. "But FYI, the word I want to hear the next time that I'm in you is *Greyson*. That's the word I want to hear when I'm behind you . . ."

"We won't . . . we won't be doing that." I can almost hear the flutters in my stomach in my voice as I try to escape.

He trails his hands up the small of my back, locking me to him. "Soon, we will," he softly promises me.

"We won't. I don't *trust* you!"

He seizes my chin and looks me directly in the eye, speaking with deliberate slowness, as if I'm an idiot. "You can trust . . . that I won't let any other asshole . . . into your sweet, tight little asshole—you sure as fuck can trust that."

I groan. "Your mouth is filthier than mine. Why are you even after me?"

"The same reason you go out there, bang the brains off some dude, get hurt and keep looking for what you want. There are three things I'm not big on. Trust. Being ordered the fuck around—I get enough of that from my father. And denying myself what I want."

"And you want me?"

I fall still under the hot feel of his lips suddenly pressing into my throat, trailing up to my ear, where he whispers, a warning, "That's an understatement, but yes. I want you." He steps back. "I want this in a way I have no business wanting, Melanie. Just don't confuse me with your prince charming."

The words, they hit me. Straight and true.

They hit me so hard, they knock the wind out of me.

"If I did, you just ruined it," I say, rolling my eyes. "Bye, Greyson."

I hate the silence that follows me out of there.

FIFTEEN

WHERE I'M HEADED

Greyson

"Next thing you know, you'll be going to fucking church on Sunday to sing choir," Derek cackles as he drives me over to Melanie's parents' house.

Why is he driving me to her parents' house, you wonder?

Because it looks like I'm doing *brunch* today.

"Shut the fuck up," I growl.

Derek chuckles and shakes his head, and I stare morosely out the window.

"Aaaaahhhhhh, god, I can't believe this," I tell myself as I rub my face and look down at my clean clothes. I took the risk of not wearing any weapons and I feel beyond naked—I feel stupid. Like some prom boy about to pick up his date.

There are some things that you just know are right or wrong. And I know that sitting at a Sunday brunch with a woman's parents is not where I belong.

My crewneck itches. I angrily tug it as I walk up to their townhome. I know exactly where their home is because I've hacked Melanie's every system, read every page, receipt, and article with her name on it. I could be a plague on legs approaching the two-story home, that's how out of place I feel as I rap my knuckles on the door. There are flower beds nearby. It smells . . . of freshly mowed lawn. I almost remember helping my mother mow our lawn thirteen years ago. In a home like this. It's been thirteen years since I stepped through doors like these, in a neighborhood like this. *I don't fucking belong here anymore.*

Derek waves at me from the car and I flip him off, then call, "I'll bring out a doggie bag for you."

He flips me back. "I chomped on a burrito at the gas station but you sure are the epitome of kindness this morning, boss."

Ignoring the jibe—because of course I wasn't my sunniest on our drive here, hell, I never am—I knock on the door a third time.

I'm not really certain how Melanie will react to my being here but I'm going to give her a little help and act like I already know she's going to be fucking delighted to see me. Period.

A servant opens the door. "Yes?"

She runs her gaze over me as if she can't help herself, then I hear a voice, similar to Melanie's. "Who is it, Maria?"

"Thank you, I'll find my way." I ease into the house and head to the noise, bursting into the dining room with ease.

Melanie's father pushes up from his chair, surprised, though not alarmed. Silver dusts a full head of hair, and he has the kind of face that perennially wears a smile. Melanie's mother, on the other hand, remains seated and wide-eyed, a beautiful woman with a pale, sensitive expression and eyes almost the exact shade as Melanie's.

"Melanie?" her father asks. I roam her body with my gaze, and when our eyes connect, I see her lightly tugging on a loose tendril of hair, nervously looking for an explanation. What? Now she's leaving me here like an idiot? Currents of electricity crackle between us, and I feel my body respond.

"Mr. and Mrs. Meyers," I say to the people seated at the dining table. "I'm sorry I'm late."

"Mom and Dad, this is Greyson. He went with me to Brooke and Remy's wedding. He's . . ."

She raises her face to me for help. Her eyes wide and bright, and god, she screws my brain. My mind flashes with images of her—the playful woman, the siren in my bed, the nurse who wrapped me up and kissed me after, and I can feel the fire in my gut blend into my soul.

Quietly I say, "I'm her new boyfriend and it's a pleasure to meet you both."

I pump her father's hand and hold his gaze. Her mother launches herself at me and almost disintegrates in my arms. "So nice to meet you!"

Uncomfortable as fuck by the immediate warmth around me, I pry myself free and head over to Melanie. My body feels charged just being near hers. Now lust, I can understand.

"He's not my boyfriend, he's just a friend," Melanie laughs, playing a role for them. With an amused smile, she looks at me, then quips, "Change of plans?"

I pull out the chair next to hers. "Looks like."

Her mother claps delightedly. "Oh, we'll have a new member to play charades with!"

Fuck. Me. Standing.

I haven't had a family-style dinner in my entire life, not even when my mother was with me. Never with both my parents at the table. I don't *eat* at tables. I don't hang out with families. In their homes.

I don't know why I followed her *here*.

Bullshit. I do know.

She's my mark, but she's marked me. Guilt, an emotion I'm not familiar with, niggles in the back of my mind when her parents instantly begin listing all of Melanie's talents for me. I guess I look like a decent guy. I look more than decent. They think if she likes me, I deserve her. Fuck, it hurts.

"Greyson King, hmmm . . . I'm trying to think of any Kings I know?" Her father scrubs his chin. "We are in King County, after all. What about the KING-5 TV station . . . ?"

"No, I'm not from around here."

"Greyson, can I just say our little grasshopper is not only an amazing decorator, she makes perfect homemade ice cream from the days when Lucas and I had a little gelato place. She can actually cook, this one can!"

"Only when forced to," she says, grinning.

Fuck me again, but she looks adorable, somehow vulnerable and playful.

She makes me fucking hot.

Hard.

Possessive.

Protective.

What the fuck?

"So how did you two meet?" her mother wants to know.

Melanie sighs. "He saved my car from the rain one day."

Her mother's eyes turn huge. "When you *found yourself standing in the rain?*" she asks Melanie, as though they've discussed the night we met.

Melanie flushes—how can I miss the way her cheeks flare bright red? The fire in my gut grows even more when I realize she'd talked about me to her mother.

"Greyson, I hope you don't think we're being overly enthusiastic but Mel's never brought a boy home in twenty-five years. Even a friend."

"*Twenty-four,*" Princess corrects.

"In a little over a month it'll be twenty-*five*," her mother says, rolling her eyes and then peers through her lashes at me. "Our Mel always throws a celebration," she tells me, her hands in prayer mode under her chin. "This year we can't wait to see what she plans!"

For the first time I notice my party girl seems at a loss for words. "I might pass this year, everything's so expensive."

"Nonsense. It's twenty-five big ones!" her father says.

Melanie's silence is weighed down with a grief that's palpable. Suddenly, I'm honed in on the fact that the three of us are watching her while she looks down at her plate, her lip caught under her teeth. My fingers twitch at my sides, and a flash of concern hits me as I realize she's sad, the flash of pain followed by a flash of determination to make it better.

God, she brightens the room. When she's sad it's almost as if a light just turned off. I live in darkness enough and I'll be damned before I let her see her light turn off.

"All right, so charades it is!" Her father claps with mock enthusiasm.

Under the table, I steal a touch of Melanie's thigh and rub up and down in a slow, soothing motion I've never used on a woman before but that she brings out in me, nonetheless, and I get high when her cheeks redden and she smiles again, her sadness forgotten. I swear her smile shoots straight up to my head like an upside-down thunderbolt.

I should feel like a thief, like I'm stealing this moment that doesn't belong to me. Instead it's too damn easy to pretend it's rightfully mine.

"Grasshopper, what do you say, boys versus girls. Huh, Greyson?"

Soon Melanie's walking around sticking out her neck, puckering her lips, and leaning forward and pecking in the air. She's sexy, and fun, and silly, and what she's doing somehow shoots like a gallon of blood straight to my dick.

So apparently this game includes cards. We picked a category. The dad went for animals. And she's acting like some weird animal.

"The team who guesses the most wins," her dad tells me, slapping my arm. "Don't worry, our little grasshopper never guesses correctly—a crane!" he suddenly yells out.

"Yes!" she cries.

"You go first, or should I?" her dad asks me next.

"By all means, sir. I'm not dying to make a fool of myself just yet." He laughs and pulls a card out and I see it's a bear.

He spreads his arms out and walks around. "Gorilla!" Melanie cries. He grins at me and lifts his arms up in the air, higher.

"Stallion!" Mrs. Meyers cries.

Mr. Meyers spares me a glance and lifts his eyebrows up to his hairline in a way that says, *See? These women are clueless.*

He continues acting until I'm chuckling, watching them, until it's my turn. I sneak a glance out the window and make sure I'm not visible—if Derek sees this, it's the end of Zero. No more respect for Zero.

I pull out a card and get dog. I start snarling and do the first thing I can think of, grab a pillow and chew on the corner.

"Wolf!" her mother cries.

I clamp it between my teeth and shake it from side to side.

"Oh dear," her mother says.

Melanie is laughing her ass off, and I feel like a dickwad. Hell, I want her to guess, but fuck this, I'm not gonna whine like some dog.

I drop the pillow and give up, and she's clutching her stomach, laughing, and so hot as she comes over and takes the pillow away, playfully running her fingers through my hair. I can see the family dynamic now so clearly.

"My grandma used to say," she tells me, with one last ruffle of my hair, "those who play together, stay together."

She's been protected all her life. Happy. Playing an innocent, fun game. She shines. They all shine. They're ridiculous and stupid and I have never in my life wanted to be ridiculous and stupid. I kill, blackmail, and con the ridiculous and stupid.

"The one who can do the best trick gets the last brownie!"

"Now, son," her dad tells me after that announcement, "any trick you can do, now's the time to do it. Those brownies are killer, I tell you."

"You go first, Dad!" Melanie cries.

Mr. Meyers begins to do a Russian dance, *hut* noises included. Her mother makes a realistic gorilla. Melanie looks at me, then she cups her mouth and starts a donkey call. Finally, they all look at me.

Fuck. *Seriously?*

This is so fucking stupid.

But . . .

It's the way *she* is looking at me, curious, happy. It brings me back to where she is. And it makes me study the dining room to see what the fuck I can do. I spot a vase with daisies on the table. They're hot pink—so princess.

Grabbing a steak knife and backing up several paces, I fling it across the room, past them. And pin the center of the daisy to the far wall.

Silence.

"Holy guacamole!" her dad cries.

"That's an incredible trick!" her mom cries.

Melanie brings me the brownie as I unpin the daisy, and as she hands over the sweet, I hand her the flower.

"That's an interesting trick," she says, surveying me and smelling the flower. "They teach you that at security school?"

"They teach you donkey speak in Decorating 101?" I want to make her flush, and it works. She laughs.

My effect on her is like a drug and it shoots straight to my head, dizzying me.

"That was one cool trick," I hear the father whisper to the mother, but I'm consumed by my fucking filthy-mouthed princess standing close, panting and excited, playful and warm and full of promises of the things I've never had in my life.

I offer her some of my brownie, and she bites into it. I start to brush her hair behind her forehead, and when I look up, her parents are watching us with these huge smiles on their faces, like they're thrilled their grasshopper has finally found a guy "friend."

And I see, right here and now, that this is what the Underground took from me.

SIXTEEN

DEBTS

Melanie

We fucked before he left town.

Straight from my parents', he followed me to my apartment, up the elevator, to my door. I stood there, starting to say goodbye. He slammed my mouth to his, scooped me up, and took it from there to the bedroom.

He threw me to the bed and ripped my clothes off, then his. My body trembled and my breaths shuddered out of me as he dropped over me.

He held me down, one hand on my shoulder, the other on my hip, and fucked me hard. I screamed and twisted, raking my hands down his back.

"Look at me."

I tried, moaning.

He slid his hand up my back, under the fall of my hair and held me by the skull, tipping my face up. "Say you love it," he commanded. "Say you fucking love it."

"I love it," I moaned.

His mouth crashed down on me and he gave me the kiss of a

lifetime, the fuck of a lifetime. When he peeled our mouths free he slowed his pace and said again, huskier, "*Look* at me," filling me to the hilt with hot, pulsing live flesh.

I looked and he looked back at me, greedy, strong, driving over and over inside me. Not holding back. Every move telling me he needed this as bad as me.

My climax took me over like a storm. With every shudder that passed through me, another, deeper one ran through him until we were both panting and undone. I clasped my thighs and arms tighter around him, holding his hard, heavy body to mine, keeping him a little longer inside me.

I didn't want to let go. My face was wet again from my orgasm but all of a sudden I felt like crying an ocean.

I'm afraid of what he makes me feel, and of the reality of my circumstances.

I'm afraid that I will owe all this money and have had no buyers for my Mustang, and when my time runs out three days after my birthday, a dozen angry mobsters will come knock on my door and nobody will be able to help me. Nobody will be able to stop them. Not even him.

I don't know what I'm going to do. I don't know what to do. But nobody makes me feel as emotionally vulnerable and as physically safe as he does when he holds me.

The fact that he came to brunch, unexpectedly, told me more than all his warnings have. He exhaled in my neck and rolled us to a more comfortable position, where he kept me to his side, and I felt strange emotions swamp me.

Don't be needy, I told myself, but I felt like an imposter. I still heard myself whisper, "Everything my parents said . . . don't believe it. They just think I'm perfect, but I fake it."

I eased away from him and clutched the sheet around me.

He sat up in bed. "I know about faking it."

"My life came at a very high price and it's just hard to live up to it."

Instantly he reached out and set a hand on my shoulder, tracing a circle on my skin with his thumb. "My life has come at a high price too. Every day of it." He brushed one lone tendril of hair back from my face, our eyes locking. "So many days trying to find some fucked-up meaning in it."

The revelation left me breathless, and I waited and waited and waited for more, saw there was more in his eyes, but he got up and grabbed his clothes.

"I'm glad to be wanted here, Melanie," he said, shooting me one of his many winning smiles.

When he started getting dressed, I turned away to the window and clutched my arms around my stomach, trying to ease the ache there. Ugh. Hate that he's leaving again. Hate that this could be goodbye.

I wanted to ask if I'd see him again, but before I could, he spoke from the door.

"Stay safe, princess."

I forced myself to answer, "Bye, Greyson."

How can I know so little about someone and yet need him so much?

He hasn't called, but this Monday morning I got another kind of call, and with it, an offer for my Mustang.

I ask Pandora as we settle in the office, "So what do you think, is it a good offer?"

Her answer is to ask me *why* I am selling my car.

Fuck. I try to think of anything but the truth, that it needs to go and I probably need to sell everything but the shirt on my back, and even then the math may not add up, but I just can't tell her. "It's impractical."

"Dude, you live for the impractical."

"It got flooded! It squeaks now."

"Which is cute considering you squeak too."

"Urgh, you're impossible."

"Melanie . . . stop buying shit and you wouldn't need to sell your car. See this shirt? I do something that's called washing it three times a week. I only need a couple of these and that's it. See these boots? They're my signature. I don't need another pair of shoes."

"This is not a shopping problem, it's a different kind of problem."

"What, like an addiction?" Her brow wrinkles with concern.

"I want to sell it, that's all," I mumble.

"*Want* to sell, or *need*?" Perceptive dark eyes suddenly probe into me in silence. "I have an idea. Sell the necklace your boyfriend gave you."

"Pfft! Don't think so!" I wave that off with one hand, then I become somber. "I want to sell my car, and I *need* your advice. Is that a good offer, Pan?"

"I'm a fucking decorator like you, I don't know shit about cars. Ask your dad. Hell, ask your precious boyfriend."

"You know what? I will! I will ask him right fucking now! He will be delighted to hear from me." I pull my phone out. "He even came to brunch."

"Wow, you dragged him off to your parents'. *Really*," Pandora says, then she clucks at me in warning.

"Oh, bug off, Maleficent!" I angrily cry, slapping her with a client's newly upholstered pillow I was checking for quality.

I'm not going to tell her shit anymore.

I won't even explain to her the complexities of two single people doing . . . what are we doing?

We're having sex, that's what we're doing.

But I don't want it to be just sex.

I don't know how many secrets Greyson keeps, but he has a secret room, and he refuses to talk on the phone near me, both of which are odd. Still, I have a secret of my own, so it's not exactly fair to feel this way. I would love to tell him, and only him, about mine. Yet at the same time I pray he's the last man to ever know.

How to relate to a guy you're dating or sleeping with or whatever, a guy whose respect and admiration you want, that you asked—that you *begged*—a group of mobsters for more time because you owe them more money than you thought you had? How to tell him that they lifted your skirt and told you they'd give you an extension—*of their dicks*—if you didn't pay on time.

I want to puke remembering the night in the alley. I could never tell this to *anyone* out loud.

I check my text messages. He was the last who'd texted me. Eons ago when he visited my apartment, and I asked who was coming to visit, and he'd said Me.

I tell myself I don't want to go through all the guessing games again. If he wants me, he wants me. Right?

But my cardinal texting rule niggles at me. Nowadays relationships are so much more equal.

I slowly inhale and text him, Will you be in town this weekend? And to my surprise, he answers right away.

Yes.

My heart starts thundering. I text back, Any plans?

I planned to look up my princess.

Gahhhh. I love that too much.

She wants to cook you dinner. Will you come?

I will. And so will you.

I grin in delight. Sexy cad.

8 pm Friday?

I could not be happier when I tell Pandora, exaggerating, "He's coming into town this weekend just to see me."

"Yoohoo for you." She sounds bored.

❤ ❤ ❤

DURING THE WEEK, I bury myself in work and in getting some of my personal belongings shipped off to an eBay store so I can liquidate, and fast. My closet suddenly seems huge since I only kept one pair of sneakers, one pair of pumps, one pair of sandals, one pair of Uggs, and one pair of rain boots. I also went down to only three pairs of slacks, two pairs of jeans, a small assortment of tops, and the most basic dresses. My accessories were the most difficult to part with. But I kept the most colorful ones to ensure I could continue wearing three colors daily, even if the splashes of color mostly come from my accessories.

On Friday afternoon, I go splurge at Whole Foods because I'm not cooking cheap food for Greyson—I just couldn't. So I bring home a brown bag full of healthy and fresh items, slip on the only apron I kept—a frilly yellow one from Anthropologie— and I cook a homemade dinner for him because it just seems like a nice "welcome home" thing to do.

Menu-wise I went for arugula and pear salad with goat cheese and a light vinaigrette, my special pasta pesto, a loaf of homemade bread, and apple tarts dusted with cinnamon for dessert.

I've always done my best thinking when I'm cooking. This time as I'm chopping and prepping the food, I think of how I'm slowly beginning to recognize my own needs, as a woman, needs I'd never realized were not being met by sleeping with a dozen different guys, needs that couldn't possibly be met until you make a real connection—scary, powerful, inexplicable—with someone. Someone you least expect. Greyson's face haunts me—serious, smiling, thoughtful. I can't stop recalling and replaying his different kinds of smiles.

The smirky one, the sensual one, the indulgent one, the sleepy one, the flat one he gives Pandora, and the one that's almost there, but not quite, as though he won't give himself free rein to give in to it . . .

I love that best.

Because it feels like I'm pulling it out even when he doesn't want me to. Like he's yielding something to me he didn't plan to give me.

"Something smells good around here and my bet is that it's you."

My blood soars when I recognize the warm, smooth voice behind me. Somehow, Greyson got inside and crept up on me! Without making a single noise. And now he slides his big arm around my waist and spins me around, the move placing over six inches of bad boy with his lips only a hairbreadth away from mine. My senses reel as I absorb his nearness and slide my hands in a fast, greedy exploration up his thick arms.

"Hey," I gasp, "I—"

He kisses me for a full minute.

A minute and a half.

Our lips moving, blending, my knees feeling mushy because his kisses are better than anything I've ever had. And now I can't think or talk or hardly stand on my own two feet.

He pulls away and I feel myself blush at his heated appraisal. "I like this," he whispers and signals at my apron, and the delighted light in his eyes makes me feel like I just won top prize on Iron Chef—and he hasn't even tasted my food yet.

"You're going to like it even more when you realize I plan to feed you dessert myself," I whisper. His dirty mind seems to get the best of him, for he looks instantly ravenous. Laughing, I urge him down on one of the two stools at the end of the kitchen island. "It's not what you *think*, it's actual food!"

"Are you taking this off for me?" He tugs the sash of my apron.

"Maybe if you finish your food like a good boy."

He chuckles, a rich, full sound, his grin devastating, taking over my brain. "You like it better when I'm bad," he points out.

Biting back my grin, I pull out the pasta dish with a glove, aware of him noticing that I'm only wearing a short dress under my apron—maybe he can even see I'm wearing *no* panties. The thought sends a tingle through me.

There's a silence and a creak of the stool as he leans back, kicks off his shoes, and there's a confused, almost amused tone to his husky voice when he speaks to me, rubbing his jaw as he watches me wind around the kitchen. "I keep wondering what you're doing all the time." He pauses, then, his voice lower and thicker than ever, "You miss me?"

"What kind of question is that?"

He gives me a roguish grin. "One I want to know the answer to."

I return the grin with one of my own as I serve us both, and when I set down his salad and pasta, he clamps his bare hand around my wrist. "Do you?"

Our eyes meet, and he gently stokes a growing fire in me as he rubs his thumb along the inside of my wrist.

"Do you?" he asks, softly.

"Yes," I whisper. I trail my free hand across his jaw and impulsively lean over to kiss his cheek. Adding, near his ear, "A lot."

He watches me like a predator as I go take my seat on the stool across the island.

We smile at each other, those smiles that seem to spread our lips simultaneously; from the moment we met it's always been like that. I notice, at last, that he's brought wine, and I watch as he pops open the bottle, searches my cabinet for glasses, and comes back to pour a glass for me, and another for him.

We clink glasses, smiling, and before he drinks, he murmurs, "To you, princess."

"No, to you," I counter, taking a sip.

"You like going against me, don't you," he purrs, still swirling and sniffing his own glass.

I laugh and suddenly I feel like the sexiest thing in existence as I start to eat. As if my every move is meant to entice him, excite and exhilarate him.

Not even my breaths escape his notice.

I feel him look at my fingers, my bare arms, my bare shoulders, my lips. I fork some salad and watch him tear off a piece of bread and stick it into his mouth. We sip quietly, watching each other, savoring each other's company. The look of each other. The energy of each other. I'm a decorator who believes in feng shui. I believe in yin and yang. I have never felt such a yang to my yin. Ever.

"Do you like the meal?" I ask him.

"Am I the first man you've cooked for?"

I narrow my eyes, sipping a bit of red wine for courage, but there's no cure for the nervous spinning in my stomach. "Truth? Yes. You are. So think very well about your answer," I warn.

"Every spoonful was as delicious as you."

I smile. "Really?" Feeling insecure, I check his plates and notice he's wiped them both clean.

He edges back, and his gaze drops from my eyes to my shoulders to my breasts. "I'm ready for dessert."

"Wait, mister, I'm not finished. I have some actual dessert that's not me, you know!" I twirl some pasta onto my fork a little faster and ram it into my mouth, licking some pesto off the corner of my lips.

Greyson watches me intently, and he looks so big, dark, and sexy in my apartment, I'm not accustomed to the deep little pangs of longing springing up inside my chest.

"How was your week?" he asks.

A flash of feelings stabs me when I remember all the nights I've lain in bed, more frightened than I want to be, and more lonely than I've ever felt in my life. Maybe it's because I know who I want to be with right now. Maybe it's because I feel vulnerable and scared.

"Actually, good," I lie. "I wanted to ask you. I got an offer for my car."

"You're selling your car?"

I gaze at him in despair and notice the sudden grim set to his mouth. "Yes, I'm selling it." I get up and go get his empty plates as I tell him how much I was offered. "Do you think it's a fair price?"

He's silent as I carry his plates to the sink, tracking me with his gaze as he asks me, "Why do you need to sell it?"

I can't help but notice he looks more than a little curious. He seems determined.

So I try going for lighthearted, including adding a casual shrug to my explanation. "Just have my eye on something else."

One dark eyebrow goes up, followed by another, and then an achingly slow, clearly smart question. "Another car?"

He's not buying it.

I wrack my brain for something to say that will be as far away from the truth as I can, until he speaks, sighing as though I wear him out, "They're low-balling you. Don't sell your fucking car, princess, not for that, not for anything."

"Why not?"

"Because," he grits out, "you *need* your car."

"Not to go to the office," I lightly counter, "and I can hitch a ride with friends to go out during the weekends."

When he continues looking displeased, I feel instantly suspicious. "Why are you so protective of my car, Greyson?"

After a rather interesting silence, during which my heart melts in my chest, I answer for him. "Because thanks to that fucked-up car, I hooked up with you."

He hikes up one big shoulder in an angry shrug. "That car is you. It doesn't go with anyone else."

I feel giddy thinking he might feel protective of the spot where we met, but I'm also sad that I can't explain to him that no matter how attached I am to that car, I'm more attached to *myself*. "My buyer is a young eighteen-year-old, she'll have as much fun with it as I have."

When he speaks again, his voice carries a unique force, almost like a command. "Nobody can ever have as much fun as you do. You *are* fun, Melanie. And life. And so is that crazy, sweet little blue Mustang."

I bring my hand up to stifle my giggles, because he's being terribly cute and protective, and when he scowls, I tell him, "I think it's adorable, Greyson."

"That word and I don't go together, princess."

"It's adorable. *You're* adorable."

He stands as though he's going to make me pay for that. I run toward my room, laughing, and say from the door, "Greyson, I know this will break your tender heart, but I really need to sell my car. I'll just ask for a thousand more. What do you say? God, even that scowl you're wearing is *adorable*."

He throws his head back and laughs—the sound rich and deep—and when I realize he won't ever get the direness of my circumstances, I excuse myself to the bedroom for a moment and call the interested party to ask for one thousand more.

The girl tells me she'll talk to her dad and let me know. When I come back out, Greyson's standing with his arms crossed, looking at me with the kind of look a man wears when he doesn't know what the fuck to do with you.

"I counteroffered," I explain, once again the word "adorable" whispering through my hair as he rubs a hand through his own in frustration.

"Ahh, princess. Really. I can't even . . ." He shakes his head in obvious frustration.

"Greyson, it doesn't matter!" I cry. "Even if the car is gone, you'll always be both my and my Mustang's hero, you know."

Somehow aching to appease him—hey, his volatile energy feels like a tornado in the room—I approach him and brush my hand through his mussed-up hair as I try to smooth it out again, loving the softness, which is just about the only thing soft on his hard head. He growls and catches me by the waist, surprising me when he drops his head and sets his nose between my breasts and kisses my cleavage with fierce tenderness.

"If you weren't going to listen to me," he murmurs, his voice muffled by my apron, "why ask me?"

"I like knowing your opinion."

"Show me you like it by proving you're listening to me, Melanie."

"I'm sorry," I whisper, rumpling his head playfully as I try to make him be happy again. The pleaser in me just can't take his displeasure. Not his. "I'll make it up to you."

"Hmm." His eyes glow like torches all of a sudden. "Make it up to me by telling me how you'd like to spend your twenty-fifth birthday," he proposes.

A moment's hesitation settles between us. What would he say if I told him I wanted to spend the day with him? Doing nothing but *him* all day? That I want him to tell me about his life, his family, that I just want to be with him because, lately, that's when I'm happiest?

Prying free of his hold and forcing him to settle down on his seat, I bring over the cinnamon apple tart on a plate, then I boost myself up to sit on the island counter right in front of his seat. Using my lap as a table, I set my bare feet on his thighs and lift a spoon to feed him dessert.

"Where did you spend your twenty-fifth birthday?" I ask, spooning a little of the tart into his mouth.

He eats every spoonful I feed him, and the act is not as hot and sexy as I'd imagined it to be; it's ten times more so. Because of those eyes. The way they watch me feed him like some predator biding his time for the *real* meal. "Probably drunk. Nowhere memorable. You braid your hair when you cook too?" he asks gruffly, tugging at my knot as I feed him another spoonful.

Something intensely intimate flares between us. Every second, he's unlocking both my heart and my soul, and there's no stopping the barrage of emotions overtaking me. Longing, tenderness, want, hunger, need, fear, happiness.

"It's to keep my hair on my head and off my plates," I tell him.

"Ahh," he says, eyes twinkling as I bring up another spoonful of tart to his mouth. Watching as his tongue takes the spoon and runs around it teases all my senses. A buttery sensation flows across my thighs as I watch how his lips close over the spoon, how he savors it, how he watches me as he eats his tart, his eyes bright and hungry and brilliant like a bastard who knows I'm wet and ready for him. I feel like he's baking me on the inside just like the oven baked my pie. As he takes the last bite, he tugs the tip of my braid and runs it under my chin, caressing me down my throat, and then . . . into my cleavage.

An instant flood of heat pools between my legs, pussy gripping greedily to feel him inside me again. Why is everything he does so fucking hot? My heart is racing and my brain is screaming—touch him! Kiss him! Straddle him and feel him, show him you want him! Make him want you back, just like this! Make him want to STAY!

But I don't move because I also really crave, I really *need*, for him to make the first move. So I boost myself down and whisper, "I should clean up."

With a low, unexpected groan, he clamps his hand over mine and forces my hand down against his erection—pulsing between his legs and as hard as I've ever felt it—then he turns his head and takes my mouth in a quick, heady kiss that tastes of cinnamon and apples and him. "Princess, I've been like that for hours. Hours. Since I boarded the damn flight on my way here . . ."

"If you've been like this for so long, then you can give me ten minutes to clear this up so I will have nothing else to do the rest of the night but *you*," I seductively whisper, then I giggle happily when he warns, a thick, raw lust roiling in his eyes, "Five minutes."

"It's not a race," I counter, and then, purposely, secretly, I start moving more slowly to entice him. He watches my every move, making love to me with his eyes as I start cleaning up the rest of the table. Playfully, I slap his hand away when he tries cupping my butt. He chuckles as I carry the plates to the sink, and I'm so affected by the rumbling sound, I can't quell the pulsing throb in my body, *begging* me for his fingers, his lips, his teeth, his tongue. He's been hard for hours but he doesn't know I've been wet and achy for just as long.

He helps me take the rest of the plates to the sink, and the gesture, along with his overpowering nearness, keeps me on edge. As he finishes clearing the table, I start to wash, our fingers brushing, our bodies connecting in so many points, every one of them sizzles across my nerve endings.

When I'm washing the last plate, he stands behind me, his body a wall of brick, his palm rubbing my butt as he starts kissing the back of my neck in the most breathtaking way. "It felt like coming home for the first time in a long time tonight, Melanie," he says, and I can detect the rasp of gratitude in his voice.

"No girl cooked for you before?"

I'm amused and laughingly turn, but when I look into his eyes, my amusement vanishes.

There's something very serious in his eyes, and very, very tender.

His jaw looks squarer from the force of his hunger as he reaches out to unhook the apron from my nape, letting it fall to my waist as he undoes the knot at the small of my back.

"Nobody has cooked for me for thirteen years," he says, knocking the wind out of me with what I see roiling in his gaze. Hunger, but not only of the physical kind. Hunger to be nurtured, taken, accepted.

I know this hunger. I hunger for the same.

Watching me like I'm all the acceptance he's ever wanted, he laces both his hands through mine and backs me toward my bedroom.

My pulse thunders as he backs me inside, letting his thumbs trail along my face. When he kisses me, his kiss is such velvet, I feel like I could fly. His body presses close to mine, filling me with yearning. I close my eyes when he dips his fingers into my braid and slowly unwinds it. I shake my hair out and run my fingers over it, and he sinks his fingers in with mine as though curious as to how I do it. I close my eyes and feel him awkwardly but very tenderly use his hands to unravel all of my hair.

Do you ever want someone to look at you, but see only the good? This is me with him. I don't want him to see that I'm a mess inside sometimes. I'm trying to be the perfect girlfriend. And I know that he's trying to be the perfect boyfriend too. I guess it's not fair. I want him to see only the good, but I want to see all of him. Even the bad. As we kiss for a while, we talk about memories from his childhood, his uncle named Eric, how they went hunting all the time at a Texas ranch. We talk about my ballet lessons growing up, my embarrassment when I fell at my first recital. We talk tonight. But I want to know more, every piece of the puzzle that is him.

He doesn't mince words and he tells me what he likes about me and how much he wants me. And I still want more, but our kisses are getting heavy, so heavy I can't breathe right anymore. He's taken off his shirt and is now in only his slacks, while he's pried off my apron and left me in my skimpy little dress.

I suck on his nipple ring. God, how I love this ringed nipple. The groan that follows my sucks. I love how the other nipple puckers in response as I stroke it with my fingertips.

"You wear a scar and yet I can't ever imagine you being broken," I whisper as I rub my hands up the muscled grooves of his chest, paying extra attention to the long, textured slash of his scar. I really value scars. The story they tell. The meaning they wear.

"My scar," I say, then I hesitate before murmuring, "Do you know what it's for? It's because I needed a kidney when I was young."

Shocked at my own revelation, I ease back, protectively curling my arms around myself. "Melanie, come here," he commands, a spark of some indefinable emotion in his eyes. I take one step to him, and he slides my dress off my shoulders, down my waist, and to the floor.

I'm so exposed . . .

I stare at my feet, feeling myself go red unexpectedly. I'm not wearing panties and I didn't cover my scar.

Greyson exhales, a long and slow sound as he takes in my nakedness, then he clenches my waist in one hand and tugs me closer, his voice low and breaking with huskiness. "You, princess, are nothing but perfect."

"Do you realize I haven't ever talked to anyone about it?" I whisper.

He fingers the scar on my hip bone, tracing it with one blunt fingertip. "I see the pills you take for this every morning."

"They're so my body doesn't reject it. But since she was my identical twin, my dose is minor. My body . . . accepted it almost as if it were mine."

Impulsively, I lean over and set my lips on the deeper, more jagged cut near the bottom of his rib cage. "Now you tell me how you got this?"

"Long time ago," he touches my hair with one hand, "my brother . . . my half brother got into a fight. Had to pull him out of there and got a souvenir. It's nothing."

Dragging my lips up his scar and toward his neck and those thick tendons I really like and the Adam's apple that makes his voice rumble the way it does, he tilts my head up by the chin and looks at me, smoldering eyes trailing down to my tits, my abdomen, my perfectly waxed pussy, and the way he looks at me as if he's photographing me in his mind sends a dizzying current racing through me.

"I want to be in you, to lose myself in you."

His energy feels as hot and erratic as a summer storm as he lifts me up and carries me up to my bed. He starts kissing me in the darkness, cupping my head and feeding only my mouth for long, heady minutes.

Then he's touching. My breathing goes with every pull on my nipples. The cup of his palm on my sex. I moan at the press and roll of his mouth over mine, and the addition of his thumb sliding behind me, slowly killing me as he caresses my little ass. "Oh god, Grey," I gasp when his free hand slips down my abdomen, lower, and lower, while his tongue takes mine. I part my thighs with a sigh, and he strokes me open, my folds slick under his fingers, and suddenly everything is gone. My debt. My dreams. My work. My to-do list. It's all gone except for Greyson's mouth and hands in me, the gentle abrasion of his stubble against my jaw. His breath going as fast as mine.

"You smell as good as you feel." His gruff whisper is hot against my mouth. His body trembles with unleashed power. I can see, even in the dark, the sheer, raw, aggressive beauty under the polish. I love the way the walls drop when he fucks me. How he peels layers of me away until I'm vulnerable and shaking. How he's as lost in what he does as I am.

"Say something wrong to prove this isn't happening," I whisper.

"I don't think so, I don't feel like ruining tonight just yet." His gruff voice resonates with lust as he looks at me, his eyes glittering, fierce. Engulfing.

"Fuck me hard." I gasp for breath as his tongue swirls wetly over my skin and he dips his middle finger into my folds, stoking, gathering my juices.

"Wet, tight, and ready," he rasps in undisguised pleasure, his chuckle dark and throaty as he presses two fingers in me.

The need for him builds and twists along my nerves, tangles in my every muscle. My heart beats furiously in my chest as he suckles one of my nipples, and when he fingers both my pussy and my back at the same time, I scream.

Hot sucking motions rock through me as I jerk my hips to his hands, my fingers burying in his hair as my body grips his plunging fingers, terrified of losing them.

"Say you want me to fuck you, long and hard and everywhere," he says, his face twisted into a mask of pleasure as he watches me.

"I want you to, I need you to fuck me everywhere," I plead. "Only you. Please."

"Here?" Face raw with desire, he caresses the outer rim of my ass with his thumb again and teases the tip back inside.

I bite back another scream of pleasure. "Greyson, I want this with you." I lick my lips as my body tightens involuntarily, a sheen of perspiration already coating our bodies, we're so hot. "You know how much I want this with you."

"It'll take us over the edge, Melanie. Over the fucking edge, are you ready to go there with me?" he warns, his tongue rasping into my ear. My flesh melts as he starts dragging his mouth down, sucking my breasts until I arch and gasp, then lower, trailing a hot, swirling path down my belly button, to my bare sex. "First I want to taste you until you're ready to convulse, princess."

He sucks my clit into his mouth and I groan in delirium. "Oh god."

"God can't help you, baby, but I can." He blows air over my clit in the most seductive way. "I want to kiss this sweet cunt, taste it, suck it." He takes it lightly between his teeth, then gently sucks me. Fire courses through my veins as he spreads his hands open on my thighs and opens my pussy lips wider for his tongue.

"Greyson . . ." I cry as pleasure bursts through my veins, my body spread open for his kiss, my hands fisting on the sheets.

It feels somehow like he's rewarding me because I cooked for him. But also like he's claiming something from me. Like he's claiming me. Every inch of me. When his thumb penetrates *there* again, I'm thoughtless, only groaning and mewing and whimpering and pleading, my hips jerking upward and backward.

"Are you ready for this, Melanie?" His eyes are dilated, but sharp and assessing as he studies me.

I squeeze my eyes shut and grind out, "Yes, please!"

He growls deep in his chest and bends over. His tongue flicks over my clit, then into my sex, probing and pushing into me. My senses open like floodgates. The tip of his thumb goes inside my backside, deeper, stimulating little nerves I never even knew I had.

Shock resounds on my body as he plays with my ass, thumbing me as he uses his other hand to hold my hips down and control the angle of us, how close we are, how his lips pleasure my wet, aching sex, every sinew in my body craving him like nothing . . .

Him.

Him.

Him.

He lifts his head, his lips wet with me, and he's the most beautiful living thing I've ever seen.

"I want to fuck you bare," he murmurs as he fiercely meets my gaze and slips two long fingers into my pussy, using them to part me. "No condom. Just you and me, Melanie."

Feel him in me? Flesh to flesh? Nothing between us?

My throat hurts as waves of lava flow through me, and I nod hard. "I've always been safe . . ."

I see a flash of something dark and haunting in his eyes. "I'm not safe, princess, but I'm clean and I want you bare just as soon as I get a lab to prove it to you. Would any other form of birth control interfere with your antirejection medications?"

"I . . . no, Grey."

"You sure?"

The genuine concern in his eyes only makes me need him all the more. "*Yes!* My doctor had once mentioned I could use a low-dose oral contraceptive if I needed to."

His expression twists with some fierce determination, as if us doing this will mean some sort of commitment for us. I sense he needs to take me, to take me fiercely and in ways he's never taken a girl before.

"Come here," he says, grabbing me by the hair. "I want to kiss you hard, but fuck you harder." He slams his mouth down, and adds, into my mouth, "But first things first."

Whimpering as our bodies grind naturally as we kiss, I run my hand up his face and slip my fingers into his soft, thick hair, and I hear myself whisper his name against his jaw. His body trembles with unleashed power. "Say it again."

"Greyson."

"Now go up on your knees and elbows," he says in a rough-ened whisper.

Oh, god . . . it's really happening.

Tremors seize my entire body. There is no man I would trust more to do this with. No man I'd ever really wanted to do this with. And I want him to take every part of me, fuck every hole in me with his cock, his fingers, his tongue. He slips his fingers over my folds again, testing my pussy first, dragging the moisture up the crack of my buttocks.

"The wetter you are, the easier this is for me to thrust in."

"I'm so hot. Grey, the way you looked at me when I was feed-ing you was foreplay enough."

"Melanie, look at what you do to me." He rubs the head of his enormous erection between my ass cheeks and presses the mounds together so I feel the friction. I feel every pulse in his long cock, how hard and throbbing he is. He uses the swollen head to spread my pussy juices up to my ass and teases me with them. I'm quivering on my elbows and knees. *Quivering.*

"Greyson . . ." I moan. The anticipation is killing me, the feel of him so close, but so far. The scent of him dizzying me, while my eyes can't see him and feel starved.

"Shh, baby I want this more than you do," he croons behind me as he strokes a hand down my spine, caressing every dent of my backbone. "I fantasize about it. I fantasize about doing this with you. To you."

I hear the ripping sound of a condom and lick my lips, staring at the wall in front of me with blurry eyes, my body throbbing for his, my pussy thrumming jealously.

"Will it hurt me?" I breathe fast and shallow as he presses the crown lightly into the rosette of my backside.

"Maybe . . ." he taunts as he trails his long, blunt fingers up my spine again before seizing a fistful of my hair and pulling my head back to whisper in my ear, "Or maybe not. With you and me, there are no givens. No rules. Just what we want. And I want every inch of you. I want what you've given no one. This fuck is mine." He sweeps a hand to squeeze my breasts, pinching the sensitive tips of my nipples. Arrows of pleasure singe me, both my pussy and the place I want him to penetrate clenching tight in response.

"Just take it, Grey," I gasp.

His thick answering murmur feels like a caress to me. "You bet your ass I will, princess. You don't tease a man about wanting a thick, long dick up your lovely, tight little butt without getting what you're asking for. Loosen up now, I'm lubing up."

I mew as he presses his thumb into me, and then . . . something thicker, so much larger, so much harder. Deliciously creamed up and pushing into me.

"Push back against me, baby, that's it, *fuck that feels good, princess,*" he cooes, softly, as he advances inch by inch, stroking a hand down my abdomen to caress my pussy.

"Oh god, Grey!" I scream, and I turn and bite down on my own arm, moaning as he stretches me so much it's almost painful, but it's too pleasurable to be painful and I like it too much, the way he does it slowly, the way he caresses my swollen sex to wet and prepare me, the way he leans over and starts to graze his teeth over my nape, primal, like a werewolf wanting to bite me.

I've never felt so full, so aroused, and so emotionally vulnerable. I'm panting to get the words out . . . "Please, Greyson. Move. Fuck me."

He grabs my hips and eases out, and he says something that shoots a new heat like a lightning bolt through me. "As you wish."

As you wish.

My favorite movie; and he knows it.

The words, in that movie, mean so much when Westley whispers them. He whispers them right now as I give him my only fantasy.

By the time he starts up a slow, careful rhythm, I'm emotionally unwound and physically unraveling. Tears stream down my face, of pleasure, happiness, and the complete barrage of sensations he fills me with.

There's a bang on the door, and my body tightens and quivers in reaction, shaking and waiting as I hold myself utterly still. He keeps his pace and remains thrusting, pulsing in me when he stays inside, easing in and out with improved ease every time. His hands tremble on my hips, and I can feel both our bodies straining, our breaths jerking out of our lungs.

"Hey, Romeo, will you answer your goddamn phone!"

Whoever is shouting outside the door is yelling L-O-U-D.

Greyson groans softly but doesn't stop, and my pulse is thundering in my veins, my heart on the verge of exploding. *Oh god please not now.*

"Hey, ROMEO!"

Greyson rubs my pussy, breathing hard in my ear, whispering,

"I'm not answering Derek until you come. I'm not pulling out of you until you twist and thrash, right now, in orgasm. Now what do you say when I tell you to come, Melanie?"

I moan as his sexy voice spills through my body, the pleasure so absolute I can't breathe, think—I can only feel taken and plowed and full and his.

"I don't know," I moan.

"What do you say to me, princess?"

He rocks his hips again, gently, as he circles my clit in delicious rubbing circles with two fingers, and I sob *As you wish* and when I turn my head and he French-kisses my mouth, slow and headily, I come, harder than ever, every piece of me shattering, body, mind, soul, heart, crying softly as I feel him jerk powerfully inside me. He clenches one arm around my waist and pins me to his body, exhaling hard as he comes with me.

When it's over, we don't move.

The pillow is wet and I'm quietly sobbing. Greyson pulses, alive, inside me, and I don't want to lose him. Still in me. Pulsing in the most delicious way. Still somehow hard. I groan when he pulls out and rolls to his back, reaching out to grab my face, searches for any hint of discomfort on my face.

"These tears. Good or bad? Good or bad, baby?"

"Good," I croak, rubbing my cheek dry with his palm. "Was it good for you too?"

"God, good's not even a word for it," he says tenderly, then he takes the rest of my tears with his lips, his eyes all liquid as he kisses my nose, my mouth, in some quiet male gratitude over what I just let him do to me. Over what we did, together.

I'm shaking a little, and he murmurs, "Stay here, princess." He stands to get rid of the condom and clean up, then he comes back and pulls me against him, brushing my hair behind my ears, his big body cradling mine. "That live up to how you imagined it would be?"

My chest is so full that I'm certain I'm going to burst. "Never in my wildest dreams could I have imagined a guy like you or how you make me feel."

"Princess, the kind of shit between us isn't normal." His lips press grimly together for a moment, his eyes darkening. "The way you invade my thoughts sometimes doesn't sit too well with me, Melanie. In my line of work distractions don't go well."

"Is that what I am?"

"A distraction? You're my fucking *obsession*. Not even a fantasy anymore. You're going to be the death of me, princess, and I don't give a shit anymore. I just don't want to be the death of you."

Fierce, glimmering eyes hold mine as I process his words.

Someone knocks on the door again. "Hey, BOSSMAN! Code 104. Repeat one-oh-four!"

He clamps his jaw as he seems to recognize what that means, then he stands with a vicious growl and slams a fist to a wall.

I swallow and roll to my back, my chest heaving as I try to recover. "Is that Derek? Is he drunk?"

Greyson grabs his clothes and this time yells out his frustration as he smashes his fist into the wall as he passes.

He comes out from the bathroom and slips into his slacks and a clean white button-down shirt but doesn't even bother to close it as he heads to the door. He slams the door behind him, and I lay here, trembling, exhaling hard.

What we did was . . .

Oh god.

I leap off the bed and go to the bathroom, clean up, splash some water over my face, then I slip into something old and comforting. A T-shirt that I pull out when I've had my worst days.

It seems my sixth sense is right.

Grey comes back and grabs my forehead and sets a quick kiss there, then looks at me with liquid hazel eyes, warm and apologetic as he kisses my eyelids. "Go to sleep, I'll be back as soon as possible. Derek will be here in case you need anything. He'll drive you anywhere, keep an eye on you for me."

I think I make a noncommittal movement of my head, but when he leaves, I scream into my pillow over our ruined evening.

I'm not hungry, but I'm an anxious eater so I have some cereal, then I watch TV as I try to calm down my raging senses. I reorganize my drawers. I even stop and turn the locks of all my windows and doors when the familiar fear starts creeping in. It's late when I fall asleep in bed, waiting for him to come back.

But in the morning, Greyson calls to tell me he's got things to take care of and he won't be coming back anytime soon.

❤ ❤ ❤

PANDORA IS HAVING a field day with this; I should've known better than to mope at the office.

"He leaves in an unspecified emergency," she's telling me as we walk to work with our Starbucks, "he gives you diamonds like on the second date. Who does that? Guys who have mistresses, that's who. Guys who can't parade their girlfriends freely across town because their wives will find out."

"Wow, you're bitter, girl."

"Imagine if he does have a mistress! You just had anal with the guy."

"I would not change it for anything, *anything*." I sip my coffee and it's so hot, I almost scald my lips and have to blow air through the slit. "Look, he was called away but he'll be back. I know he will."

"When? Your birthday's *this* weekend."

"So? Who cares about my birthday when . . ." My voice drops, and I whisper, "He's the *One*. He is *so* the One that when I'm with him, I feel like pinching my own arm to see if it's real. And yet in all this time, Pandora, not *once* have you been happy for me. Why? Why are you being such a fucking party pooper?"

Pandora stops walking in the middle of the sidewalk and just gapes at me.

Which forces me to come back and plant myself at her side to explain.

"You've said every bad thing you could think of and then some," I remind her. "You want me to talk to you and want to be encouraging, but guess what? All you make me want to do is not tell you shit because you judge and you judge harshly, Pandora. Nobody likes being around people like you."

She blinks, then scowls and starts walking again, her face downcast and her voice apologetic. "I'm sorry I'm not Brooke."

"I don't want you to be Brooke, I want you to be happy for me," I clarify. "Or at least, like, only half as mean!"

"Bullshit, you want me to be Brooke, and guess what?" She stops and grabs my arm so that I stop with her, looking at me with eyes that glow fiercely with determination. "I'm sorry I can't be like your best friend forever but she's fucking gone, Mel. So text her all you want and wait two hours for her to answer because she's too busy with a real man and a real baby and a real life! I'm the only real friend you've got right now and I'm trying to watch out for you."

"Thank you for watching out for me, but what you say *hurts me* and you don't realize it. It hurts my optimism. It fucks up all the hope I have for us—for me and him. Did you know that I feel awful every Monday when he leaves? Did you? I have this strange paranoia that I'm never seeing him again and every Monday at the office you only make me feel worse. Like I'm not worth him returning to."

I wait for her to answer, but she doesn't answer, so I go on, "I get what you're trying to protect me from, but it's too late, Pan. I'm already *falling in lo*—"

"Shit, don't say that! Don't. Fall."

I plunge my fingers through my hair, close to pulling it off at the roots. "God, please, for your own health, tell me the name of the guy who made you like this!" I beg her.

She hesitates, scowling down at the sidewalk for a moment. "Look him up in the Guinness Book of World Records under World's Greatest ASSHOLE," she mutters.

"Just tell me his name so we can go make a voodoo doll for him or something!" I cry.

She groans and clutches her stomach. "I can't. I can't say his name."

"Why?"

"Because it's fucking everywhere and it drives me insane. Insane! I won't speak it. Ever."

"Pan," I say softly, but she shakes her head.

"Look, I'm sorry for spoiling your fantasies, but I'm being realistic here and you're going a thousand miles an hour, Melanie. You meet the guy, you get jewels. He tells you his driver is here for whatever you need and the dude is following you—" She signals to where Derek is clearly driving around the block. "You have kinky, wonderful sex, then he disappears. And you don't question this? You meekly wait for a call? Where's the Melanie I know? The Melanie I know has ants up her butt and she wouldn't take orders from some dude she just met. Your birthday is two days from now. For the first year in your life, you have nothing planned. You have to celebrate. Period."

"I'm saving this year, all right? Next year I'll blow the roof off the house, but not this one, so bug off."

We both become morosely silent as we ride up in the elevator and head to our desks, and that's when Pandora informs me in her typical monotone voice, "Check your text. Your BFF is not happy about no celebration happening. We've just been sent tickets."

"What?" Confused, I pull out my phone and see Brooke's message.

Mel!!! Come to Denver! It's your twenty-five years, I want to see you, and Pete's already taken care of tickets for both you and P.

I gasp, then blink three times and swing my chair around until I'm staring at Pandora. She's smirking, the closest she gets to grinning. "Brooke got us tickets! PLANE TICKETS! We're going to see Brooke!" I cry.

"Yep," Pandora says, nodding and nodding.

Grinning, I text Brooke: Holeeeeee sheet! Thank you! I miss you so much!

Brooke: I miss my BFF and Pandora told me you're having man troubles.

Me: Sort of. ☹ I'm just terribly confused and terribly hooked on him and worried that he's not. I need my BFF! I can't wait to see you.

I tuck my phone away and grin at Pandora.

"Yeah, I know, you love the hell out of me," she mumbles.

"Well, I do," I say. "I love you and Brooke so much. Are we watching a fight?"

"Of course, ninny! Who do you think paid for our tickets?"

Smiling at that, I turn back to my computer and absently stroke my diamond necklace, and suddenly the feel of Greyson's diamonds under my fingers makes my heart wrench with new pain. A fresh, wild hope claws at my insides as his words come back to tease and torture me.

Melanie, when you're waiting for me to call, look at these stones and know for certain that that phone will ring.

SEVENTEEN

MORE

Greyson

Seething inside, I look past my shoulder at my half brother Wyatt.

I shouldn't even be here. I've got better things to do than babysit him, and the thought that I ended up driving around town for twenty-four hours with C.C., looking for my "lost" brother instead of spending the weekend in Seattle makes me want to hit something.

Slamming on the brakes, I park the SUV, turn around, and slam my fist into Wyatt's face.

"Ouch!" he cries.

I then get out and go around to pull him out of the car and shove him toward the old bar-turned-warehouse where tonight's Underground fights will take place.

"You can't hang out with our fighters, much less with that twisted motherfucker Scorpion," I growl as C.C. climbs out of the front-passenger seat and follows us. "There's no such thing as friendship between them and us—only business. Do you understand me, Wyatt?"

"I understand you're a fucking asshole, Grey," he says, wiping blood from his nose.

"I'm not running a grade school here. You either get the gist of things or get off my fucking floor. C.C. won't be bailing out your ass anymore—nor will I. I've got fucking stuff to do."

"Yeah, why don't we talk a little bit about that because you're moodier than a chick with fucking PMS!" He smirks. "So, what's her fucking name, huh?"

I grab him by the shirt and lift him so our eyes are level, my patience at its limit. "You can't rough up the police chief's son over a fucking *cockfight*! He was drunk, you were drunk, and the Scorpion was stoned out of his mind. We've got something much bigger going on here, Wyatt, and you're going to get us all exposed." I let go and jerk the door open while Wyatt storms inside.

"Those weren't even my fucking roosters, I was just helping attach the bladed claws."

"That's just sick, Wyatt," C.C. says as we enter.

"Nobody gives a shit what you think, C.C.," Wyatt snaps.

I look at my half brother. Banged up. Reckless. Careless. If it weren't for C.C. bailing his ass out the years I was gone, Wyatt would be either dead or in jail. "I'm so sick of you trying to prove yourself to him," I tell him with an angry shove. "Now get inside and get to work before our father finds out about this."

"You won't tell him?"

I clamp my jaw and shake my head in angry silence. God knows I should. I should tell him. But watching the kind of punishments my father would dole out to him would give me no pleasure.

"Don't tell the Big E either, bastard hates my guts. Hell, I can't see why since you're the one who poked his goddamn eye out."

We watch him storm away, and C.C. looks at me. "Sorry I called. Figured he needed to get the ultimatum from you or E. But E's got his hands full with your father as it is."

I head over to stash the cash from two of my latest marks into the accounting records in the vault, ready to get out of there and work on some of my last targets.

I need the job done, and I needed it done yesterday.

Outside the long hall where we're set up, the screeching of dragged scaffolding blends with the noise of men working to set up the space. The Underground's fighting season has started. Two or three fights per week, each week a different location. Before my flight to Portland, home of one of my last targets, I check on the team.

Wyatt is surveying the cameras while a half dozen men set up the fighting ring.

Through the monitors, I see Leon is helping make sure the stands are set.

I can also see Zedd is out by the entrance, making sure the exit doors work.

Harley, he's eating pizza.

Thomas's voice is audible down the hall, along with some female voices of a couple of groupies, I suppose.

In one of the biggest rooms, Father sits quietly, all his medical equipment surrounding him. I pause as I walk by. A nurse is feeding him, and he looks slimmer. A slither of remorse hits me as I wonder if this man—a man I saw torture and kill, yet also protect me—is actually dying. I stand by the door and Eric rises. He's been by my father's side for days, and he looks beat. "Didn't expect you here."

"How is he?"

Why do I fucking ask?

Why do I fucking care?

"Weak. But still hanging on. He really wants to see you succeed," Eric says.

I feel my jaw muscles work at that, because I don't want the Underground, I want my mother's location. But I walk over and say, surprised by the fucking mercy in my voice, mercy he certainly didn't teach me, "I'm almost done, Father. Only four more and you get every name and what you're owed. And I'm waiting to hear from my mother most of all."

He smiles weakly. "This place was your home. We lived like gypsies, but it was your home. My dream is for you to show me . . . you're man enough to make it yours. Good or bad. You've shown me you're my son . . . but you're also your mother's son, aren't you? Which is why Wyatt doesn't cut it. Only you do."

Once again, I see the respect in his eyes, and I grind my molars.

"Good or bad, you'll get every name on this list scratched off," I vow.

COCKFIGHTS, HANGING OUT with one of our most disreputable, dirtiest fighters, one who'd had Wyatt rough up the police chief's son? I do not like this side of Wyatt.

My brother is still glaring. Guess we never got along. When I came on board, he was younger and had been my father's toy until my father decided it was more fun to play with me. If I'd let him break me, maybe he'd have left me alone, but when I didn't, he grew obsessed. Wyatt doesn't know how lucky he was—he doesn't get it.

"Tina stopped by," he grumbles. "She's got something for you but she refused to leave it with me."

"I'll make contact, but I can't right now. Do me a favor and make yourself useful." I want him out doing something, not sulking around here, nursing a grudge. "Book me a meeting with her for this weekend so she can deliver what I need."

He glares and nods.

I steal a slice of cold pizza from Harley and chomp it down as I make sure Wyatt makes a note of it.

"All right, thanks," I say, slapping his back. "Put some ice on that." I signal to his nose.

"Fuck off."

"Fine, Wyatt, have it your way."

I slip on my gloves and head to the airport.

One flight later, just as the sun is about to start setting, I hop into the back of a cab while I stare unseeingly out at the street, wondering how my princess is. Suddenly I see an image of my mother being taken, Melanie's face superimposed, and a new kind of rage simmers in me. I need to get back. I need to finish my marks and get back, soon. Derek is good—he can protect Melanie. But he's not *me*. Now Wyatt is asking why the fuck I'm so wired—what her name is? Soon he'll find out. They'll all find out.

I pull out two of my phones, add her number to my newest prepaid device, and before I disable the old one, I text her, Got new number. Call you at 9.

Disabling the old phone, I text Derek a numerical code from the new one so that he knows it's me and I have a new number. He answers with another number. Another code that says everything is good and Melanie is at work.

When the cab drops me off at my location, I ease out, pull the black hoodie over my head, keep my aviators hooked into my collar, and head into the office building. Harley and Wyatt are black-hat hackers. They've got me booked on my mark's appointment list under one of his acquaintance's names. The marks? They hate when you're in their homes or their offices. They feel vulnerable and threatened that a man like you would steal into their space.

And that's what you need to do: you need to make them feel unsafe. Like there's nowhere to hide from you. No way to escape you because of the fucking money they owe.

I murmur my fake name to the receptionist, get a pass, and slip on my aviators as I head upstairs. I'm aware of the security cameras everywhere. I'm gloved, wearing new sneakers, clean clothes, my body scrubbed dry, my hair protected under my hood; no trace, I'm like a ghost. The key is to keep my head down so no camera can see my face.

Easing out of the elevator, I repeat the name to the tenth-floor secretary. By the time I enter my mark's sumptuous office, he's grinning behind the computer, thinking I'm a young college friend of his son who's going to discuss internship.

He lifts his head and stands. "Daniel," he explodes in glee, extending his arms.

My hand curls around my SIG. "Sorry, Daniel got caught up. Don't even try it." I've got my gun aimed straight at his skull. "Trust me, old man. You don't want to die over this."

His face paling somewhat, he slowly moves the hand he'd started to dip under the desk back to his side. "Who the fuck are you?"

"Sit down, relax," I tell the man.

He sits down behind his desk, his back stiff as a board, and I sprawl comfortably before him on one of the two chairs facing him, my gun propped on my knee and aimed right at his heart.

"Who *are* you?" he asks in a combination of horror and dread.

"Nobody you should be concerned with. But this?" I pull out a copy of a paper with his signature on it and slide it across the desk surface. "This is why I'm here. It's a paper my employers own. A paper where you promise them, and me, a lot of money. Two hundred grand to be exact. Today I'm collecting. You've had two months of warnings, so I hope you're finally ready to pay."

The guy goes mute.

He also doesn't make any quick move to pay.

Sighing, I produce one of my video cameras. "*Or* I could also make this little movie public." I pull the small chip out of a handy pen camera and play a video of him being royally blown by some-one I know with certainty is not his young wife.

"You're on your third marriage, correct? I believe this third wife wised up and had a prenup drawn too, didn't she?"

The images keep playing to the man's complete and utter horror.

He puts his hands on his head, groaning.

I quietly remove the card and toss it over the top of his desk. "Here. You can keep that. I've got my own copy."

He pulls out his checkbook, writes the sum, and hands it over with a trembling hand. "You let someone else see that, and I'm ruined. Do you hear me? Ruined," he whispers, sweat popping up on his brow.

I grab the check. "My interest isn't in ruining you. We appreciate your business. But if anyone follows me out? Any word about you and me here? The video still goes live, check or no check."

A morose silence follows me outside and to the elevator. They don't get it. These rich men don't get it. They think they're untouchable, that they'll be exempted because of their names. Of who they know.

They don't get that the Underground wins. The Underground always wins.

❤ ❤ ❤

I CHECK INTO a cheap motel under another fake name. Tomorrow I take another flight, hit up another target, and then I'm almost done.

Shit, I'm exhausted. My muscles weary, my neck stiff. I drop my duffel next to the bed, shove my gun under my pillow, push my knives under the mattress, then I roll over to my back and exhale as I stare at the ceiling.

I think of the way she cooked for me.

The way she gave herself to me.

The way my body surged inside hers and she instinctively pushed back for more of me.

And then—the fucking way I felt when I had to *leave*, like I just got punched and my girl took the brunt of it.

My life has been the Underground. The Underground as a life and also as a means to find my mother. I've blended into it like black blends in the shadows. Nobody needs to tell me—*me*, king of the fucking Underground—that the *Underground* wasn't made for lively little princesses. I. Fucking. KNOW.

Christ, but I want her with me.

I have lusted after this girl for months, but it's not the lust that keeps me coming back. Somewhere in my gut I've always known that she was born for me. In some place, maybe long before I was born and long before I even killed, before my soul was dirty and broken, I was given this angel and I would bet everything I am on the fact that she was given to me so I could protect her. She was for me, and me for her. I've had no girlfriends in my life, not even an interest in any. Only fucks. Only whores. Only bar flings. Nothing that lasted over the few hours it took me to be done with them. As if a part of me knew and I was only biding my time for this one girl to look at me across the rain one day with those eyes—and that right then nothing else would matter even a fraction of what she matters.

It's two minutes to nine and, though I like being exact, before I know it I'm grabbing my new phone and hitting her number. One ring, two, and she answers, breathless. My stomach rips open when I hear her voice.

"Hello?" she says.

"Don't ever answer a call from an unknown number unless I warn you beforehand."

I can hear the laughter in her voice, beneath the scowl, of course. "Then don't call me from a strange number, you dick."

I chuckle. "A change of device was in order."

"Why? Don't you have enough?"

I shut my eyes, relaxing my muscles for the first time in days. God, she's special. Made specifically for me.

We've been raised differently but it doesn't matter. She was taught to play games while I was taught to play with things.

And yet here we are. I'm obsessed with her and she sure as fuck isn't too far behind. Now it's up to me to take our relationship to the next level. It's up to me to trust her enough and respect her enough to let her know that I'm not a normal man. Fuck. Me. Running.

You don't really want to do that, King. You tell her the truth about you and it'll be permanently OVER.

No. Hell, I won't let it be over.

"So. Did you just call to hear me breathe?" she prods.

"No, that's not all." Last time I heard her voice, she cooked for me, and then she gave herself to me in a way she hasn't been with another guy. She welcomed me home, ruffled my hair, smiled at me, wanted me, gave me stuff I never dreamed I wanted and I'm now fucking starved like a rabid dog for.

"You mad I haven't called?" I ask huskily, dropping my voice in case I'm going to have to do some explaining.

"I hardly noticed!"

"So you *are* mad. Princess, I didn't want to leave you, not like that." I drop my voice as a shit ton of regret tightens my chest, and I stare out the dingy motel window and think of my new Seattle apartment. I want it bad. I want my bed with the thousand-dollar sheets and the million-dollar girl cuddled right beside me. "Baby, *talk*," I hear myself plead.

"What for?"

"Just talk." Exhaling, I press the receiver closer and cling to her voice. All the sunshine in it. The way it squeezes my heart, my gut, and my balls, all in one fell swoop. The way I need it to remind myself that what I did today was just a job. A role. An act. Not all of me. She's the only one who gets to see all of me.

"I don't know what to say," she finally whispers. "I want to know why you left, how you are." Her tone gentles in a way that sends all the yearning in me spiraling outward like a hurricane. I exhale through my nostrils, trying to keep the blood in my body out of my already straining cock.

"I had work to do, but I'm good now," I explain. "Come on, princess, *talk to me.*"

"Okay then. I'm lying in bed in my panties and bra."

My brain nearly explodes. Fuck me with that. My heart slams against my rib cage and my dick punches into my jeans. I instantly picture her: lying in bed, her hips hugged by those panties, eyes heavy lidded, and suddenly I'm in that bed, right with her, and I'm holding her braid to keep her still while I fuck her sweet, hot mouth with mine.

"Isn't that why you called me? Aren't you horny?" she asks when I don't reply.

I throw my head back and roar with laughter. I've laughed more with her in months than I have on my own in years. "Princess, I'm horny with anything that has to do with you, but that's not why I called."

"Oh. Why then?"

I keep picturing her in that bed. Yeah. With me right next to her. "You wearing your braid yet?" I have to know. I still can't figure out how she so easily grabs so many strands of hair and winds them all perfectly together, silken, gold and lovely when they fall in that braid against her slim white neck.

"Yes, I am."

"You chewing your lip?"

She giggles softly. "Yes."

I smile in wolfish delight. "I want to suck that lip, baby, but what I most want right now is to be there, kiss the shit out of you, and fuck you without a rubber. I'm going to get tested, so next time I fuck you, I'm not wearing one. Would you like that?"

"Yes, please. One Greyson without a rubber, and can you make that an express order?"

My chest floods with tenderness at how playful she is. "Yes, baby, I will, but I didn't call to hear myself talk. I want to hear you. So talk to me, princess."

"What about?"

"What else? About you, baby."

"All right, so that girl who wanted my Mustang? She went up a thousand and I accepted."

I groan and slam my palm to my forehead, then drag my hand roughly down my face. "Princess, I'm telling you . . . sell something else. Not your car. You need your car."

"It's all I have to sell, Grey."

"Are you sure about that?"

"Yes, I'm sure. My car is all I have to sell."

"The necklace I gave you, that's not sellable?" I bluntly come out and say it.

"No."

"No? Why *not*?"

"Because it's all I fucking have of you!"

My heart thuds once at that admission, then keeps on thudding from the frustrating urge to assure her, in person, that's not the case. "Nah, that's not true."

"It's all I have, Greyson. I spend days alone and all I have to know you exist and remind me you're going to call are these stones. They're all I have of you."

"You got me, princess. Jesus! Do you not see what you're doing to me? You have all of me, Melanie. I'm states away and I feel like half a man, I feel like I'll tear something apart if I don't see you soon with my own two eyes . . ." I trail off.

What the fuck am I doing? Is this fucking *Oprah* here? I press my palm into my forehead and breathe. *Shut the fuck up, you fucking pussy!*

She softens her voice like she understands. "Greyson, when are you coming home?"

Home.

God, I love that she calls wherever we are together "home."

"Not yet. I have work to do," I whisper, rubbing the pang she just caused in my chest.

"But when are you coming back to me?"

Holy god, she's going to be the end of me. "Soon, baby," I concede. *On your birthday. When I want no more bullshit between us, nothing between us.* "I'm coming home soon and next time when I leave, I want to bring you with me," I gruffly whisper. "Just answer me this. Are you my girl?"

"First tell me you're my guy."

She misses me.

It's in her voice, in how she speaks to me.

"Yeah I am, which officially makes you my girl. And, Melanie?"

She's quiet on the other end of the line, breathing hard.

I add, my voice low but uncompromising, "I'm going to eat YOU UP when I get in. As long as I have breath in me, you're going to be my princess."

"Okay, Grey. Then you'll be my king," she whispers.

Oh, yeah, she'll definitely be the end of me. "I thought we said no majesty jokes."

"It wasn't a joke," she counters. Then she adds, "Grey?"

"Yeah?"

"I knew you'd call. *This* is why I'll never sell the necklace."

"I'll always call, necklace or no necklace. Let it go, baby, and I'll give you something better."

I hang up and try to get a grip on myself, but my blood runs hot from talking to her. I remember the first day I saw her screaming for Riptide in the Underground. She was bouncing up and down, clamoring for another man, and I just stood there feeling strangely assured, and a little voice in my head said, *This one's mine.* I knew I'd been had in the same way I know when I've got my marks in my pocket and a debt slashed—*I'd been had.*

All of me, part of me, whatever piece of me she wants, she can have.

I've got it all perfectly planned.

Two more marks . . . aside from princess. I'll retrieve the evidence for that second-to-last one in Denver, and I'll take care of shit that night while the team makes sure the Underground fights are running smoothly. Then I fly to Seattle just in time for her birthday. I'll surprise her. I'll get to tell her that *no, baby, I wasn't spawned from the devil, and soon, you'll actually get to meet my mother . . .*

I groan as the first flicker of hope I've had in years takes root inside my gut, and I flip around in bed, trying to get some sleep even when I already know I won't. Not until I know both my girls are safe and sound and with me.

EIGHTEEN

UNDERGROUND

Melanie

The Underground is exactly as I remember.

Crowded.

Noisy.

Stinky.

Nervous about encountering any mean men, but happy about Brooke expecting us, I tug Pandora toward our ringside seats, and that's when I spot her.

My best friend. Dark hair in a ponytail, skinny jeans, spaghetti-strap top. She's staring up at the ring as the two fighters work each other to the point of collapse.

"BROOKE!" I call as I start running over, and she leaps out of her seat.

She's been my best friend since we were old enough to wear halves of a locket that said "Best Friends" and broke right in the middle. Naturally I still have my part in a little box under my bed, but Brooke's part fell during a sprint and we never got it back. Which is fine, because our friendship itself has never broken. I've never fought, loved, or had as much fun with a girl as I've had with my best friend, so there's naturally squealing involved when we hug today after months of separation.

After a tight squeeze, we both push each other back to make a thorough inspection. I want to make sure Mr. Riptide is taking care of my girl, but, holy shit, Brooke looks . . . there are no words for the shine in her eyes and in her hair and in her smile.

"Look at you!" I cry. Shit, of course he's taking care of her, he freaking adores the Jesus out of her.

"No, look at *you*!" she counters as she hugs Pandora even though Pandora doesn't like to hug as much as I do.

Pete comes and greets us as we settle in our seats. He starts chatting up Pandora about his romance with Brooke's sister, Nora. I loathe Nora, so I'm glad the bitch is in college and away from here. Pete is so good for her, but I secretly hope he'll fall for someone nicer and sweeter and smarter and break up with her for good. Nora used to be the girlfriend of one of the Underground's grossest fighters, one with a scorpion tattooed on his big fat head—enough said.

I squeeze Brooke's hand so that she updates me on everything possible. "How's Racer? Am I going to get to see him tonight or is it going to be too late?" I demand.

"You can come over to our suite, of course! He's so big, Mel. But tell me—" She stops talking and her eyes widen when we hear the word *"RIPTIDEEEEEEE"* shoot out from the speakers.

And the arena knows it's that time. Riptide. Remington Tate. Brooke's husband. God of sex—in case I haven't mentioned him a little, let me just say I know for sure that every vagina in this arena is crushing over him.

The fights in the Underground are never as alive and intense as when *he* comes out—there's just something about him. He puts it in the air, excitement, intensity, raw strength, and boyish playfulness.

"My ovaries just exploded," Pandora mumbles to my left.

Brooke jumps to her feet as Remington "Riptide" Tate leaps into the ring, draped in a boxing robe that is redder than red—and I'm so excited to be here, to see this, to get my mind out of my own insecurities and that stupid debt that I can't help it, and my body can't help it, and my vocal chords can't help it—so I *scream*.

"Remmyyyyy!!!" I'm on my feet with Brooke, where I can't resist hugging and smacking her simultaneously. "God, you fucking whore, I can't believe you do that every night!" I say, shoving her.

She shoves me back, yelling, "*Several* times a night!"

And that's when he winks down at her from the ring.

She stops goofing around with me and grins back at him—all her attention on only him. Her husband now. And as he waits for his opponent, he keeps his smile and his sparkling blue eyes on her. And that look? It's a clear You're Mine look, but it's so fucking tender I feel it melt over me. *Greyson . . . Greyson . . . Greyson . . .* suddenly he's in my head, his own version of this look swimming inside me. His own version is a little less tender, a little more guarded, a lot more raw, a lot more dark, like there is something painful inside that makes him hurt more when his eyes meet mine. My body feels like a huge void just opened inside it at the mere memory of him. Of us.

"Oooh god, you guys are going to kill me," I tell Brooke, watching as a big-ass man comes to take the stage. I'm concerned for Remy for a moment as the fight begins, but then, *wham*! He takes control so thoroughly that I'm not concerned anymore.

"YOU'RE THE SHIT, REMINGTON!" I squeal, pulling Brooke's face to mine. "Look at you. Wife and mother, dude, he's so fucking in love with you, I can't even take it!"

"Oh, Mel." She sighs and sags against me like she can't take loving this man any more than she already does.

They bring another man up for Riptide, and I swear these opponents get bigger and bigger as the seasons pass by.

"Remy!" I scream again as the men start fighting up on the ring.

Brooke squeezes my hand, and I squeeze back and lift her hand in mine, high in the air as we watch them fight. "Remy! Your wife is hot for you, Remy!" I scream.

Brooke has always been the reserved one of us two, a little shy about speaking out with conviction, but I know that she loves it when I do the screaming here.

"Remington, you're so fucking hot!" I scream on her behalf.

And then Brooke stuns me when she leaps up to her feet and cups her mouth so her voice carries farther, and she starts screaming with me, "YOU'RE SO FUCKING HOT, REMY, KILL IT, BABY!"

And he instantly kills it.

The public goes wild as his opponent falls down with a thud, and I stupidly blink at my best friend. "Omigod, so you scream now? And how well trained is Mr. Riptide to immediately please his sweet little wife?"

I'd go on, but Brooke is too busy grinning up at Remy because he's grinning down at her, all sweaty and lickable, and I fall quiet while something squeezes hard in my heart.

I will never be the first person Brooke turns to now when she wants to cry, or talk something out, or vent, or go out for a run. My best friend is deeply, madly in love with this man who I know would go through hell and back for her—because he already has.

So, in a way, my best friend has a new best friend now. And he's a husband too, a father to her baby, a lover to her.

But me? My guy likes to fuck me. He says he's bad for me, but I sense he needs me. I sense he misses me. Is it my gut talking to me, or my silly hopes? All I know for certain is that I'm falling in love and I'm so far in deep now that the sheer gravity of it all makes it seem impossible to stop myself from continuing deeper and harder into this dark, unknown, scary plunge.

God, I'm so fucked.

Brooke seems to notice I've fallen quiet, and I hadn't realized she'd been watching me intently.

"Do you want to talk about him?" she asks me softly, surveying me with the keen perception only a best friend could have.

I nod and I have to lean closer to her in order to be heard through the crowd. "When I don't have to scream over these assholes!"

When the fights are over for the night, Pandora and I take a cab to our hotel, which, unfortunately, is not where the Tates are staying—their hotel is much too expensive. Pandora didn't want to take anyone's "charity" and I'm a world past broke, so we're staying at a small three-star hotel a couple of blocks away.

Pandora, however, decides to opt out of visiting Brooke's suite for the evening.

"Why?" I ask her, nudging her in the back of the cab. "Come on, it'll be fun. I need to see Racer! Last time I saw him he was growing just a little buzz of hair and he smelled like talc and grinned at me with this one lone dimple that's going to kill a lot of ladies someday. Come on!"

"Nah, I'm tired. You two should catch up. I'll order pay per view and wait for you later."

"You sure you don't want to come?" The cabdriver seems to be getting impatient, so I open the door and wait for a second longer.

"Yeah I'm sure. You know I'd rather pet a dog than a baby."

I nod slowly because I think I get it. I get her more than she knows. She thinks because I try to have fun, that I don't hurt, or want anything, or take anything seriously. I laugh away my hurts, but she uses anger as a barrier. And I know it hurts her too when she sees Brooke sometimes, because Pandora used to be in love.

All I can guess is that she loved him very much. "Pan," I say softly, "the guy who hurt you so bad . . . he wasn't the only guy you'll ever love."

I don't even know what else to say because I'm no expert on feeling like this—I can barely stand the way I feel for Greyson and I'm afraid to call it love. I feel even more awkward when we stop at Brooke's hotel and the cabdriver complains, "Ma'am, you either in or out?" so I quickly step out and shout at her, "I'll see you later. Watch a comedy!"

She flips me off as the cab takes her away, and I smile and wave. But as I get on the elevator, I just don't know. I don't know anything anymore except that a couple of months ago I didn't know Greyson King. How can I miss him so bad now?

You're in my veins, you fuck.

You're in me one moment, you're lost the next. You take me, you leave me, and I still wait, trembling for you to come back and do it again.

Ugh. *When are you coming back?*

Brooke swings the door of her suite open and babbles out, "I want deets and I want them now!" pulling me into the first bedroom, away from the group of guys in the living room.

She sits me down at the edge of a bed and then plants her hands on her hips like some demanding angel-bitch, her eyes gleeful with excitement. "Tell me. Tell me all about him!"

I laugh in excitement but then I groan and jab a finger into her chest. "I'm experiencing some déjà vu, except the poor sucker thinking she'd fallen for a guy who may be wrong for her was *you*."

"Omigod, you love him, Mel?"

I can't believe how hard it is to talk about him, even with my best friend. Sighing, I drop on the bed and pat the place next to me so she settles down close.

Love didn't feel like this when I imagined I'd fall in love. Love was exciting and precious in my mind, not frightening and unexpected.

Brooke and I lie on our sides facing each other, smiling like we've done the thousand times we've spilled out secrets and fantasies and more. "Brookey, am I lovable like that? The forever kind? I'm good for fun, but do you think . . . Sometimes I think Greyson just doesn't want to involve me in other parts of his life. I wonder if I'm just a sex toy to him, like I've been to every other man, but then he calls me, or then he gives me this . . ." I touch the diamond necklace hiding under my silky shirt. "He just looks at me in this way . . . I don't know, there's not even a word for that look. But Remy gives it to you too. It's the BEST look. It gives me heat and heart palpitations and butterflies. And if you saw him with my parents, how he was laughing while we did our stupid Sunday games. I just refuse to believe that I don't mean something to him, you know? He says I'm his girl."

Brooke laughs and sits, hugging me briefly. "Mel, you're fun and sweet, loyal and honest. You've got so much love to give. You love everyone, even strangers. You're my little love bug. He's lucky you not only get to love him, but you get to fall *in love* with him." Her eyes light with excitement as she squeezes my shoulders. "Melanie, you've found your prince. He's not even a prince, turns out he's a *king*. Do you realize you've talked about this faceless, nameless guy since you were seven?"

"Dude, I've waited all my life to feel like this and now that I do, I don't want to. I feel unstable, unsafe, vulnerable, happy, and yet worried it's not going to last."

"No! No, no, no, don't hold back. Is Pandora poisoning your head? Mel, OWN THIS. Own how you feel. Tell him. Go after him. Go after what you want. You've always gone after it—you won't back down now that you found it!"

"You say that now 'cause you're no longer a *chicken*! You know Remington loves you. You know he loves you so much he's never letting you go. If something happens, you'll work it out and you both know it. He'll fight for you and you will for him. But me? I don't know what Greyson feels. He wants to be with me and then he's gone for days. Whatever we have, it could be real or it could be something passing like—"

"Lust," a low voice by the door says.

I lift my head to spot Riley Cole at the threshold, Remington's coach's second, looking cute as ever. Riley and I are great friends. We've gotten into a lot of mischief in the few times we've met after a Riptide fight, and not just sexually.

He's a guy used to guarding secrets. I know, because when I tried to dig out all of Remington Tate's secrets when he was pursuing Brooke like a battering ram, all Riley said to me was that he'd never seen Remington go after a woman the way he went after Brooke.

So Riley's definitely a man who knows how to keep a secret. Including, thank god, *mine*.

Brooke has always said he looks like a sad surfer boy, and she's right, he does. Which works for him. But tonight he looks more like Pandora's angry blond twin brother, scowling at me with the same scowl he wore the day he first met me.

"What's up with you?" I ask him, returning his scowl with one of my own.

"If this boyfriend of yours ever hurts you, we'll take care of it." He cracks his knuckles, and instead of making me scared on Greyson's behalf, the sound makes me laugh.

"You mean *you'll* take care of it, or Remy?" I say as I stand, hearing his quiet, familiar chuckle.

"Okay, you got me. Maybe I'll bring Rem along just for intimidation purposes," he says jokingly, but his smirk fades into a flat line of displeasure. "No one hurts you, Melanie. Or I punch him. I don't care how many times I need to punch him to make him bleed, but I'll make him bleed."

I laugh as Brooke pulls me out to the living room so I can see her precious baby.

"Barbies don't hurt, remember. Don't worry," I toss past my shoulder at Riley, kicking him playfully as we pass. He'd called me Barbie when we met, and not in a nice way, so flinging it back at him makes him simmer a bit.

Then I hear a baby sound and am filled with glee. I spot Racer proudly sitting on the curled arm of the bodyguard-nanny, Josephine. But he doesn't want to stay there. Racer throws himself at his father, who was chugging down a blue sports drink, but when he sees his son coming, Remington catches him in one arm and slam dunks the empty sports drink into the kitchen sink.

Lifting Racer up high, he makes a growling sound, then carries him in a football hold, which makes Brooke groan at my side.

"Remington, he's going to puke up all his dinner," she chides.

"Ahhhhh," he says, the sound incredibly cocky as he twists his son into a sitting position and avoids the catastrophe. Looking at Brooke, his smile flashes two sexy dimples at her, making her forgive the transgression, and I swear I'm almost dead.

And then Racer grins and flashes his mom one dimple too.

"Urgh! You're both killing me!" I tell them. "Remington, I need to touch this baby or else!" I go and grab Racer and as I hold him to me, I make cute baby sounds as I nuzzle his little tummy.

He protests like he's not exactly thrilled about it, and he looks at his mother, then at his father, then at Pete, with a new, sad dimple in his chin.

"What? He doesn't like me?" Racer looks at his mother and

his father again and makes a face that deepens that dimple on his chin. "OMG, I'm making him cry!"

I pass him to Brooke. "What a failure!" I laugh.

"You're fine," Remington says as he drops on a chair and pulls Brooke to his lap with one arm while he passes a nearby squeaky toy to Racer with the other.

Racer looks at the toy and his Melanie-induced cry morphs into a squeal of delight. Remy smiles down at him and then his eyes slide to Brooke, and what I see there truly, deeply kills me as he kisses the top of her head.

It's that true, *real* I'd-die-for-you love that I've always dreamed about.

"Mel," I hear from behind me, and when I turn to the sound, I realize Riley has been watching me all this time. He steps closer to me and whispers ominously, "Can I talk to you?"

I nod. There's no mistaking the look of lust in his eyes. I sense that he wants me, aside from the fact that he also wants to talk to me. The old me would've wanted nothing more than another night with a fuck buddy. I can rarely say no to an attractive guy who wants me, but every pore in my body wants just one man now.

But I still nod at Riley, because he's the only one I can talk to about the one thing that's been plaguing my thoughts other than Greyson King.

❤ ❤ ❤

"HERE." RILEY SETS a check atop the white linen of a small round table by the bar of a chic little restaurant just blocks from the hotel. "I've been saving up," he explains.

"No!" I gasp. "Riley, don't be ridiculous! I couldn't!" I push the check back, feeling flustered as the waitress sets down our drinks. I wait for her to leave before hissing out, in a whisper, "It was my decision. I chose to do it, okay?"

"But *I'm* the idiot who suggested it in the first place," he counters on another hiss, and he seems so genuinely mortified, he won't stop shaking his head. "Remington never loses, Melanie. Never. If I'd known he'd throw the fight for—"

"Urgh, to save stupid Nora because he just loves Brooke too much not to do anything. But even if you'd told me he would lose, I'd never put my money on Scorpion. NEVER."

"Then let me help you pay this debt off." I ignore his pleading look and push the check back to him yet again, shaking my head too. "At least let me tell Rem," he urges. "He'd pay on your behalf if he knew. If I hadn't given you my word I wouldn't tell anyone . . ."

"Riley, I'll kill you if you tell anyone. We were *drunk*, out in town, you were making a bet, I was nosy and asked about it, thought it was such a great idea to make a bet of my own, especially when it seemed like such a sure thing! Then we went to your room and celebrated by thinking it cool to get in bed together. I feel stupid as it is. I don't know what I was thinking!" An image flashes across my mind of a beautiful apartment—the apartment of my dreams—and my car debt paid off, and I add, "Well, I *do* know. I could've made a handsome down payment on my very own apartment and maybe even have the balls to start my own design firm."

"Then let me help, Mel."

I look at the check and a part of me screams *Take it! Take it, Melanie! Please just save yourself from those monsters!*

But what will Riley expect in return? How can I take money from a man when I'm in love with another? "This is very sweet of you, but no. Really."

He cocks one blond eyebrow. "What about your new boyfriend? Will you at least let him help?"

My chest aches as I think about him and all the reasons why I can't bear for Greyson to know. I gulp down the rest of my drink and admit, "I think that . . . if I ask for help from anyone . . . he'd be the last."

"Why?"

"Because I don't want him to know I'm *this* stupid! He knows I'm a mess already. Riley, he met me out with my convertible parked on a rainy night without the top—enough said. It's a miracle he stuck around long enough to get to know me. I don't want him to . . . lose respect for me. Think less of me."

Riley's scowl is getting darker by the second. "I can see he's tossing diamonds at you already?" He nods to the necklace half-dipping into my top. "You know men do that to *buy* the women they sleep with? It has nothing to do with caring about you."

"Yes, it does," I counter. "It means he took the time to go and look for something pretty he thinks will make me happy."

"You can use that necklace to pay, Melanie. Just tell him you lost it or something and get rid of this debt. Those men kill for five bucks—they're fucking gangsters! Even the guy Pete deals with, Eric, looks sharp and polished in that suit, but they don't trust that guy for shit. He just kisses Rem's ass 'cause he's their prime moneymaker, but everyone knows his boss Slaughter makes Scorpion look like a teddy bear. They say he's got an enforcer that's like some demon straight from hell, and he'll come collecting whether you want him to or *not*!"

He looks around warily, then leans closer, across the table, lowering his voice. "Pete heard rumors the only guy with a lick of sense was Slaughter's eldest, but he didn't want shit to do with the dad and apparently dropped off the Underground years ago. Not even his *son* wants anything to do with a man like Slaughter. I swear I don't sleep thinking you still owe them."

My heart starts stampeding in my chest with renewed fear, and I hold my hands up, palms out, to pacify him. "Riley, I asked for more time, okay? We have to just . . . breathe here."

"What? What *the fuck*? When'd you ask for more time?"

"Last time I came to see Brooke. It's okay. Really! I just sold my car and can buy more time if I maybe give them half the payment."

"No you fucking can't, they'll take it as interest and demand you pay fully before you can even walk out the door! Don't ever approach men like these alone. Jesus, just trust me and get out of this, Mel. I paid my debt and I want to pay yours, and if you won't let me, then at least promise me you'll let your new boyfriend help. If you're too proud to ask, just pretend you lost those diamonds on your neck and get rid of this debt; *trust me*."

I guess I look as hopeless as I feel, because he adds, more direly now, "I vow, Melanie, if that debt isn't gone before you leave, I'm telling Tate and we're taking care of it for you, him and me."

I gasp in outrage. "I will not let you or my best friend's *husband* step into this, do you hear me? And I will not involve my boyfriend either. This necklace means something to me." I touch my diamonds with an awful wrenching sensation in my chest as I wonder—*Is this the only way I'm going to be free, letting go of the only thing the man I want with all my heart has given me?*

"Riley," I whisper, almost plead with him, "I'm just not this girl who swindles her boyfriends out of expensive things to turn them into money."

He glowers at my precious necklace, and my stomach starts to hurt just thinking about parting with anything that has to do with Greyson.

"That gift didn't mean to him what it means to you, I assure you," Riley says with annoying self-confidence. "I've never seen a guy more in love than Remington, and he doesn't need to throw dollars at Brooke to show it."

"Well, Grey has a different style, so what? The end is the same. I feel pampered and taken care of and he gets a look in his eyes when he sees me wearing them that I absolutely *adore*."

I can't stand having another person in my life criticize Greyson to me! So I stare at him narrow eyed and add, so that he at least gets the true depth of my feelings for my man, "When he looks at me like that, I swear it's all so perfect I sometimes have nightmares that I dreamed it all, that he's too good to be true."

"Maybe he is, Melanie. Maybe he's two-timing you right now, meeting with some chick in secret as we speak."

"Ha!" I lift my glass and sip my drink. "He's a workaholic. If I have anything to worry about, it's that mistress of his called Work Myassoff."

Riley smiles at me, a chilling smile, a very unfriendly smile, and he nods to the entry of the restaurant.

I turn about ninety degrees to get a look . . . and that's when I see *him* walking into the restaurant.

Him.

Grey-fucking-son.

All my recognition flares into disbelief, excitement, and then, anger combined with a bolt of nearly blinding lust.

It feels as though an energy source clings to his skin, for the entire air shifted the moment he materialized in the room. Over six feet of pure male perfection. Greyson. Fucking. King. My hormones burst awake when he starts walking forward, following the maître d', his eyes directly on a table at the far end.

I can't believe it. My eyes run up and down his form. There is no word for the way Greyson walks, with a hand in his pocket, his face somber, his cheekbones chiseled, his jaw smooth and tan, his mouth perfection, his dark hair carelessly tousled; I swear that awesome hair is the only thing careless and playful about him. The rest of him is Bond 007 perfection, even those narrowed, hazel-green eyes, which seem beautifully self-contained and remote. Even now, two months after going out with him, I can sense he's still holding back the most crucial part of him, *but* I can visualize an "us" and what we can be so perfectly, and I'm determined to make it happen. Greyson and Melanie, living Happily Ever After.

Then I see the woman at the table. Waiting. A redhead.

My blood pools at my feet when Greyson bends to kiss her cheek.

Riley and I only stare.

And I'm certain it's not him. He's working . . . somewhere. It can't be him.

But it sure looks like him.

He's wearing all black, his hair shining under the light, and he settles down in his chair, leans back in that self-assured way of his, and starts talking over a fucking candle to a redhead. A fake redhead. One who looks older and expressionless.

Mrs. Botox.

OMIGOD!

It cannot be Greyson!

I never get cheated on, I'm the one they cheat *with*.

My belly muscles are rigid with anger as I try to breathe and force my lungs to expand. I scan the restaurant around me for something to throw, but the best thing I can think of is throwing myself at that no-good whore.

My eyes blur and ache with the sudden urge to cry. It's almost midnight. In fifteen minutes, I am twenty-five years old and my boyfriend is sitting at another table with another woman. I really, really want to cry now.

No. And let him see me snivel and cry like a hurt baby girl again? My mind churns with ways to make this hurt go away.

How does it go when he's in your veins? How?!! I laugh out loud, hard, and grip Riley's hand, but Greyson's not even looking in my direction, he's not within hearing distance. He and his elderly whore are deep in conversation in their own little world. Their own Melanie-less world. A part of me still refuses to believe he would do this to me.

An idea occurs to me and I grab my phone and text him an angry face.

Then I tell Riley, "If it's him, he will at least look at the text. He's a slave to his phones."

As if on cue, the man at the table edges back and slides his gloved hand into his pocket, looks at his phone, stares at it for a long, long moment, then he tucks it away and continues talking to the redhead.

My heart just got quartered.

I don't know how long we sit there, Riley fuming in his seat, gripping it ferociously. They'd met briefly at Brooke's wedding, and I could tell neither of them liked the other much. Now veins are popping up in Riley's neck. "I'm going to go over there—"

"And *what*?" Stopping him, I pull him back down by the sleeves of his suit. "She could be a client. He never did really tell me where he would be this week . . ."

I trail off when she gives him her hand over the table, and he takes it and whatever was in her hand. Then he gives her a box with a bow and all. A blue box. She peers in, looks delighted, he smiles back at her, they have some wine.

"Waiter!" I yell. "Another round, please!"

I'VE DOWNED A lot more cocktails by the time Greyson takes care of the check and they stand to go. Riley stands too. I foolishly turn around in my seat, my heart pounding as Greyson and the woman head for the door.

And that's when he sees me.

A current, electric, runs through me at the way he looks at Riley, then at me, and I see a dozen expressions in his eyes until he shutters them, turns to the woman, whispers something and pulls her toward the exit as if he hadn't just seen me.

All this time lying his gorgeous ass off.

All this time probably laughing at how stupid I am.

As he walks off with her, I see him turn his head the merest fraction. Straight toward me, and our eyes catch again. He searches my expression for a moment, the remoteness in his eyes flickering for the briefest moment with . . . *jealousy*? Anticipation pulses through me like a live charge at the way his eyes darken in . . . fury? He tingles my extremities, and it's just that, a stolen look, and then it's gone and he's gone, taking HER—another woman—with him, at exactly the stroke of midnight.

Happy birthday, Melanie . . .

Riley remains standing, then he looks at me with a what-the-fuck look. "Your boyfriend . . ."

"*Ex*." A sudden raw and primitive grief overwhelms me. "Ex-boyfriend. God, not even a text necessary. Not even a . . . Riley, please, let's go. Please, please let's get out of here."

The tears are going to come whether I want them or not, and I don't want them to be here. I grab Riley before he sits down again. "Please just get me out of here. Will you take me to your room, please—let's just walk back to your hotel, please," I whisper.

He pays our tab and ushers me out of the restaurant, tucking me close as we walk the couple of blocks to the hotel. I'm cold, cold down to my bones. We get on the elevator and I'm grateful that no one else is in here with us. My throat is on fire as the feelings of being a fool swim in me, and the necklace—his necklace—feels like a steel weight around me, choking me with his lies. I tear it off me and press it into Riley's hand. "I can't see this anymore. Let's just do it. Sell it, get anything, take it please."

My throat aches with defeat as I replay Grey looking at me, walking away . . .

Looking at me . . . walking away . . . like I am nothing.

Like we meant *nothing*.

"Do you think he's got a wife? A family?" My voice breaks and I can't ask any more questions as we head to his room.

"Dude, I don't even know what to think. He didn't look happy to see you, I'll tell you that."

I continue fighting my tears, fisting my hands at my sides as my whole body starts shaking. "He can go fuck himself *and* that whore. That fucking liar, that . . . I hope she gives him crabs. In fact, I hope they both have alien babies together."

Riley ushers me into his room and shuts the door, and a sensation of intense desolation and betrayal sits deep in my gut. I've never in my life hurt like this. Never. I want the hurt to go away. I want the image of Greyson walking away with another woman to go away.

Blinking back the tears, I grab Riley's shirt and pull him to me. "Riley," I beg. His eyes widen when I press my lips to his.

"Mel," he protests, but I can't bear to hear it, so I press my lips harder.

"Please don't say no," I beg. "Please don't say no. I swear every man-whore in the world should be castrated. You said you'd punch him if he hurt me. This hurts, Riley. This really hurts and I'm so done. I am so done with him."

I kiss him. He kisses me back with only lips, soothing his hands down my arms. They feel warm, familiar. He holds me to his body and he feels good. Safe. I kiss him and wonder if maybe this is why one-night stands have been all I'm worth. Because I can't deal. It hurts too much. And always someone else comes along, and for whatever reason, my guys stop seeing anything of interest in me. For some reason Greyson has lost interest in me. I lost him.

No. I never even had him.

The realization wrecks me, so I try kissing Riley on the mouth a little more and he lets me. His arms aren't as thick, his lips aren't as fierce, but I need them so much. Anything to try and stop thinking of . . . *Grey pulling on my nipples with his teeth . . . tugging . . . sucking . . .*

There's a knock on the door and I groan in protest when Riley sets me aside.

"Pete could need me," he explains, and I watch quietly as he heads to the door, his image blurry through my tears.

I unstrap one of my shoes and wipe my eyes. One night with Riley and in the morning it won't all look so miserable. I will realize Greyson King isn't the only man in the world. My heart will still be broken but I'll glue it back together any way I have to, and I will be happy again.

I *will* be happy again.

Sniffing, I am quickly starting to unbutton my top when I hear a low, familiar voice speak.

"Where is she?"

I have never, ever heard anyone speak so quietly and at the same time sound so pissed.

My skin pricks and my gaze snaps up to the door.

Greyson's tall, lean, black-clad form covers the threshold, and I hate how my systems go haywire at the sight of him.

I'm partly undressed in the middle of the room. Drunk. My hair a mess. My face a mess. Anger and hurt coil in my stomach as he comes forward with a blazing, territorial gaze.

I grab the shoe I'd been removing and throw it at him. "Get away from me!" I yell.

He ducks, and the shoe hits the wall and falls with a stupid thud to the carpet. Then, slowly, he straightens and comes the rest of the way over, grabs me by the arms, and hauls me up against him. Every inch of my body feels his. He looks at me with a fury I've never seen before as he starts to button me up, all the time those eyes looking at me until my stomach feels heavy as a rock. He jerks off his suit jacket and drapes it over my shoulders, forcing my arms inside and buttoning that too. Then he reaches for my strappy ankle boot lying across the carpet. Before I can stop him from putting on my shoe, he slips it on, efficiently straps it, and then he speaks to me in a low, cold voice. "Put your arms around me."

"Where's your fucking redhead?" I demand.

"I said put your arms around me."

I don't obey.

He doesn't care.

He lifts me in his arms, his coat huge on my frame, and I have no choice but to hold on to his nape. Suddenly, I smell him. I smell him on the coat he put on me, and in the scent of his hair, and on his skin. Forest and leather and mint. The pain in my heart becomes a fierce and fiery gnawing as the stinging in my eyes returns.

As we pass Riley at the door, he flatly says, "Stay away from her."

"If you fucking hurt her—" Riley starts, but Greyson cuts him off.

"No, if *you* touch her again, I'll kill you."

Greyson's words—*if you touch her again, I'll kill you*—send a chill through me.

Riley takes a step forward but I lift my hand to stop him and shake my head in a frantic no. I can't bear to risk Riley and I've never—ever—seen Greyson like this. His whole body crackles with unleashed energy as he carries me to the service elevators, holding me in one arm as he murmurs into his phone, "Back service entrance," and then he tucks the phone into his slacks and presses me even tighter to his chest.

Tighter than ever.

We're alone in the elevator, and though he's quiet, he's wearing an expression I've never seen before.

I think I'm going to vomit.

We exit into the underground parking lot, the cool air biting into my legs and cheeks, and I close my eyes and duck against the cold, feeling utterly miserable when the heat of his body rises up to warm me. I wonder if she licked his skin. Slid her fingers into his hair. If he calls her princess too.

I briefly hear a car motor start nearby, and when I look up, Greyson is looking at me. When our eyes lock, my nerves sizzle down to my toes. My body is screaming possessively for me to claim this man from any other woman. But no. Greyson might drive my body crazy, but I just realize he can never, ever be the man for me.

He's a cheater.

A liar.

And he's very, very mad right now.

A car pulls over in front of us and he yanks open the back door and as he guides me into the backseat, all this confusion rears up in me, and all the alcohol in my system isn't helping.

He climbs in behind me, settles to my right, and slams the door, then a gloved hand cups my face and forces me to turn, where he looks at me with frustration carved on his hard jaw. "Sometimes I won't be able to tell you everything about my work. I do it to protect you."

"Fuck you! I saw you holding her hand. I saw you—"

"You saw me *working*, Melanie. That's all you saw."

"I saw you giving her a present, motherfucker! How on earth would a security job involve that, huh?" I push him away and he curses under his breath. "Do you feel like a big man, having lots of women panting after you? All of them deluded? Thinking they're *special* to you?"

"Jesus, listen to you!"

"That's right, and hear me well, Greyson, this is the last time I'm played! Do you hear me?" I rap on the limo ceiling, hoping Derek hears, but he doesn't stop the car.

Greyson laughs in dark disbelief, then he rakes his hands through his hair and stares outside, his hands in fists, and I stare unseeingly out at the passing storefronts, stubbornly clinging to my anger and insecurities.

"I'm on to you, Greyson. What's in your secret steel room? Porn? Is that where you Skype with . . . *who the fuck is she*?"

Until he interrupts, softly, "I saw your lipstick on another man's mouth and I can still go back and break it until he can't find his fucking teeth. Hell, I want you to *watch me* break it if only so you know, once and for all, that you're *my* fucking girl and the only lucky bastard getting a piece of my girl is *me*."

"Was!" I drunkenly correct. "Was your girl."

He laughs more darkly. "You are so fucking mine you don't even know how mine you are," he says in a soft, threatening voice, and in my drunk brain, I suddenly register that he's trembling with rage. He's not worried about me having just caught him cheating. It seems all his thoughts are on his selfish jealousy. But I can't even remember what happened in Riley's room, all I keep remembering is Greyson and that bitch.

"You walked past me like you'd never seen me before!" I cry, hitting his chest.

He catches my wrist and squeezes. "Because I don't want a woman like her to use you against me—anybody to use you against me. Do you understand me? Do you, baby?" he asks, lowering his voice, tender, almost pleading.

"I understand you are a liar and a cheater and you didn't want HER to know you also had ME waiting on the side!"

"Fuck! Seriously? You were in *another guy's fucking room, stripping for him*! Were you trying to drive me insane?" Suddenly the vivid pain in his eyes is real. The pain in his voice is real, so real my chest cracks open like glass. "Were you really intending to go through with it? Were you honestly going to let that motherfucker inside you?" he asks, every word like a shard inside me.

"YES!" I cry.

He shudders as if he's breaking, and I start sobbing for real.

He releases me like he needs some distance, his voice trembling with more than anger. It's pain, and it wrecks me. "Do you think you can fuck someone to replace me? Do you think he'll make you feel the way I do? Was I nothing special to you, Melanie? Do you fall in love with every asshole you date?"

A tear runs down my cheek.

He slams a hand to the window and curses. "Fuck this."

"It hurts," I sniffle, talking to myself as I lower my hands. "You hurt me like nobody's ever hurt me, Greyson! I can't stop thinking about it. Do you call her princess? Do you spend your weekdays with her and your weekends with me?"

He stays silent, gazing out the window, his shoulders tight. "I don't call anyone else princess. I don't spend time with any woman but you. Hell, I work my days around just so I can come *home* to you."

"Then why are you here with her? I'm not big on second chances, you know! But I've given you every fucking chance you've wanted!" I cry.

"She is nothing." He grabs my face with his free hand, hissing through ground teeth, "She is nothing but a work contact. You are *everything*, you've been everything from the moment I saw you, screaming for Riptide. You didn't see me, you didn't see me, Melanie, but I've watched over you ever since—you are everything. Can you say the same about me? Can you say the same about him—that he's nothing?"

I stare blankly at him for a moment. "He's nothing, he's a friend, I swear. He was a fuck buddy when I came over to see Brooke sometimes, it meant nothing!"

He stares at his hands. "But he's touched you."

I suddenly can't stop myself from touching my boobs. So much smaller than the redhead's. "Who was she? What's her name? How do you know her?"

He rubs his face with both hands. "Just a business contact. She gets the dirty on men I need to negotiate with. I've never had a relationship with her. I've had a thousand fucks, but she hasn't been one of them. My every single fuck for weeks has been you." He looks out and curses, and I wipe my tears.

I see his face and remember the way he smiled at her and my stomach roils with fresh jealousy. "I wanted to pull her fucking hair out."

"I want to pull his guts out!" He grabs me by the shoulders. "What part of you being my girl didn't you understand?"

"I refuse to be yours if you're not going to be mine. If you fuck around I'm going to fuck around—an eye for an eye!"

"Stop being a stubborn-fool drunk and listen to me. I am not cheating on you—but you *were*."

I fall quiet.

"Were you?"

"You and I were over the moment you walked past me and I realized all this time you've been lying to me," I cry, sniveling.

"Come here," he rasps out.

"Why?"

When I edge a little close, he opens his arm, and my eyes blur more when I think about explaining to him what Riley knows about my secret. "I'm fucking sorry, Melanie," he says.

He pulls me into his chest and the familiarity in his embrace and the comfort I feel in his arms unexpectedly opens my floodgates.

"I'm sorry too, Grey," I cry.

I start sobbing harder as he presses a very firm, almost desperate kiss to the crown of my head and squeezes me with almost enough force to break me and says, "It's going to be okay. You'll never have to run to another man again because I'm going to be right here. Right here for you, if you still want me after I tell you what I have to tell you."

I try to wipe my face and look into his eyes. "You made me feel unworthy, Grey. Like you're hiding me. I don't know who you are, your parents, your family, I don't know anything about you. Please, I want to know you. Can't you see I want to *know you*," I sob.

His eyes look haunted as he looks at me. "I hide you to protect you, because you're my princess." He strokes my nose. "I'll tell you about me. Just let me enjoy the way these eyes look at me a little longer."

He kisses my wet eyelids almost desperately, like what he is telling me is going to be bad, real bad, and like he thinks I won't be able to stay after I hear it.

I cry harder. I'm used to his touch. His touch is unique, delicious, and I've felt it for eight weeks, but I knew one day it was going to break me.

NINETEEN

LOST

Greyson

Melanie slides her hands around my waist and buries her face in my shirt, and I pull off my gloves and shove them in my pocket so I can run my thumbs down her cheeks to track her tears.

Peace.

She's the most restless woman I know, but she gives me peace. Things were perfectly planned.

Melanie was in Seattle. I was here in Denver gathering the evidence for my second-to-last mark. I was going to steal into his place at midnight, blackmail and harass him for payment, so that by tomorrow, I'd be able to fly back to her.

But hours ago, Derek texted me that she was at the airport. By the time the incompetent fuck parked, she'd checked in and he lost her past the security checkpoint. I barked at him to buy any fucking ticket, get past security, and find her. He got a ticket, but failed to find her. So I asked C.C. to search the flight records while I finished the damn appointment with Tina and got to things myself.

But no. Melanie ended up here, at the same fucking restaurant, at the same time as Tina Glass and I were here, and she saw me. I couldn't afford to have a criminal like Tina Glass get any wind of us, otherwise Melanie would be exposed to Zero's world, and she would be vulnerable.

God, but the hurt in her eyes? If that wasn't enough to bring me to my knees, it almost was when I saw her in that asshole's hotel room.

You can't hurt a woman like Melanie and expect her not to react. You can't expect her not to try to peel away the hurt so she's the happy girl again everyone knows.

I feared I'd lost her.

I feared the determination in her eyes when the door to that hotel room opened and I saw her.

And I saw the hurt in her eyes.

And I was angry, so fucking angry, but the most gripping, surprising, infuriating emotion in me was the fear.

Fear of never again tasting those lips, never feeling those eyes on me, never playing her stupid games with her . . . The only times I ever feel good are with her. Good not at killing, blackmailing, and doing what I was taught to do. Just good.

She moves now, and fire in my veins sizzles and smokes as her hair brushes against my neck. The curves of her body fit perfectly against me. She's sitting on my thigh, and her hip is against my cock. When she shifts, I groan softly into the crown of her hair, my muscles knotting. Lava flows over me at the mere feel of her.

I want to fuck her so hard, punish her for thinking any other bastard would do.

Her hair is messed as if she's rolled out of that asshole's bed, but she'll never be satisfied until she rolls out of mine.

Her eyes are glazed with tears for me.

Every muscle in my body tight, I brush her hair aside and kiss the back of her ear. "I want to taste your bare skin very, very desperately," I murmur.

She jerks my shirt out of the waistband of my pants and sets her hand under my shirt, over my heart, touching my nipple ring. We remain like this, her eyes closed, her cheek to my chest, her closeness turning me inside out.

I duck my head and she holds her breath as if she'd been praying for me to, and she tips her head up so we can kiss. Our lips meet, softly. There's the tightening in my cock, the rapid beat of my pulse, the taste of her on my tongue. My hunger spins out of control as I open her wider and kiss her slow, but deep.

Each repetitive flick of her tongue sets loose a wildness in me, that elemental pull between us stretching and strengthening.

She eases back and I look down at her, absorbing the feel of her as she slowly lifts her eyes to mine, pure green, and I feel like my chest is being torn open and she's squeezing my heart with those dainty white hands. I feel more for her than I've felt for anyone in my life. I never thought I could be capable. I lost something I loved too young. I built a fortress around myself, and it's been there, not allowing anyone a fraction of real, raw emotion from me.

But what I feel for her . . .

Nobody has ever had the power to hurt me like she now has. Since my mother left, nothing has been truly important to me. I've never let myself care for anything or anyone. Not for my father, my uncle, my brother.

Now a little girl whose father calls her grasshopper has the power to break me in two—me, a fucking criminal, alone most of his life. And if any one of my enemies knew, they'd use her to take Zero down in a heartbeat.

And now we're too far in for her to stay in the dark any longer. I need to know if it's me she loves, or the idea of me.

She will leave you. Despise you. Reject you.

I'm already mourning the loss of her as her hand wanders to the zipper of my pants, and the merest brush of her fingers gets me hard while my chest throbs with the loss.

She's fucking lost to me already.

I groan and close my eyes as I battle my own urge to take her, right here, right now; instead I stop her wandering hand and kiss her. I want to dip my hand up her skirt, edge the panty aside and slip in a finger. She's already panting hard and clinging to my neck, her head falling back in pleasure against my shoulder. But she's drunk and I'm angry, and I'm jealous and want more than her body. I want her fucking soul, and I want her to give it to me knowing who I am.

Fucking fool, she won't.

Groaning in pain, I lean into her mouth, and she kisses me hard.

She mumbles my name, and I hear myself whisper that she was an angel in the rain . . . the only woman I've ever spent the night with, bought a home for, followed around just for a glimpse . . .

A new tear slips down her cheek, but I'm the one undone. What shakes me is the tenderness in the way she curls to me even as she's crying.

I press a kiss to the top of her head and I can't seem to stop pressing kisses into her hair, my own self-loathing growing by the second.

Just one more mark now. I've got the evidence to nail him. And then I just need to whisper in her ear, to give me that fucking necklace I gave her because I'm going to give her another one, a better one, and that this one will take care of everything.

I'll get control of the Underground. I'll be smarter, better organized, I'll make sure my mother is safe, and as for Melanie . . .

I tap on the car roof and lower the partition separating us from Derek. "Drive over to get her friend, the happy one," I say with sarcasm.

Mumbling some sort of protest under her breath, she shakes her head. "Don't go. I've been dreaming about you."

"And call one of the guys," I tell Derek. "I'll need you to stay with princess while someone drives me to the airport." I pull up the partition between us and Derek and groan. "Don't say that now," I whisper.

She grabs my hand and puts it on her tits. "When I see you, my boobs hurt."

God. She's so fucking drunk. "When you're sober, I'm going to tell you some shit you won't like," I whisper, a gruff warning. "Don't say anything now."

"Greyson . . ."

"I'm going to tell you something about me but I don't want you to try to fix me. I can't be fixed. You either need to accept who I am or tell me you want to leave, and I give you my word I'll let you go if you ask for that."

She stops and blinks, her voice emotional. "You sound like you think you're bad for me."

"I am." I glance out the window and grind my molars, tightening my hold because this might just be the last time I hold her like this.

"You're not. What you did for me in the rain is one of the nicest things anyone has done for me."

"Fuck. Stop saying that; you've said that before and that pisses me off."

"Why?"

"Because you should be inundated with people doing nice shit for you. To you."

She smirks. "I don't like them doing nice things to me, I like it when they're a little bad. Like you."

I laugh. "Yeah, you're so drunk. You wanted to kill me just now. Then fuck me. Now you want to canonize me?"

"Because you're a bad boy, but a good man, and I'm in fucking lov—"

I shut her up with my mouth because I can't take it. I can't take her sincerity, the thought that she might seem to have forgiven me now, but she won't when I tell her what I do, is something I can't take. It's grown too big, the way I feel for her, the way I respect her, like her, admire her, the way I want her to be happy and the torment of knowing that every moment I'm with her, I could be putting her at risk. I can't risk her. She has to know.

And Greyson King will have zero future with her.

❤ ❤ ❤

SHE'S ASLEEP BY the time Derek brings her angry friend, who's fucking fuming as he loads her and Melanie's suitcases into the trunk.

She slides into the car. "What the fuck did you do to her?" Immediately she signals to Melanie's neck. "She never takes off her precious necklace. It's always under her shirt and today it was right on top of it. So, what did you do to her?"

For the first time I notice.

Melanie did take off my necklace.

There's a roiling in my gut, a feeling like I'm sinking as I brush my fingers regretfully over her bare throat. I wanted her to use it, didn't I? I wanted her to sell it.

It shouldn't *hurt* like this, it shouldn't even fucking matter.

"I'm driving you two to a suite at a better and safer hotel," I say in a cold, emotionless voice, low and keeping my eyes on Melanie. "I'd appreciate if you kept her company until I can return."

"I'll do it for her because it's her birthday but not because you asked me to, asshole."

TWENTY

CONFUSED

Melanie

I wake up disoriented, and then, like a brick to the head, it hits me.

I'm drunk, still.

More like hungover.

A fierce pounding in my temples makes me squint my eyes as I try to place myself. I groan and shift in bed, and I realize that I have a braid and I don't remember doing my hair. To think that Greyson may have put his hands on my hair makes my stomach hurt.

I push to my feet and peer around the room. It's three a.m.

I fell asleep in the car?

There's an enormous bathroom and I feel so filthy, I go around the room in search of my stuff—and see my suitcase. Quickly I tear off my clothes and pull out a T-shirt and cotton undershorts, then walk around, parched. I guzzle a bottle of water and peer around. I've never been in such a big room. It's lavishly decorated, and very cozy. There are pictures on the wall of wildlife next to wooden boomerangs.

Books run from side to side on one wall in a living room, and there's another closed room. I see Pandora's shoes by the bar and I frown in confusion.

I hear a noise from a third room and peer inside, and I see him. My insides tighten when he doesn't see me.

He's got glinting silver things spread out over the bed. He looks freshly showered and is slipping into a shirt, sleek black slacks hanging low on his waist.

The lamps to both sides of the bed are made of onyx, each with a lightbulb glowing warmly at the center, filtering through the onyx in an incredibly elegant way. It kisses his skin golden, it runs through his hair, it touches him in a way that makes me fist my hands at my side.

The sight of him reminds me so much of other mornings. In his huge, empty apartment. When we were fooling around, sometimes taking a bath together. It felt like he was mine.

But he's not.

Instant emotion swells inside me when I think of him and that woman.

Then I remember Riley.

Our fight.

What else happened?

As I try to decipher what's on the bed, I notice he's begun observing me with a quiet, narrowed stare, and something passes across his face, a wistful kind of longing that makes my own yearning slice me up in quarters.

"Where are we?" I croak.

"A hotel."

"Not my hotel."

"It is now."

The sight of his nipple piercing glinting in the lamplight as he starts buttoning his shirt mocks me. I want to suck it as I ride him. Tug it and play with it as he fucks me, loves me. No, he'll never love me.

"Zero . . ." I whisper. "When I was falling asleep, I kept hearing someone saying that number over and over, what is it? You were telling Derek to call someone to come pick you up at the airport, and several times he said Zero . . . What is that?"

He sighs and turns, then spreads his arms out and watches me cautiously. "Me."

"Zero?" I nearly choke on the word. "Is Greyson not even your name?"

Greyson waits it out.

Which only makes me more confused, more frustrated.

"Zero?" I repeat. "What the hell does that mean? Certainly not the number of women you've fucked. Hell, I thought I *knew* you!"

"You thought *you* knew *me*?" His outrage is like a tangible thing in the room. "I thought *I* knew *you*! What the fuck, Melanie? Your necklace is missing! I find you in a room with another dude! *You* tell me what the *fuck*. You have a whole Underground in yourself, princess, I'm not the only fucking liar here!"

There's a knock, and a guy with a sleek head peers inside. "I'm ready when you are. Derek will keep his post here—your reservation's—"

"Leon, I need a fucking moment here," Greyson interrupts as he stalks across the room, slamming the door shut on his face, but not soon enough. Not before I see the man. Recognize him, that tall, lanky man.

From the time I visited Brooke one weekend and stole away alone to the Underground, begging for an extension.

Extension? We can make you an extension of our cocks, how's that, lady?

I glance at Grey and an even more terrifying realization washes over me, and with an awful wrenching in my gut, I finally, finally get it.

Greyson, that skinny guy he called Leon, and the other group of guys who laughed at me when I'd asked for more time; they are the gods and lords of the Underground.

The lanky, ugly one looked at Greyson like he's a god, and he's the guy who wanted to fuck me as payment. Payment for my debt. I gasp at the realization and I clutch my stomach as a weakening wave of nausea roils over me.

"Omigod, you're one of them."

His eyes flick to the closed door, then to me, and he tells me, "If he sets a finger on you, I'll cut it off so help me god, I'll cut off every single one of them—"

"Omigod!"

Cupping my mouth, I sit on the edge of the bed when my legs fail me. I rock myself to and fro, because he's not just a liar, he's . . .

He's . . .

I don't even know what he is.

Suddenly, I think of how he met me . . . god, was he following me?

The men? Was he the guy . . . the guy who drove me home then left me, drenched with his blood?

I can't. Can't. *Can't.*

I curl forward and hold my stomach as I try not to get sick.

"Oh god."

"Princess." He whispers the word almost reverently as he starts for me.

Motherfucker!

I leap to my feet and whip one hand out to hold him at bay. "No! Stay. Stay there, don't you touch me. Just tell me one thing . . ." I'm assaulted by my pain as other memories keep piling up in my brain.

Lies . . . lies . . . lies . . .

I can barely make myself speak. "Were you collecting?" My eyes blur with tears when I look at him, as if the bastard hasn't already made me cry enough today. "Were you collecting from me?"

"Is that what you think?" he asks, softly, standing a few feet away with about a tornado's worth of energy simmering around him.

A rage unlike any other bubbles within me as I reach for the hem of my T-shirt. "Here we go then!" I jerk it off my head, drop my shorts, kicking them in the air—in his direction. "Let's collect. Let's get this bet over with. Surely you've received partial payment for all the other times I fucked you?" Then I start slipping off my G-string. "So how many more do we have left? How many? Huh?" I kick my panties aside and stand naked before him. "Huh, Greyson?"

He's frozen like a statue, his eyes brilliant as I gather my T-shirt in one fist and toss it in his direction. "C'mon—let's get this over with. Just tell me how many fucks it's going to take."

He grabs the shirt and in one lightning-fast second, covers the distance between us, pressing it into my chest, calmly murmuring, "Get dressed. We'll talk later today. I have *one* man left to see, and I don't have much time, Melanie. My father is very ill . . ."

"There's nothing to talk about."

"Just put this on *please!*" he roars.

Angry, but suddenly scared, I start slipping back into my T-shirt as he goes to stand by the window, staring outside in bitter silence at a distant green mountain.

The silence is deafening.

I'm suddenly . . . heartbroken.

Not even angry. I feel like he gathered all my dreams, all my hopes, and all my emotions and put them in a blender, and now they're pureed into nothing. They'll never, ever be pieced back together again. Ever.

"Who *are* you?" I ask dejectedly. A ball of fire is gathering in my throat. "At least tell me that. At least tell me that, Greyson."

"Zero is an alias. Because I'm . . ." He turns around, spreads the arms that have always made me feel protected out to encompass the room. "Untraceable, supposedly."

A tense silence settles between us.

His gaze shutters as he murmurs, almost as though he doesn't want to say it but some decent part of him is forcing him to, "I was retired, but now it seems that I help collect gambling payments owed to my father. Forty-eight collections. That's all I had to do in order to retire again. I've got one more . . . and you . . . and then I'm done with this. And he'll tell me where my mother is."

And you, I silently repeat, the blender spinning my emotions again.

"What's your real name?" I ask thickly.

"You already know my name," he says, his voice low and gruff as a spark of tenderness steals into his eyes. "You've moaned it. Screamed it. Whispered it. It's Greyson, Melanie." He starts for me as though he suddenly needs to make some sort of contact, but I can't bear it if he touches me. I back away, shaking my head from side to side.

"So you're one of their leaders. Leader of these mafia Underground men," I say.

His eyes burn with some unspeakable emotion. "If that's what you want to call me, yes."

"My necklace. You didn't even buy it. Did you?" I can hardly speak, my voice is so pained and raw.

"Some payments are made in substance. And we keep them on hand for bribes—so yes, princess, I didn't buy your bauble exactly."

"Wow. My friends were right, it meant nothing to you."

"Which friend? The one you were kissing last night? Where is that necklace, Melanie?" He stalks toward me faster and I back away until my spine is flat against the wall and he presses into me, a big predator with eyes that somehow own me as they look down at me.

He curls a hand around my neck, and his hunger reaches me, weakens me. I feel my knees wobble at his nearness. His scent. God, I missed him and I hate that I did. That I do.

He's standing here and I still do.

Miss him.

Want him.

"You kill people," I rasp.

His hand circles my throat, and the pad of his thumb slowly, sinuously, begins caressing my pulse point as his eyes drop to my lips. "Sometimes." His voice is a low rasp.

"Do you torture them?"

I'm breathless.

I'm breathless and hurting and why can't I unlove him? Why can't I *unlove* him?

"I do what I have to," he murmurs as he strokes my neck with his thumb and keeps staring, keeps hungering openly for my mouth, his gaze so powerful I lick my lips nervously, and it only makes his eyes darken even more. He hungers even more.

My breath is no longer mine. But I keep trying to get air into my lungs, because all the emotions in my chest are too painful to hold back. "Stupid little bimbo, is that why you chose me?" I ask thickly.

"Chose you? If I'd chosen a woman, I would never have *chosen* you." He rubs the back of one knuckle over my lips as he keeps fucking my lips with his eyes. "You're a hot mess, Melanie," he rasps. "You're a hot, innocent little mess and I would never willingly tie myself by the balls to someone as fun, merry, innocent, and happy-go-lucky as you. I didn't choose you, but I sure as fuck can't free myself of you. You're in my head, you're like some demon in my fucking heart."

"Fuck you!" I push him, but he grabs my wrists to halt me and pulls my arms over my head, causing my body to arch instinctively and the tips of my nipples to brush against his hard chest. The instant bolt of arousal I feel sparks my own anger at myself.

"Use me," I yell, squirming in his hold, "discard me. That was the plan, right? Fuck her and then fuck her over. Get some blonde who doesn't think too much and won't ask a lot of questions! One you can get rid of easily!"

"Do I look like someone who's trying to get rid of you?" he grinds out, tightening his hold on my wrists, pressing his erection against me. "I want you like I want a new *life*, Melanie," he grits out. "I have files thick about you and men, I know about your debt. I knew about your twin before you even told me, Melanie."

I choke when he mentions Lauren. My eyes blur as he softly continues, easing his hold on my wrists and slowly, caressingly, dragging the cup of his hand down the delicate inside skin of my bare arms. "I know your parents lost her, and you blame yourself because you lived. Don't you?"

I think there's not only a fireball in my throat, but it's in my eyes and in my heart.

"So all your sweet life you've tried to make up for what you feel you took from your parents. You've tried to make them happy, you've tried to make everyone around you happy, because maybe, deep down, you don't want anyone to believe you didn't deserve the chance your sister never got."

"Stop it," I say quietly, but a stream of tears pours down my face because nobody has ever seen so clearly into me before, and I'm scared, and hurting, and his hazel eyes just won't let me go.

He tightens his hold on my shoulders now, his gaze fiercely tender and still hungry for me as he adds, "I know you've used sex to stop feeling lonely too long, Melanie, and I know you're the loveliest thing I've ever seen, always trying to make the best of everything. Giving every frog a chance, because you were given that chance, right? So why would you deny a chance to someone? Anyone? Even a fucking asshole like me?"

He slides a hand down my face and caresses my cheek, the kind of caress only he gives me. The one I feel under my skin, down to my nerves, my bones.

"I know that you quit a semester in college to stand by your best friend when she was injured," he adds, "and you never told her you postponed the semester because you wanted to keep her company. I know you're the sort of girl who'd buy a Mustang in a city where it rains almost every day of the year because it's worth it to ride with the top down for the days where there's sun. I know you, Melanie. Fuck, I know more about you than I wish I knew because I would not change one thing . . . one thing . . . one *word* . . . of the ten-inch file I have of you . . . on my fucking desk."

I drop my gaze from his with a quiet sob, and he tips my head back and forces me to look into his face, which is fierce with conviction, as fierce as his hot, penetrating gaze. "Your saucy 'I got this' persona? I *like* her. I know her, but I see the glimpses of you, Melanie. The *real* you. The one who's frightened. The one who doesn't like being alone. The one who's vulnerable and makes me want to say I got you. Come here, I fucking got you, princess."

"You know all this about me and I don't even know *you*!" I cry.

"Yeah you do," he counters, and he cups my head and crushes my mouth with his, and the hunger in the kiss sizzles through my nerve endings, lights me on fire.

Hot lips. Taste. He's not the only one hungry for the taste. I want it too, badly.

Please, please, be smart, Melanie!
Leave, Melanie!

"God," he growls when my mouth seems to part of its own will and I somehow find my fingers digging into his biceps. "I've been taught to con and blackmail, lie, cheat, anything it takes to get what I want."

The hot suckling motion of his mouth makes my toes curl, my body burn and arch closer to him as he wraps his arms around my waist.

"And I want you. These sweet little teacup breasts. I want my mouth on them again." He cups my ass with one hand, and one tit with the other. "I love when your nipples bead for me. They bead at my voice. At a glance from me. I love your ass. I love your fucking mouth." He seems to be going crazy, doing everything at once. Massaging my ass. Massaging my tit. Gobbling my mouth. Then he kisses my neck, flicking his tongue out to taste me. A shudder rockets through me. *God*. It's ecstasy. Agony. Both.

" 'Zero'—do you know what he does, princess?" he dares me, taking a hot, sensual bite out of my lower lip before easing back to look at me with hooded eyes. "He looks for a weakness and pounces on it, wrecks the prey, and makes it pay."

I shudder over the sensual tone of his voice and whisper, "I'm sorry for them."

"Hmm. You should be." He heads to my ear, his breath hot as he grinds his erection against me. "I think I know your weakness, Melanie. I know your weakness. Your weakness . . . is me."

"Stop."

"I'd stop it if you meant it. Mean it," he commands, then cups my face and looks at me, waiting for me to mean what I say, his eyes electric. "Right now. Mean it," he whispers seductively, his breath hot on my face. "Tears?" He edges back, his eyes sober and yet relentless. "Tears . . . why? I haven't made you come yet."

I want to pull free.

But I'm shaking and craving and wanting. It's true that I want his body, every hot, delicious inch, but more than anything I want to know who he is—who the man who has this effect on me *is*.

He. Is not. Real, MELANIE!

He is a liar, a player, a fucking scoundrel and a rogue. You don't need him! You don't want him!

"Tell me who you are!" Suddenly my voice rises with my bewilderment.

He looks at me, dark shadows crossing over his eyes, then he surprises me when he leaves me and sits on the bed. Setting his elbows on his knees, he leans over, looking at me, every inch of him tormented. He runs his hand through his hair and, slowly, I watch as each copper-streaked strand falls into place one by one. Silence drags on, the tension palpable until he breaks the silence, a low, hard bitterness spilling into his voice.

"I was raised by my mother, Lana King. She left my dad when she got pregnant, to protect me. One day when I was thirteen I came home and she was tied up in a chair, gagged, among a group of men—among them my father. He offered . . ." He trails off, then smirks coldly. "He told me if I killed one of his men, she'd be untied and set free. I didn't know he had a deal with her, that she'd told him I wasn't a killer like him—that he'd promised to let me go if that was true. I didn't know about that fucking deal when I took the gun he offered, aimed it, fired it, and killed him. And I never saw her again."

His voice turns empty and cold, like an echo of an old tomb. I'm not sure if it's the tone he uses, the words he tells me, or the lack of sparkle in his usually brilliant, beautiful eyes. "My uncle Eric told me my father had made a deal with my mother. He would take me if I proved to be his son. My mother promised him that I was nothing like him. And then I shot a man. I didn't hesitate. I shot him."

A war of emotions rages in me, my feelings toward him becoming confusing and as painful as anything in my life has ever been.

"I doomed myself to a life of this." He signals around him. "Maybe I should've shot my father. It could've been over, right then and there. But blood is a curious thing." He looks at me, a slight confusion in his hawklike eyes. "It ties you. Even when you loathe your kind, something here . . ." He puts his fists to his chest. "Somewhere here you're still loyal. I spent eight years with him, believing he'd let me see her. Until I realized he wasn't ever letting me see her so long as he knew I didn't really give a shit about him. So I went rogue, dropped him, and tried to find her, doing little jobs in between. I followed every trail I could find. Nothing. She vanished without a trace."

His bearing is stiff and proud, but I can finally see the chaos in his eyes. I imagine him, a young teenager, torn in two. Using his smarts to survive, while still trying to find and protect his mother.

His every disquieting word races through my mind, his childhood so different from mine that I don't understand it, almost.

"He's summoned me back now that he's dying. He's got leukemia and he wants me to take the reins of the Underground." He laughs sadly. "A man like him, I can't even imagine him sick. But he needs to pass on his torch. Wyatt—I know he's been more of a son to him than I have. But he wants the alpha." He pulls out a piece of paper. "When I saw you on this list, you were supposed to be something I worked out of my system. That blonde in my dreams. Then there you were. There you were in the fucking bar with that fucking asshole trying to take you home—and then there you were, a fucking devil of an angel in the rain."

"Don't even talk to me about the rain!"

"You wanted to talk, so I'm talking to you now." He walks forward, stopping in front of me, the faint smile tugging his lips holding an infinite amount of sadness. "This isn't how I wanted to spend your birthday, Melanie." His voice is a tender murmur, squeezing my heart.

I won't cry, I won't fucking cry. I blink and swallow.

"All I ask is that you let me celebrate you when I get back. If I only get to spend one day with you, I want to spend *this* day. With you."

I can't stand the way he knows me. The way he understands me. The way he makes my every dream come true and breaks my every fantasy. If there were a day I'd need him in a year, it would be my birthday. But suddenly I desperately need to go home.

"You're leaving right now?" I whisper.

His eyebrows rise inquiringly. "I have to. Just one more mark. I owe it to my mother."

He comes over and wraps me in his arms. I close my eyes as his heat envelops me, his scent, him. When he tries to pull away, I pull his arms closer, suddenly just needing this a minute longer. "Why do you want my arms?" he whispers in my ear. "I just told you they've done more harm than good."

"Not to me."

"Because you fell for me, you fell for me and all my bullshit, and even with everything I just said, you're still falling, aren't you," he rasps. He kisses the back of my ear. "I'm right here to catch you." He kisses the back of my ear, harder. "Let me catch you."

I duck my head to compose myself.

He ducks his dark head too and glances at my toes. On each foot, my toenails spell, in perfect blue and hot pink all the way around, GREY ❤

"Nice toes."

I curl and tuck them into the rug. "I got a pedicure. At the best place in Seattle."

All for you . . . I think miserably.

His grin gives me butterflies in my stomach, and I wish I had an ax and I could literally kill them. "That someone could get you to sit your restless little ass for a while to get to do that is a testament to their abilities." He looks at me with those eyes that reach strange little places inside me, and my stomach starts to feel heavy from the complete overload of my emotions. "Or to your conviction to wear my name on your feet?"

He kneels, and I hold my breath as he takes my toe and kisses it.

"Grey, you're kissing my toe," I say, voice thick and cottony.

"It's got my name on it."

When I pry my foot loose, he exhales a long, long breath and rises to his feet, to over six feet of beautiful lying man, then he quietly starts getting some of the stuff on the bed into his black jacket. I stare into the shadows, watching him slip on his gloves, feeling like this innocence I just lost will never, ever be recovered.

"I feel like my boyfriend just died. I will never, ever, have Greyson anymore."

If I sound sad, he looks *wrecked*.

"I feel like my alias just killed my girl. And she'll never look at me the way she did before."

We stare the way we do, except we usually smile here.

This time we don't.

Go home, Melanie, I think miserably.

He steps forward cautiously, and I remember how obsessed he is with my eyes, and I feel a strange sadness for him when he somehow cups my face, thinks about kissing them, but drops his hands instead.

"I'll be back. Stay here with your friend for the day tomorrow, and *think*, Melanie. When I'm back, I dare you to look into my eyes and tell me you don't want me."

I don't know what he's going to do, but terror, lust, love, every emotion swims in me as he crosses the room to leave. "Greyson, swear to me that you won't kill anyone!" I cry. "Swear, or we will have nothing to talk about. Nothing."

My heart pounds in my temples, my chest, my fingertips as I wait for his answer to my impulsive ultimatum. He stands by the door and laughs softly, then he pulls something from his jacket, pulls off the cartridge from his gun, sets it down, and swings the door open. He didn't give me his word, but I believe him.

I don't know why, but I believe him.

I wait until he shuts the door behind him to have the mother of all nervous fucking breakdowns.

TWENTY-ONE

THE LIST

Greyson

It was an easy mark.

I slip inside the darkened home, wake him up with the tip of my SIG right on his temple while he startles up in bed. He shook like a flag in the wind as he opened the safe, gave me the money.

He'll probably never again sleep.

Welcome to the club, old man . . .

But I'm not thinking about that anymore. His name is scratched, the fights were good tonight. Riptide owned the ring— and that's fine by me. Riptide is money, and the Underground is all about money.

But I'm not thinking about that either.

I'm thinking about her. Wondering if she's sleeping. Or even half as tortured as I am. It's six a.m. at the hospital, and I've been sitting here, hating what I already know.

Hating that I already know what she's going to tell me later on today when I go to see her.

That I don't deserve her, am a liar, a con, and not the man she wants and it's fucking. Eating. Me. *Alive.*

Can't sit still. Can't stop going over shit in my head.

I've sat all night at the hospital watching my father struggle to breathe.

I feel choked myself, the air clogged in my lungs. I knew what my life was, what I wanted. It was all clear.

Nothing is clear anymore except that I can't imagine continuing a day without her. If she won't have me, I already know I will be obsessed. I will stalk her. I won't be able to let go of her. I will need to be sure that she's safe, that she's herself, that she's laughing. I'll have to see someone else touch her. The man she wanted—the man I couldn't be. My heart thrashes in my chest. A firestorm rages in my body at the thought of anyone touching her but me.

But I won't be the Hades that drags my Persephone into hell with him.

She's not Persephone. She's Melanie Meyers Dean, and I love her.

I exhale and put my face in my hands, shuddering as I try to get a grip on myself.

I'm sick and she's the only cure.

I'm sick for her, as sick as my father.

I glance up and he's hardly moving in bed, the sound of his breath low and even. Yeah, it hurts. I hated him all my life. He took everything good from me. And it still hurts that he's weak and mortal, and still, the motherfucker clinging fiercely to where my mother is.

Rage, impotence, it all swells in my chest. I've just worked my last mark with the help of Tina's information. I carefully worked around my numbers so that only one mark remains . . . number five.

"The list?" Eric anxiously asks me after conferring with the doctors and realizing my father only has hours left. *Hours*.

"I'm going to get the payment," I lie, pushing the chair back and rising.

But I won't. I'm going to get back my girl, and then I'm going to come back here and tell my father that he failed. That he failed in making me like him. In making me completely selfish and evil.

I'm going to get back my girl and I'm going to fetch some of my cash and buy back my girl's paper. He can put any price he wants on it. He can put my own life on it. Or the price of the Underground. But he's going to tell me where my mother is, and he's going to watch me scratch off Melanie's name while I hand him the cash she owes.

He will think me weak. He will die thinking me weak.

I don't give a shit anymore.

I'm fighting for what I care for and I'm going to fight for it if I spend the rest of my days in the shadows, making sure my girl's all right.

TWENTY-TWO

DECISION

Melanie

❝I want to go home."

Those are the first words that pop out of my mouth the next day when Greyson stands at my hotel room door, all in dark clothes, freshly shampooed hair. Not my prince. Not my knight in shining armor. Rather my villain in black.

"I really want to go home," I repeat in a hoarse, broken voice. "I've thought about . . . our conversation and I just want to go home today."

That's all I say.

Not, *hey.* Not *good morning.* I don't even comment on the box he holds, or the gerbera daisy he's loosely holding in his hand, like the one he pinned to the wall in my parents' home. Emotion seizes me as I remember that day, how real he was, how fun it was.

Those who play together, stay together . . .

That's not true, Nana. Sometimes men just play with you and break you.

I can't even say Greyson didn't warn me.

I feel like a vampire just sucked all the blood out of my heart as I open the door wider to let him in. The room shrinks as he enters, his gaze never leaving mine as he sets everything down on the coffee table as if he's probably just realized I don't want any presents. I don't even want to have a birthday.

"Hey," Pandora greets him from where she was having coffee at a small dining table. It's the first time she doesn't sound so hostile toward him. Maybe because we talked all morning about it, she finally convinced me, and I convinced myself that he IS ALL WRONG FOR ME.

But now that he's close, it's so hard to believe that.

I can feel his grief as he follows me to my bedroom.

My insides scream at me to launch myself into his arms and work it out. How can we not work it out? He's owned me. For over four months, he, and everything he is, has owned me. But I need him to let me go or he will break me.

I'm too much of a romantic; he's too hardened, too cold with what he's done all his life.

When I close the door to my room, suddenly I turn, and he pulls me to him and kisses me. We kiss, not fighting it, instead melting into each other's mouth as we kiss longer than we've ever kissed. Minutes and minutes and minutes. My wanting body sinking into his hard one, his hands holding me by the small of my back tightly pinned to him. Our tongues move faster than ever, starved, as we memorize each other's taste, the silkiness of our kiss. Until he groans and yanks himself free and heads toward the window.

I see him struggling to pull up his walls again. Walls I wrecked because I wanted him to love me. He does. I know he does. It was in his touch and the desperation in his eyes right now, like he wants to let me go, but can't.

He stands facing the window, hands in his pockets in that take-on-the-world stance of his that I love. Every inch of me knows he's aware of me, but he doesn't acknowledge me until he speaks, without turning, his voice so raw it scrapes my insides like a saw. "Are you sure leaving's what you want?"

"I'm sure," I say, my voice also like sandpaper.

His voice breaks with huskiness when he adds, "Derek can drive you to the airport then."

"I can take a cab." I take a step toward him and stop. What am I going to do? Hug him? I can't. I need to break this.

I see the gloves he threw on the bed and lovingly take them in one hand, needing to feel them one more time. He turns and looks at me, and it cuts me to look into his eyes. His proud Greyson King eyes. I drop my eyes to the ground and start blinking.

"Whoever you end up with, just know you were mine first. A part of you will always be mine. When you find your prince charming, the one who has everything you're looking for, perfect, you'll still be my fucking princess and not any other's."

My eyes water because his words hurt, the truth in them hurts as I press his gloves into his hands. "Please let it go, even that part."

"I could make you love me, Melanie. I can make you choose *me*."

I start crying and set my head on his chest, and he inhales my hair. "Is it what you want? I'll be your plaything and you'll be my playboy, and every night you'll do bad things and then come back to make love to me, and I'll be in heaven when I'm in your arms, and in hell when I'm out of them and these arms are doing something terrible."

"I own this body, Mel," he says, rubbing up my curves. "Every inch. These hands know how to love you more than they know how to do what they do."

I wipe my tears. "I've liked you owning it. Every inch. But the love of my life can't do what you do. He can't."

He cups my face. "He does," he says, tenderly.

I swallow as I have to acknowledge it. "But I wish he didn't."

I shake my head, but he looks at me with those piercing hazel eyes with little flecks of green that seem to glimmer right now. "And yet it's a part of me," he says huskily, stepping forward. "I'm not your prince, I'm everything you don't want and you still want me. You need me, Melanie, you've been *waiting* for me. Let go of the idea of who I should be and—"

"No! No, I don't want to be in love with you! Not you!" I push him away.

"Baby, I won't let it blacken you, it only needs to blacken me. You won't know about anything that needs to be done. Anything . . ."

"No! I couldn't bear to know you're doing anything like that, Grey!"

He lets go and steps away to face out to the street, the sunlight hitting his face in every beautiful angle, and my brain still seems to have enough cells working for me to register what is happening. Grey and I are breaking up. I wanted love, and I found it, and I'm going to let it go because . . . it's not like in the dreams, the stories, it's not like I imagined.

I feel stabbed in the chest by what I'm doing, but every instinct of self-preservation in me tells me I have to go.

Which makes it hurt inside when Greyson turns to me, cups my face, and tips my head back to his, his voice resolute.

"The Underground will be more organized than it was with my father. Melanie, I'll keep a cool head . . ."

"You can't ask me to stay by your side while you blackmail people, intimidate people . . ."

He groans and closes his eyes. "It will be *business*. Nobody will get hurt. Understand that I can't just drop this. There are livelihoods . . . fighters who live for this. Your friend . . . her husband, Riptide . . . they thrive, they breathe, they adore the Underground!"

"I know! I know it's a dark that has to be, I just can't be in it. I'm *afraid*!" I cry. The admission clouds his eyes with torment, and I don't know if he realizes maybe what I'm most afraid of is the way I feel for him, and the fact that he's everything I never wanted, and suddenly all I want.

My chest aches as I touch his cheek and look into his eyes and absorb the way he's looking at me. "You are so heart-stoppingly beautiful and such a good man, in here. When I think of you I want to think of who you were when you were with me, Greyson."

"You'd rather love the fantasy than the real man," he says, and it clearly hurts him.

"No, it's a real man I'm hurting for right now. It's a real man I'm in love with." I swallow. "Brooke said you were my Real. That's what she calls the love of *her* life now. But you are not my Real, Greyson. You're my knight in leather gloves who went rogue."

"God, you're tearing me open, Melanie."

I swallow and take his palm and put his gloves there, quietly accepting the fact that I know who he needs to be, and as he curls his fingers around those gloves, he curls his fingers around me. His eyes fall to my lips, and then he kisses my lips, a sudden brush, as if he can't help himself, then he pulls me back.

"You have three seconds," he says, "to go."

It hurts, as if I'm ripping a little piece of my heart, and I can't know of anyone else but my sister who could take me from this man's side. The opposite of my every dream and fantasy, and suddenly all I want. "Two seconds, Mel."

"Grey, stop me . . ." I suddenly say. *Omigod I can't believe I'm leaving him!*

"One."

God, he won't stop me.

For all his criminal ways, he won't subject me to this life. His life.

I turn around and grab my suitcase with everything I'd brought here and shut the door behind me. Then I stand there, crying against the utter silence in the room where I left him. Pandora stands and goes to get her own suitcase in silence.

I have slept all over Seattle, and I've never once felt like a whore until I broke this man's heart.

In an ideal world you only love the perfect man.

But it's not an ideal world. I love an imperfect man who sins, lies, steals, blackmails, and how odd to know already—even though the years have not passed—that not even my Mr. Perfect or Prince Charming will ever, ever live up to the one I just left.

PANDORA AND I don't talk on our way to the airport. Derek ended up insisting that he drive us, and I'm too devastated to protest. I found love, and I left it. I found all I wanted, and it was all wrong, and I left him standing in a hotel room he paid for, staring out the window like he'd chain me to him if he so much as glanced at me.

"I'm texting Kyle to organize something for tonight," Pandora says.

"No," I say.

"Mel, it's your birthday."

"No!" I say. "Please. I want to be alone."

We board. I even go as far as sliding my suitcase into the top plane compartment. And I remember him in the rain. I remember every single thing he's done for me.

"I've got your car."

"Be home tonight."

"My life has come at a high price too. Every day of it. So many days trying to find some fucked-up meaning in it."

"Am I the first man you've cooked for?"

"You got me, princess. Jesus! Do you not see what you're doing to me? You have all of me, Melanie. I'm states away and I feel like half a man, I feel like I'll tear something apart if I don't see you soon with my own two eyes . . ."

"I know you've used sex to stop feeling lonely too long, Melanie, and I know you're the loveliest thing I've ever seen, always trying to make the best of everything. Giving every frog a chance, because you were given that chance, right? So why would you deny a chance to someone? Anyone? Even a fucking asshole like me?"

He carried me . . . I suddenly remember how he carried me, home, while bleeding from a cut I gave him, and set me on my bed, filled up my bathtub, and squeezed my hand. He protected me. Held me. Tried to warn me against him because he didn't want to hurt me but somehow, like me, he couldn't stay away. I see it so clearly. The LOOK he gives me? That's what's real. That look is real. None of that other bullshit matters.

The gratitude and ferocity in his eyes when I cooked for him and he felt . . . accepted.

The times he opened up to how he felt about me. *Him!*—a man who's not used to probably feeling anything at all.

The way he knows me. All along, he has known every good and bad thing about me, and still he looks at me like I'm the most precious diamond of diamonds.

Suddenly I remember Brooke telling me OWN THIS, MELANIE! You've been looking all your life, fight for it!

"Pan," I whisper, my feelings for him intensifying until I feel like screaming or imploding because I won't, I refuse, to live with this bottled up. To live alone when I can have him. Will fear keep me from my guy? My man? My rogue? My hands are shaking as I unlatch my seat belt and almost stumble out of my seat before they close the door. "I'll see you in Seattle."

"What do you mean? Dude, I'm afraid of flying and I just popped a fucking sleeping pill and you know it!"

"Don't stop me. I don't want you to stop me. Please. Please, Pan! I want him. I *love* him."

I don't let her convince me of how stupid I'm being, or how reckless. I feel a lurch of excitement within me at the mere thought of running back into his arms, and my insides are jangling and out of control as I barely get out of the plane before they shut the door. I sprint down the airport terminal, trying to find Derek.

"Derek!" I call, hurrying in the hopes of catching him. I'm bounding through some sliding doors when another man in cowboy boots and a checkered shirt stops me.

"Holy shit, that's you!" he says.

"What?" I blink and take in the young man. He has the sort of face I remember seeing on many other men, plain and friendly, but a pair of sunglasses shields his eyes and for the life of me, I just don't remember meeting him before.

"Melanie. You're Melanie," he repeats, speaking the word like he just found gold.

"Do I *know* you?" I ask, glancing past his shoulder while praying to see a glimpse of Derek's big, broad back. Suddenly I can't stand it; I want to go back and stand before Grey and say, *I love you. I love you and I trust you and we're going to make it work. Somehow. You fucking asshole, you're my prince whether you want to be or not!*

"No, you don't know me yet." The young man grins and extends his hand. "I'm Greyson's brother, Wyatt. I overheard that you were leaving. I even thought I'd missed your flight, and yet here I was hoping I'd convince you to stay." His eyes twinkle as though he knows about Greyson and me, what we have between us. What we just lost because I'm a chicken and he was being . . . noble.

Noble.

And letting me go.

The anxiety to see him increases by the second. "Are you going to see him now? Where are you going? I was hoping for a ride."

"Actually, first I was going to see Greyson's mother."

"*What?*" The joy I feel almost doubles me over. "You know where she is?"

"I just found out myself, but shh. Don't tell Greyson first, it's a surprise. My father's not doing so good . . . he's been in the hospital for days and doesn't have much longer."

I'm nearly bowled over by the news. Bowled over with happiness, hope, anticipation. "Omigod." My eyes blur as I think of what this will mean for Greyson. After how many years will he finally see his own mother?

"Wanna come and bring her to him?" Wyatt suddenly offers.

"YES!"

TWENTY-THREE

NEWS

Greyson

The text comes from Melanie's phone, but immediately my gut freezes when I realize whoever is writing is not her.

Congratulations. You won.

I text back, And you are?

Melanie forgot her phone in the plane. This is Pandora. You won, I hope you're happy. She's on her way back to you. She's blindly, hopelessly in love with fucking ole you.

The words wrap around me like some sort of blanket, heating me. At the same time, an oddly primitive warning sounds in my brain. I punch Derek's number. "Where the fuck are you?"

"On my way back from dropping your queen. Why?"

"Get your ass to the airport and bring her back to me. Bring her back to me RIGHT FUCKING NOW!"

All my protective instincts have kick-started with a vengeance, mingled with the wild, primal excitement of what I just read on my phone.

She's coming to me.

She's coming back to me.

Twenty minutes of pacing later, I get Derek's call.

"She's gone. Taxi dispatcher saw her leave with a guy in a checkered shirt and boots."

My stomach roils, and suddenly it all clicks, and my blood turns to ice in my veins.

Wyatt.

Eric's familiar voice rings behind me. "Son, your father wants you . . ."

I'd been waiting outside his hospital room, waiting to talk to him, my checkbook handy, ready to settle things for Melanie, now I glance at Eric and grind my molars in rage.

"Tell him I'm gone. Tell him I'll be back!" I run down the hall and pull out the keys to my rental, punching C.C.'s number. "Wyatt's got her. Go to the south of the city, I'll take the north, spread Derek on the east, get the rest of the team on it. FIND WYATT, HELP ME FUCKING FIND HER!"

Thirteen years I've looked for my mother.

Thirteen.

If Melanie disappears for longer than a day, I'm going to become a monster, a full-on monster on a rampage with one mission and one mission only.

Find her, protect her, keep her, mate her. NEVER LET HER GO AGAIN.

I've never prayed but I throw myself up to a god I've never believed in and yell at him to take anything, anything of mine he wants, but not her.

TWENTY-FOUR

REVELATION

Melanie

"So where is she? Where has she been all this time?" I ask curiously from the backseat.

Greyson's brother just smiles and keeps driving deeper into the bad neighborhoods on the outskirts of Denver. He's a shorter guy, with a manner of dress that says I-wanted-to-be-a-cowboy.

I don't know if it's the sixth sense they say women have, or the chilling look in his eyes, or the way my heart speeds up in my chest, but something is very, very wrong here.

And suddenly I know—I know—that Wyatt is not taking me to Greyson's mother, like he'd said he would.

"Take me back," I say softly.

He laughs. "Seriously? You give orders now?" He clucks and meets my gaze. "Let's just make him come to you, hmm? Don't all girls like that? Being rescued? My brother's definitely going to want to rescue his 'princess.'"

"Listen, he doesn't care about me right now. He and I are over . . ."

When I reach over to open the door, he pulls out a gun. "Sit down and shut up."

The shock of having a gun trained on me makes me slam back against the seat, instantly silent. My heart is hammering now, my breathing ragged. I don't want him to know I'm afraid, but I feel a shudder of fear as I remember hands pulling me . . . taking me away . . .

It was *him*.

"Oh, trust me, he cares. Hell, I've made studying him a religion. My fucking father wanted me to be just like him." He sneers. "He's in love with you. He's had your name on that list for ages and he worked his way from number forty-eight downward, instead of upward, all to postpone the time he'd have to collect from you. In the meantime he'd disappear and I saw him watching you through the cameras of the Underground. All those fights you've come to? Greyson has been watching you. He pauses you, rewinds you, replays you. Oh, he fucking cares more than he has about anything else in his life—and I wanted his mind *fucked*! I wanted him to think he'd lost you too. So fucked he can't finish the list—and then the Underground would be where it belongs. In my hands."

He laughs to himself, a laugh that conveys some unnamable fury in him. "He even made my father promise no one would touch his marks . . . all because the bastard couldn't have anyone getting close to you."

He gives me a sideways glance and his smile is the fakest thing I've ever seen. "You trust me, *princess*, he gives a thousand shits about you, more than he's given about anything. It used to be impossible to bargain with him. His mother was gone, nowhere to be found. He doesn't give two shits about our father. He didn't even give a shit about being alive. Until you . . ."

That laugh again, making every alarm bell in my system ring even when I have nowhere to go—and I'm trapped, trapped, in broad daylight, in the backseat of this car.

"Greyson's smart, methodical," his half brother says, his eyes narrowing on my face. "But *he doesn't have what it takes*. He wants to keep it too clean, too nice, gentlemen doing business. This is *my* world. He doesn't even want it. He's just doing all this to find out where his mom is."

He smiles again, laughs again.

I hate that smile.

I hate that laugh.

"Yeah, pretty boy Grey thinking Dad is a bad guy. Always saving people. Kills for the wrong reasons. It's a dirty world, the Underground. When my dad's gone, Zero's going to turn it into a legit enterprise. What? Are we going to sit down at a committee table and fucking negotiate?" He laughs. "That's not the way the Underground runs—as long as I live, it ain't running like that. Now I have you, so I got him. Now I'm the one taking the woman out of his life."

"You can negotiate without me. He doesn't want me anymore," I assure. "Why don't we go to his mother . . ." I suggest.

"Bitch, nobody knows where the bitch is but Slaughter, and he won't say SHIT!" He jerks the wheel so we weave to the side, then he glares at me as he straightens the car back out. "God! It's beyond interesting to me that my brilliant, talented brother would fall for a bimbo like you. But I'm sure you give good head."

I remain silent, too scared to speak now.

Greyson thinks I left. He let me GO.

He won't come for me.

I know the exact shade of Grey's eyes when he looks at me.

How he sleeps with an arm under a pillow, facedown with his head turned to me.

I know he smells like a forest I want to get lost in, forever, and never be found.

And I don't know shit about his stupid criminal actions.

Except that he was hiding them all from me.

And now I don't even know how dangerous his brother is. If he's a rapist and a killer in addition to a kidnapper. If he's just holding me for ransom or planning to torture me simply because he can . . .

I don't know what *the fuck to do*!

"Go ahead. Judge me. I don't give a shit," the guy spits out.

He pulls the car into an underground garage and slides a gate closed behind us, and pulls me out of the back of the car, pressing the gun to my temple. Cold. Hard. Steel.

My stomach roils as he clenches my arm and drags me to the underground elevator.

"Tell me," he says as we ride up, and I can hardly hear him through the pounding of my own heartbeat. "Who was doing Slaughter's dirty work when his precious Greyson took off? I was sure he'd never come back, but oh, no. Julian was willing to practically beg. He was too afraid to lose his golden child. When Julian learned he was sick, he couldn't sleep thinking he'd never see his precious Zero again, his Underground—all the fights, all the gambling, the lucrative business, the prestige among fighting leagues—it would all go to waste if Zero wasn't behind the reins."

I hear his words, but most of all, I *feel* the sick resentment that he's venting out on to me.

Kick his nuts, Melanie! But I'm frozen.

"See, I'm not jealous."

Melanie, twist around, run away!

It looks so easy on television, but my stupid knees . . . my stupid knees feel like Jell-O and it seems that, apparently, I can't run to save myself.

"When Slaughter dies, Greyson gets nothing so long as I got you," Wyatt continues as he opens the elevator gate and shoves me into an abandoned loft, littered with old wood, dried-out paint cans. "Sit on that fucking chair or I shoot your legs."

I drop down on the chair without question, clenching my jaw to keep my teeth from chattering.

"He's dying right now. And I got you. Greyson loses. The list is incomplete and he loses. Even if he were to fight me for it, if he wants you back, he's going to need to give it up in exchange for you, and I'm going to have to kill him. And you—you want to live, then give me a juicy little fuck and we'll see." He looks at me. "That's right, Melanie. You see, I've been watching you lately too. All those videos he plays. I've been watching you. Your tits bouncing. You screaming, 'Riptiiiiide!' Yeah, my brother's not the only one with a hard-on for you."

Wyatt starts tying my arms behind my back with thick hemp rope.

Fear. It's eating me alive now. I can hear the chatter of my teeth knocking.

The wind whistling outside.

He straps me down and I blink my eyes because, no, I don't want this asshole to see me crying.

"He'll kill you when he finds you," I rasp, hating the fear in my voice.

He laughs. "Darling, I'm already dead." He leans over. "And he won't. Kill me. See, that's the thing about him. He doesn't like to kill. He does it only when he has to. But I'm the only family he'll have left. He still feels responsible for me. Bailing me out of my shit. He'll feel, in that part of him that hates being a Slater, that it's my father's fault I'm like this too. He'll let me live."

He ties something around my mouth and leaves for a moment. Suddenly it's so still, and the silence frightens me most of all.

My eyes burn from the need to cry.

My throat is raw, my tongue is dry and sticky under the cloth he wrapped around my mouth.

I may die today.

I failed myself, my sister, my parents. And it gives me no pleasure that the last time I saw the only man I've ever loved, I threw our love away. *Oh god.*

I told him how wrong he was for me, but never how right. He never knew that I was happy, blissfully happy—even if afraid—to be in love with him. I didn't say that I think I fell from the moment he charged into the rain to spare me getting wet. I never told him that deep down I think it's hot that he's bad, and even hotter that he's so good at being bad. I never told him that even after he lied, I trusted that he'd never, ever hurt me. I never told him any of that, only that I was scared. A fucking pussy.

He will never know that I believe, without a shadow of a doubt, that either by a cruel twist of fate or a blessing from heaven, he's mine. And that I was his before he even touched me.

He is what I never knew I wanted and now all I need.

I believed it enough to come back to him. Enough to leave my fairy-tale land and follow him right into his exciting and frightening Underground.

He might never, ever know this.

Noises shuffle across an adjoining room and my stomach pulls and wrenches into knots as he approaches again.

Uncontrollable quavers seize me as I try edging my nails into the rope knot biting into my wrists. My hair is all over my face. I hate it. I. *Hate.* It. All my muscles are cramped as my blood rushes through me in an effort to make me move, to help me escape. The chair screeches beneath me and I wince at the sound.

Wyatt marches to a small, cracked window and peers outside, then he cants his head in my direction and stares at me, his eyes raking me on the chair.

The lust in his gaze is unmistakable, and it sends my fear spiraling out of control. *Oh god, this can't be happening!*

A jolt of adrenaline kicks through me. Holding my breath, I press the inside of my wrists tight together and wedge my thumb in between the knot, using my nail to try to catch a tiny opening to get the knot to creak open. The rope loosens as I jam my thumb inside, followed by my other thumb, pulling it open on opposite sides, and I pretend to stretch and arch my back as I finally jerk one of my hands free, then wiggle the other one out.

In less than three seconds, he's back on me. He grabs my hair with one fist and pulls me off the chair, then jerks me facedown on a rumpled makeshift mattress. "What are you trying to do? Huh? Escape?"

I'm scrambling, fighting to get free, but he flips me around and straddles me with his hips as he grabs my breasts and squeezes. My blood pounds, my face growing hot with humiliation as I fight him.

"Don't touch me, asshole!" I cry as I buck and try using my knees.

He pins my arms above me and I turn my head and bite blindly, pulling out a chunk of meat.

He wails and I squirm free, panting as I get my bearings while my heart keeps pounding frantically in the middle of my throat.

He roars and lunges and I clip him with my heel, the gun clattering to the floor. Spitting out the blood from where I bit him, I grab the gun and swiftly turn when he kicks it away from me.

"Bitch."

He smacks me.

The pain rips through me, then he grabs me by the throat and lifts me up in the air, and pain and the urgency for oxygen screams with every breath wheezing out of my throat. He grabs the gun and I kick in the air and raise my knee, ramming it in his nuts. "Ooof."

He drops me.

I start running to the elevator, but when I spot the exit stairs just three steps away, I sprint over, grab the door handle, and jerk hard, trying to open it, yelling at it, "Come on, come on!" But it's jammed, and I'm about to kick it open when I hear the elevator gate open and angry bellows behind me.

"Get over here, you fucking cunt!"

Which is when the door I'm struggling to open finally gives. It swings open, outward, and I'm so attached to the knob, I follow it, taking a giant step forward—only to find there are no stairs, only a five-story fall, my body plunging into nothingness as I hear the most blood-chilling, desperate call I've ever heard in my life—"NO! PRINCESS!"—and I crash into blackness.

TWENTY-FIVE

FALLEN

Greyson

My world bottoms out.

I watch Melanie disappear through the gaping hole of the open door. Something takes over me. I hear myself yelling one more time, "PRINCESS!" as I charge for the empty space. My brother lunges at me, tackling me against the wall, grabbing my arm where I'm holding my gun. I overpower him easily, slide my SIG between us and aim it right in the center of his rib cage.

BOOM!

He howls, and I drop his writhing body to the ground and drop the gun as I run to the empty doorway. My chest is tight. I can't breathe. Five stories below, I see a pool of golden hair.

"MELANIE!"

No response.

Derek steps out of the elevator and is instantly by my side, unrolling a piece of rope as I bark, "Lower me, I don't want to crush her." I grab one end of the rope as he slowly lowers me one floor, and then two, until there's no more rope, and from two stories up, I leap down, crashing to the ground with a curse. "Call an ambulance!" I yell at Derek.

"Princess." I roll to the side and crawl over to her. "*Princess*."

She's pale and lifeless. Streaks of blood cover her cheeks, streaming from her lips and nose. She mumbles something unintelligible.

"Baby," I say as I reach out to touch her neck for a pulse.

I feel it, fluttering faintly under my fingers. My heart hurts in my rib cage. It hurts so fucking bad. For the first time in my life, I feel impotent.

"Melanie, stay with me." I sound like a pussy. Begging. But holy shit, she can't leave me. She can't fucking leave me.

I check the back of her neck; it's not broken, but I'm not moving her. I don't dare. I simply cup her head in my hands because I thought I'd never see this fucking face again and I stare at it. And stare at it. Her eyes closed, her smile gone, the blood trailing from her lips. Before I know it I duck my head and press my lips to hers, kissing her bloodied lips, my voice roughening as it starts breaking, "Baby, I told you to stay away from me."

She's not moving. I can't breathe.

The room closes in on us, sucking out the oxygen. I can't fucking breathe. "Melanie, look at what I've done to you." I brush her hair back with my gloved hands. I growl in anger then pull my gloves off, shoving them into the back of my jeans, then I take her hair, silk in my hands as I tug the strands into a braid so that she won't have to worry about her hair on her face.

I feel like I'm losing control, like I'm about to snap and nothing will ever hold me together again.

"Stay with me," I still beg, lifting her hand to my lips and kissing it, over and over. "Don't leave me again. Stay with me."

I want to see her eyes. Those save-me green eyes. Holy shit. I need to see her smile at me. Laugh at me. Call me an asshole. Tell me she loves me.

When the basement elevator doors open, I'm shaking with

rage as I look up to watch Derek shove my brother in my direction. My god, I'm going to fucking kill him.

I charge across the room to where Wyatt stands, arms tied behind him, stomach bleeding out. He's hurt, but it does nothing to calm me. I want to grab all my knives and start cutting up his limbs, bit by bit. I want to hear him scream, I want to spill his blood, I want REVENGE FOR WHAT HAPPENED TO HER.

Raging in pain, I smash my fists into his face. "Why'd you take her? Why? You motherfucker, WHY HER?!"

"To fuck YOU!" he yells back, spitting out blood from his mouth.

"What did she say?" I shake him hard before I slam my knuckles into his jaw again. "Her last words before she fell, what did she say?"

He grins a bloodied grin, and I slam him with my knuckles, blood spurting from his mouth. "What did she say, asshole?" I demand, the pain so deep I feel like an animal. Soulless. Lifeless. A killing machine, nothing more. A brutal rage beats through me.

I'm a raging maniac, stewing inside, hurting inside.

I'm inadequate for her but it can't stop me.

She's the soul I don't have.

I thought I was dead before.

No.

I was only dormant.

She woke me up, but now, if anything happens to her, I'm dead. A walking corpse. He groans in pain when I slam him again.

"You make her beg? You make her beg you to let her go?"

Wyatt sucks in a breath. "Yeah, asshole, I made her beg."

"How'd she beg you? For how long?"

"Look, I was angry."

"How long did she beg for her life? Did she say please? Did she?"

"Minutes. Only minutes!"

"Did she tell you I would kill you? Did she tell you I would *skin you alive for harming so much as a hair on her head*?" I slam my fist again and he groans and rolls uncomfortably to the side, bringing the chair with him.

"Z, she fell on her own . . . !" he begs. "I was just keeping her to keep you from finishing the list!"

"You touched her, you fucking cunt, didn't you?"

"YES! I grabbed her tits, I wanted to piss you off!"

I slam my fists into him, repeatedly, yelling, "Congratulations, I'm *pissed*. And now. You're. DEAD!"

I pummel him, then curl an arm around his neck and start squeezing the life out of him.

Promise you won't kill anyone. The words come back to haunt me. My eyes begin to sting as I remember the hope in her eyes that one night. *Promise me you won't kill anyone.*

Growling in defeat, I let go, panting as I catch my breath and drag my arm across my wet eyes.

Promise me you won't kill anyone . . .

"Zero," I hear someone yelling. "The ambulance is here."

I walk to my unconscious girl, still fallen in that same spot, and I drop to my knees, taking her hand in mine. "Remember when I told you I didn't beg?" I whisper. "I'm begging you. Come back to me."

❤ ❤ ❤

WHEN I WAS thirteen years old I lost the most precious thing in my life.

Then I built a fortress around myself so that I'd never again lose anything I cared about. Never again feel lost, betrayed, alone, or kidnapped.

I became as cold as ice and as calculating as a robot.

I let no one in.

Loved no one, not even my family.

And it all works out great until you let down your guard.

And you finally do let someone in.

A blonde, green-eyed girl who just laughs about everything.

Who loves everything and everyone.

Who connects with people like she was born to it.

And you start wishing in the deepest part of you that she'd connect with *you*.

And no matter how demonic you are, what an asshole you are, that you lie to her, refuse to share the truth about you with her, she does connect with you.

She opens up the gate and walks inside you before you know it, and you feel so fucking full, so fucking blessed, you slam the doors closed and lock her inside, protecting yourself, protecting her.

Until you realize you're done for.

Until you're no longer cold, no longer a robot. You carry your weakness deep in your heart and her pain is your pain.

Until her smiles are all you live for.

Until you sit in a hospital chair and wait and pray for the first time in your life to a god that never heard you when you prayed for him to let you see your mother.

You still pray because Zero has no power here. Your money holds no sway here. Nothing counts except your will, and you can do nothing except pray, please, not her.

But it *is* her.

The doctors walked out to speak to me. To let me know the news.

She's in a coma.

She's barely breathing on her own.

She's somewhere far away where I don't exist, where I can't get her, can't protect her. And I still see her, feel her, hear her. Need her. LOVE THE DAYLIGHTS OUT OF HER.

She never knew that I did.

Hell, I didn't know.

Neither of us knew.

I brush my arm over my eyes when they keep burning, then stare at the text message from C.C. I got several minutes ago, numb to what it says.

Your father just passed.

Without a word, I stand and go stare through the window at her, my one and only princess, then I head down the hall to plan my father's funeral.

❤ ❤ ❤

"CONGRATULATIONS, Z."

"Congratulations, Z!"

"Zero, congratulations!"

I scowl when we reach the compound the day after my father's funeral, watching Eric cautiously approach with a large, closed steel box.

"What's this?" I ask. I'm not only thrown by the reception of the team, but by the items he's holding outstretched in his hands.

"Everything, Greyson. Ownership to the Underground. Something that belonged to your mother. And this."

I'm confused as he hands me an envelope, but then my mind is worth shit now. *I'm* worth shit. I feel like roadkill. I haven't eaten in forty hours. Haven't slept. Haven't taken a bath.

"I didn't finish the list, Eric," I feel obligated to specify.

"Yes you did. By the time your father died, every last name on the list was accounted and paid for."

"Not Melanie . . ."

"Her friend brought in her payment for her."

He pulls out the necklace from his pocket, and I almost unravel at the sight of the familiar jewels, sparkling like mad.

The diamonds glitter, and I touch the necklace she used to wear on her neck.

Memories assault me. Melanie asking what list would this be? Melanie wanting to go inside my steel room. Melanie cooking for me. Melanie Melanie Melanie. I want to see her eyes sparkling bright. I want to see her eyes open and LOOK THE FUCK AT ME LIKE SHE ALWAYS DOES! With life. Like I'm her god. Like I'm her guy.

Princess, do you realize what this means? I want to tell her as I take her necklace in my hands and stare at it while I feel poleaxed in the gut, chainsawed in my chest. *You saved me, baby. You fucking saved me. I can find my mother now.*

But there's no joy in my heart, not even at this news. There will never be joy in my heart if those green eyes don't fucking open and see me. Please just see me if only to tell me what a fucking asshole she thinks I am. Tell me I'm the reason she's like this right now.

"So this is it? This is where she is?" I ask Eric as I look down at the sealed envelope, my voice rough with the emotions I'm trying hard to keep concealed.

He nods toward that envelope. The one containing the information I've waited over a decade for. Things claw and knife at me as I grab the note and tear it open. I've waited thirteen years for this. Thirteen. I have done unspeakable things for this, for her. To find her. Try to protect her.

Pulling out the paper, I read the address written down in my father's handwriting, and that's when it hits me. Like a torpedo slamming into me, it hits me.

My mother is in a cemetery.

I stand there, absorbing it without swaying, without even a muscle in me twitching. I'm motionless, while at the same time, there's a nuclear destruction within me. Here it is. The answer to *why* I could never find her.

My mother. Is dead.

The death certificate is dated several years ago. Around the time I left the Underground to look for her. She was on an island, a *private* island. That's where she died. Natural causes, the autopsy reads. My mother died, alone, on some sort of secret island that will now belong to me.

My mother is *dead*.

My father is dead.

And my girlfriend is . . .

The thought of her in that hospital bed sends a fulminating, raging pain through me. The way I found her, unconscious, her skull banged, bleeding to death, her body small and pale and lifeless.

MY. FUCKING. GIRL.

Barely a pulse beating in her throat.

Pale and motionless on the ground when all I wanted was to lift her in my arms.

I stalk toward the bar and yell as I slam my fist into the wall.

I WAKE UP to an eerie silence and dozens of bottles are scattered across the floor. This shithole can't be my room. The fucking mess can't be where I slept.

I groan as I push myself up and the pounding in my head rolls to expand across my entire skull. I blink and take in my surroundings while instinctively pulling out my gun from under my pillow. I cock it as I stand and kick aside a fallen pillow. The place looks destroyed, like some motherfucker didn't have the intention of anything in here surviving.

"You alive, man?"

I groan and tuck my gun back as I spot C.C. Apparently one thing survived, the one the motherfucker didn't want to: me.

"You have anything else to break in here?" he asks me.

"So I did do this?"

So I destroyed my place. Great.

I'm so fucking proud of myself.

"Hell, it could be worse. Bro, you're a fucking legend, the king of the Underground, rich as fuck . . ."

"My mother is dead. My mother is dead and my girl is . . ."

I can't say it. My heart rips open at the thought of her. I put my head in my hands.

"I'm sorry, Z. I'm fucking sorry we didn't reach her in time."

"She was coming back to me, C.C. She was coming back to me even with this . . ." I spread my arms out and look around at the mess I look like—I finally look the part of the criminal I was born to be. "I may be revered in our own little dark world, but out there I'm shit. Out there there's something very wrong with us, C.C. And a girl like her can do much, much better than me. And she was coming. Back. To *me*."

He's silent.

I start picking up my knives from where they lay scattered all over. "If I'm doing this, C.C., if the Underground is mine to deal with . . . things are going to change."

"What do I do about Wyatt?"

"Jail him. Pin everything wrong there is with the Underground and my father on him. We start with a clean slate." I look at him. "C.C., I want to be the man she wants. The man she needs. The man I could be."

"Z, she may never wake up. She could stay like this for months until her family decides it's time to turn off the artificial . . ."

I grab him by the shirt and warn, "Don't fucking finish that sentence!"

C.C. quiets, and I start putting all my weapons aside.

"Grey, the Underground will fucking thrive with you. Your father was weighing it down. You can take it to another level. You can give our fighters more, our clients more."

"I'll take care of things. I'll take care of things like I always do, but not now. Not now. I can't now." I start packing some stuff.

"Dude, where are you going to sleep?"

"For now, at the hospital."

He signals to the box, my mother's box, on my bed.

"Aren't you going to open it before you leave?"

It's a steel box, rather large. I stare at it for a long time, haunted by the sight of it. I rub the top and wish I could talk to her. *I'm sorry I failed you. I'm so fucking sorry I failed you.*

I failed proving to her that I could be good and tempered when I shot a man. I failed finding her in time. I became the thing she had been running away from for as long as I can remember. She died thinking I was a killer and probably never wanted to see her. She died thinking me a criminal just like the man she hated, my father. The reason I lost my mother is the same reason I lost the woman I loved. The Underground.

C.C. leaves, and I fist my hand around the key and eye the slot. The box is old, larger than a shoe box, made of steel.

"*Fuck this.*" I force myself to shove the key into the slot and crack it open. I peel open the lid, and it's heavy, creaking. Then I stare inside. There's a pendant with a diamond I remember her wearing. So simple. The scent of her lingers somehow. I pull out a set of pictures of me. Age fifteen? Check. Age eighteen? Check. Age twenty? Check. In all of them, I'm training with my knives

or at a shooting range—unaware of the camera. Fuck me. What a
way to say hello to your mother.

Next I find a bundle of letters tied in a white sash. Hand delivered, maybe. No addresses. Just her name on them. I open all
three and immediately recognize my father's handwriting.

Lana,

    *I've been told you've been uncooperative as of late. Let me
assure you how cooperative I will personally be if you stop
trying to leave the island . . .*

J

Lana,

    *He's doing well. How else would you expect a son of mine
to do? He thrives under pressure and he's thriving now. If you
mean to ask me if he's been asking about you? He has. I've
assured him you're all right. Don't make me a liar.*

    *I cannot guarantee I'll let you see him and risk all the
work I've done so far, but it's in both his and your best
interests that you get on my good side.*

J

P.S. There's a cook on the island for a reason. Eat.

Lana,

    *As you requested, it's at the Waterfront. The deal was this
for your cooperation; it will be gone in an instant if you ever
defy me or my wishes again.*

J

Mother*fucker*. Even with keeping her locked up, he still wanted her to accept her fate without quarrel? I'm gritting my teeth as I go to pull out the rest of the box's contents.

And a set of keys falls out and to the ground. I'm about to bend down and grab them when I see, at the bottom of the box, another letter.

And this one's addressed to me.

To my son, Greyson,

I remember you. Every day I wonder what you're doing and how you've grown. I ask for pictures, and as you can see I've gotten quite a few. You're as handsome as I imagined you'd grow up to be. I look at these, wishing all your inner strength will be able to stand living with a man as hard as your father. But I try pretending that you're all right. I try remembering how strong you are, how resilient, and I tell myself, one day you'll outgrow your father and then you'll be unstoppable. You will make yourself to be exactly what you want.

I've written you countless letters, none of them ever reach you. So I stored this one away to make sure that, somehow, it will.

I remember all our years together, I cling to them. And of all those years, I remember our time in Seattle most. You liked it when we walked to the waterfront.

We used to stare at the yachts out on the water and we'd wonder what it would be like to have a home that gave us that kind of freedom.

We both wanted to stop running, remember? We were tired of running from city to city, home to home, and yet every time I told you to pack, you did so quietly and without complaining.

I've never forgotten what a noble son you were, and I never forgot those days. Not when we moved to Dallas, Ohio, Pennsylvania, or Boston.

I'm surrounded by water now.

Since I got here, I've seen these lovely yachts sail by, and I became obsessed with finding a way to make sure that one day you have a boat of your own, where you can sail far away from any trouble, away from all those bad men around you.

In the end, I couldn't see another way to do this except to cooperate with your father.

Escaping has been futile. And even if it were successful, who's to tell me he won't take his anger out on you before I reach you?

I've stayed put and tried to make the best of what I have.

The best of what I have is you, Greyson.

In this box you will find the little that was of value to me, most especially the keys to the boat I wanted you to have. It's not much, and not nearly everything I would have wished to give you, but I hope that the ocean can give you the kind of comfort it has given me all this time.

Your loving mother,

Lana

TWENTY-SIX

IN DARKNESS

Melanie

Blackness. Cold. Beeping sounds. I feel alone. I feel empty. I want to move, open my eyes, as I hear voices around me. Why can't I move? I don't remember it. I see faces. A woman. A man. Familiar. Familiar voices.

"Melanie?" she asks.

"Sweetheart, do you remember us?"

I blink and the lights burn through my retinas.

Who . . .

WHERE . . .

Panic starts setting in, and that's when I see the large figure at the other end of the room. My body trembles in reaction, not from fear but from some innate emotion and my heart starts beating really hard. His face is strained, there's remorse there, and anguish. Seeing the pain there cripples me. I start hurting in places other than my body. Deep inside. I don't understand how a pain could go as deep as this.

My lips part but I can't talk, and then the woman presses a straw between my lips. I swallow coldly, my throat raw. The man—he, he is all I want to see—pushes himself from the wall and starts coming over, his eyes taking me in, forehead, eyebrows, nose, lips, cheekbones, neck.

Heat prickles through me hard and fast when he is close enough that I can smell something other than disinfectant. Forest. Forest. My brain screams thoughts at me. Forest. Kisses. Forest. Love. Forest. Danger. A tear trails down my cheek as I open my mouth again, and nothing comes out.

"Oh, I think . . . maybe you should leave," the woman whispers to him. Not the woman. My mother. My *mother,* holding me when I was three, ten, fifteen . . . what happened after?

The man hesitates.

THE MAN looks at me like he lost himself and doesn't think that what he lost can ever, ever be recovered.

"No," I rasp. "Don't go."

His eyes bounce from my parents and back to me, and behind the depth of those hazel-green pools, there's a roil of feelings in there. Frustration, regrets, and another more powerful feeling . . .

This man loves me . . .

His eyes red, this man looks proud as a rock and nothing will convince me he has not sat in that chair in the corner and cried for me.

He waits and they step back to give us a moment. He starts to whisper achingly softly to me, and the low timbre of his voice torments and heals me, both at the same time. "Hey, princess," he says, gently running a hand down the length of my braid.

I'm wearing a braid. Someone braided my hair.

Hey, princess . . .

The way he LOOKS at me, I almost can't take it. He stands there, his body vibrating with tension as he tries to hold himself together. He looks helpless. As broken as I feel. All my senses ache and hurt and my body itches and my arms ache and my soul burns for me to wrap my arms around him. To get closer to him, comfort him, but I can't move and the wanting to be close is choking the breath out of me, making my heart race.

"Do you remember?" he asks in that achingly soft voice that makes me close my eyes and remember hearing it. Loving it.

"The doctors said you might . . . or you might forget a couple of things."

I'm mute, desperately trapping his voice in my ears, it's so beautiful.

"You're Melanie Meyers Dean," he says in that low, deeply tender voice, "The couple that just left are your parents. You're a lovely twenty-five-year-old decorator. You love wearing three colors at the same time. You love things that are bad for you, you love laughing, and you love . . ."

You, my mind screams.

He's fallen silent, as if he has no words for me, raking his eyes over my face as if he hasn't had a drop to drink and I'm an oasis in his desert.

"Melanie," he rasps, searching my face for any sign of recognition, reaching out one hand, but then thinking better of it and easing it away. "I'm Greyson King and I'm your *man*."

He waits in silence, flexing that hand into a fist at his side as though that's enough to keep him from touching me. A huge lump of emotion gathers in my throat, and as we keep staring at each other, he looks more and more desperate. He takes his shirt out of the waistband of his slacks and slides my hand underneath, over his smooth, warm chest, past his scar, to his nipple ring. I feel his skin, his warmth, seeping into me, the beat of his heart against my palm. It beats as fast as mine, and streams of tears streak down my cheeks.

Tears of joy.

Of feeling safe, of not feeling alone, as all the love I feel for him floods me.

"Greyson," I sob.

A breath shudders out of him as if he'd been holding it in all this time, then he brushes my eyelids with his lips. "Do you remember me? Do you, princess? Do you know what I do? Who I am? What you mean to me?"

Thoughts jumble in my head, one after the other. Me running away from him. Me running toward him. Me, and him.

Me and HIM.

Black gloves . . . diamond necklace . . . kisses in the dark . . . almost-there smile . . .

I feel unexpectedly weak, but not even this weakness can stop me from slowly sliding my hands up to his chest, his thick neck, his dark, stubbled jaw as I look into his eyes, eyes looking at me the way they've looked at me from the beginning.

The way Greyson King looks at Melanie.

"Remember you?" I croak. "I came *back* for you."

TWENTY-SEVEN

PERFECT

Melanie

It's the perfect night for a party.

The perfect night for a kiss.

The perfect, most *perfect* night to be in love.

I'm sitting on a thick limestone terrace railing, my dress hiked up to my waist so that Greyson can wedge his body in between my thighs.

He thumbs my nipple, and I try to keep from moaning as I visually devour him before me—his body clad in a black suit, his hair mussed by my hands, his lips a little red with my lipstick. He stares back at me as he slides his large, warm hand up my thigh and tugs off my panties. I'm breathless as he tucks them inside the pocket of his suit jacket, his hand coming back to cup my sex while the other plays with my aching nipple.

Can you die of pleasure?

Can you die of the way your boyfriend looks and looks and looks at you?

I am. *Crazy.* About this man.

I would do anything for this man.

And I've been waiting for and fantasizing this moment for months.

Behind him, I can see the party getting under way—a party he organized to celebrate my twenty-fifth birthday, an event well over three months old. But trivialities like that don't matter to a man like Greyson King.

What matters is getting his way.

And from the brand-new Harry Winston diamond necklace dangling from my throat, to the lavish party behind us, to the glimmer in his eyes that tells me almost to the last detail what he plans to do to me tonight, there is no doubt in my mind my boyfriend is getting his way tonight.

And all I can think is, *It's about fucking time.*

I'm so anxious that I'm not sure I can wait for us to find our way to our bed.

Maybe if I unzip his pants and get him close enough to ride him . . .

But now hundreds of our friends mingle inside the Ceres Ballroom. These people include my boss and coworkers, my parents, my friends, and Greyson's old and new business partners. The old ones are the dangerous ones who work for him at the Underground fighting circuit. The newer ones comprise the committee of his King Yacht Corporation he's founded in honor of his mother.

Anyone could step outside and see us. Him standing before me in his elegant suit, and me . . . my blow-dried hair now in disarray as it flaps in the wind, my body shivering under his hands and his lips, and the way his beautiful hazel eyes look at me.

"Greyson . . ." I say, a plea. He uses his body to shield me from the ballroom doors, towering over me as he ducks so he can trails his lips over my jaw. "You look delectable, Melanie, you taste delectable. Who is it that you're panting for?"

I grip his shoulders to brace myself from the delightful dizziness taking over me. "Who do you think?"

"I've been waiting for this for months, princess. Months." He tweaks my nipple in his big hand and lifts the swell of my breast to his lips, covering the peak with his mouth.

His tongue rubs against the hard little point, and I die. I die as he suckles, gently first, then harder, causing a rush of desire to shudder down my spine.

I know Greyson is not a man used to loving. I don't think he's ever loved another human being since his mother got taken away from him over a decade ago. A decade of feeling nothing . . . until he met me.

He's hungry now. I have felt his hunger building in him as our return to Seattle approached and my release from the hospital finally happened. He's hungry and male enough to not give a shit about anything but this hunger of his tonight; for without thought or hesitation, he tugs down the sleeve of my dress to bare my breasts and moves to suck on my other breast. Quaking in a mass of lust, I grab his thick, copper-streaked hair and pull his head up so his lips meet mine. "Kiss me," I groan.

He surveys my mouth first—already very well kissed by him. He rubs his index finger across my lipstick, rubbing what's left of it off.

He takes his goddamned time—his sweet, long time—and I whimper and then sigh when he lowers his mouth to nip my lower lip. We groan and start kissing, his mouth melting everything around us but him.

He takes my hand and slips it around his neck, where he wants it, forcing my fingers to curl around his nape. "Someone could come out any moment . . ." I whisper.

The breeze caresses me softly. The salty scents of recent rain and damp cement and grass reach my nostrils. But more than anything, I smell him: wet forest. Metal and leather. His scents.

"I posted Derek by the doors. Nobody's venturing out here."

His whisper is more breath than voice, more groan. He edges back just a fraction, only enough to take me in with hazel eyes that sparkle like all the stars in the sky above.

"What if my friends want some fresh air," I counter.

"Well, my girl's taking up all the freshness there is out here." He smirks and takes in my state of complete disarray. My hair is whipping around me, I can feel tendrils of it on my cheeks. My dress is exposing everything indecent. My heels are digging into the small of his back, my legs curled around him.

"Look at you, all sexy and undone just for me," he whispers huskily, visually devouring me.

Shivering, I whisper, "What if I forgot how to do this?"

"Then I'll just have to teach you what goes where. My tongue . . ." He rubs it over my top lip. "You see, my tongue goes here . . ." He eases it, wet and scalding, into my mouth. "My fingers like it here, where it's warm and wet and clenching around me. Greedy for me."

"Oh, Grey." I rock my hips when he fingers me with one long, knowing finger.

"I have no problems teaching you. You have this beautiful, perfect cunt that was made for my cock. You're not bedridden anymore, Melanie," he murmurs between kisses, rubbing that finger deep inside me. "You're very alive . . . as alive as you've ever been, those green eyes sparkling with life, this body pulsing for me. And this lovely bare pussy . . . ." he murmurs as he bends down . . . lower . . . and lower . . . and his head dives between my legs.

He flicks his tongue over my clit and pleasure rockets through me. He's stroking a hand down my back while pulling my clit into his mouth, rolling his tongue over the sensitive flesh, playing with me.

I'm burning and I need him, need him desperately. I fist my hands on the back of his head, locking him against me by the hair.

Now I feel his lips nipping on my clit, lightly tugging, and my heartbeat gallops faster as he inserts two fingers into my pussy.

It's been weeks, over three months . . . in the hospital; first the coma, then the rehabilitation. All this time, he was there for me. He was there for me when I woke, and there every time I fell asleep. My eyes sting as I feel an overwhelming desire to climax at the same time I feel an overwhelming need to make love to him.

"Grey!" I cry out, pulling him back by the hair.

He eases back and meets my gaze, straightening his black tie and smiling at me.

"I love you like this, all fucking hot and wet for me." He slides his hips between my thighs and pulls me into his arms, raining kisses on my face as he embraces me in his thick, muscled arms.

My eyes drift shut. He's hard against my bare pussy. Straining the zipper of his dress slacks. But I know he's waiting for something special tonight. He's been telling me how he craves to sink in me . . . lose himself in me . . .

So do I!

My pussy is still damp and gives a little squeeze at the thought of my guy, the only man I've ever loved, making love to me. Finally. After months of what feels like a whole life waiting. He's told me he needs to make love to me without a condom. We've talked to the doctors, and I'm on low-dose birth control for a while. They mentioned it could only be for a little while because I'm also on long-term kidney transplant reject medication. But that's okay. We will make use of these months like nobody's business.

I'm so ready to feel him, to be with him . . . I didn't want the party. I just wanted to come home and lie in bed with him. But Greyson can't seem to get past the fact that he missed my twenty-fifth birthday and he's making up for it in style.

He helps me arrange my dress, pressing one hot kiss on the top of my ear. "Ready?"

"I used to solve everything with a party. Sad? Party, girl. Mad? Party, girl. Bored? Just party, girl! How come it's lost its old allure?" I scowl at him, then poke his hard chest with my finger. "It's your fault, you know. The best parties now are the private ones with only you and me." I slide down the railing and to my feet, my voice playful to hide the lust winding inside me. "Don't look at my ass when I walk away."

"Why, can you feel it?"

"Yes!" My limbs tremble as I head to the arched doors leading into the ballroom.

"Your princess looks fucking edible," Derek says as he opens the door for me.

Greyson smacks the back of his head as he passes. "Apologize."

Derek looks at me with a silver-toothed grin and I wave a hand in dismissal, laughing. "You're forgiven."

Greyson slaps the back of his head again. "Don't think about her, don't look at her, and definitely don't tease her. That's my fucking job."

I'm terribly amused by his jealousy as I sweep into the ballroom. Long white columns welcome us and I can already see the crowd inside, all of them curious about the CEO of the new King Yacht Corp—rumored to also be the head of one of the top Underground fighting circuits. He's like some sexy JFK Jr. figure and suddenly, I'm his Carolyn . . .

I spot Pandora and Kyle by the champagne fountain, helping themselves to a new glass. They spot me almost at the same time. Kyle waves; Pandora smirks and lifts the glass in toast, her eyes shining warmly. The room's only spot of color tonight, apparently, is me. Everyone is dressed in black and white, while

I'm wearing red. "It's a black-and-white gala?" I'd asked Greyson when we arrived.

His lips quirked. "It's never black and white for you."

Greyson rubs his hand up and down my back as he reaches me, and my pulse starts accelerating as I remember little glimpses of our past.

My name is Greyson, Melanie . . .

I close my eyes, savoring this memory. When I was in a coma, I didn't remember anything, but when I came to, all my memories slammed me almost to the point I couldn't peel apart one from the other.

I love my memories now. What a treasure to know who you are, who you love, what you did yesterday, what you hope for yourself for tomorrow. What a treasure to remember the day I met the man I love.

And I remember it—every bit of it.

When I finally open my eyes, I feel his gaze on me.

As if he's waiting for something . . .

That's when the canopy that makes an artificial ceiling high above our heads, white and elegant, bursts open and a mass of white, red, and black balloons starts raining down on us.

Squealing, I tip my head back and watch them fall on us, stretching out my arms so I can feel them bounce on my palms. It feels magical, special, unforgettable.

Some of my friends take the long, sleek feathers adorning the tables and use the tips to start popping the balloons. Greyson is happiest when I'm happy—I've noticed this. Now he watches me with a curl to his lips, leaning back with his legs spread apart and his arms crossed, watching as I join the fun and start popping balloons. The music starts up as most of the balloons have fallen on the dance floor, and as the band starts playing, people try dancing around them while others are making a game out of popping them with their feet.

I'm laughing and lifting my dress, digging the heels of my shoes into a balloon.

Pop!

Pop!

POP!

When I look up, he's still watching me.

I sense his happiness like it's mine.

The song "This is What It Feels like" by Armin van Buuren rocks around us, and I start dancing to the music in the middle of the room, feeling it run through me, and I watch as Greyson pulls out a chair and sits down, leaning forward, elbows on his knees, brilliant, narrowed eyes fixated on me as I dance by myself.

He fills his jacket perfectly. I see the muscular arms, the perfect triangle of his wide shoulders, narrow waist, and I want it all. That mouth that seems a little bit pinker than normal due to my kisses. Those hungry eyes. That beautiful man.

He watches me come over with a stare that glimmers with love, and I feel like there's a fist gripping my stomach because I suddenly want these people to pop away like these balloons so it's just us. Him and me. He smiles, and I smile back, a tingle deep in my belly.

Even before we met, he'd been watching me and I didn't know it. I had something that belonged to him—to his father— and Greyson had become a shadow I never noticed, but boy, did he notice me. He *likes* watching me. So I let him watch his fill as I sway my way over, and when I stop a few feet away, he lifts his hand and crooks his finger at me.

I start up again, laughing when he grabs my waist and hauls me down on his knee. "Do you realize how fucking beautiful you look tonight," he whisper-growls into my neck, and in that dark suit, I'm Buttercup and he's Westley who defeated the one with five fingers and now . . .we can be happy. We *are* happy.

He draws me closer to his chest, clearly savoring the feel of me, the scent of me. "You couldn't be possibly any sexier, princess. Any fucking sexier. I could watch you until you wear yourself out, but I need you to have energy for what I have planned."

His sexy voice so close to my ear ripples through my body. I start kissing his hard jaw. "When?"

"When we get back to the apartment," he promises, his voice tight with lust.

He brushes my hair back from my face, and tingles race from the roots of my hair to my toes. He's all I breathe and see. All I want and need. His eyes, hazel green and fiery. His mouth. Lips that look soft and firm. A jolt runs through me when he caresses his hand along the length of my bare back, and my pulse skitters at the caress as he roughly adds, "I adore you. Treasure you. Cherish you. I think I'm damn well keeping you."

My entire body responds. I feel so cherished. *His girl*. Me. Me. Me. "Yes. Keep me. Love me. Ride me hard tonight, Grey. As hard as you ride your men," I tease.

His men respect him, are in awe of him, maybe a little in fear of him too.

But I'm not afraid of him.

He may make men twice my size tremble, but not me. Okay, yes. He makes me tremble. He makes me tremble in love. In lust. But never in fear. Because I know that he'd never hurt me. In fact, he's the only one who can truly make me feel *safe*.

He chuckles a low, deep sound. "You don't rule a snake pit gently, but I'd rather use a firm but gentle hand on my princess."

"Mm. And I hope you know in my instance, one hand won't do. You have to use two!"

We laugh, and he nuzzles me as we do. I love how he calls me princess even when he's *no* prince. But in my heart, he's so much more. He's my King.

❤ ❤ ❤

IT'S PAST MIDNIGHT when we reach our apartment building. Of course it was *his* apartment, but he asked me to move in, and now it's mine too.

We're crossing our building lobby, his hand laced with mine, when he presses the elevator button and then surprises me by scooping me up in his arms. "Um? I can walk?" I say.

"I know you can do many things, including driving me crazy with that very walk, but you're going to need your energy for what we're about to do. So sit tight and hang on."

I grin up at him and do exactly as he asks, whispering in his ear as we ride to the top, "Nothing makes me feel as alive as you do. Smelling you, feeling you, loving you." I kiss his thick throat and the back of his ear, glad we're alone in the elevator so I can nip and lovingly kiss any part I can reach. "I love you," I whisper, closing my eyes and inhaling him, rubbing my hands up the plackets of his suit. "I love you so much, I missed the smell of your skin and your hair and your shirts."

He cups my skull and tips my head around to his. "Melanie." My heart hurts from the way he looks at me, like I'm a living, breathing dream of his.

He takes my mouth in a long, hot kiss until we reach our floor. Then he carries me out of the elevator and into our apartment. I play with his shirt collar and whisper, "Set me down so I can take off my shoes and hang up the dress you got me."

He drops a kiss on my mouth and sets me down, then locks the door behind us. "One minute. No more."

I love the feel I get when we walk into this place. I've decorated it because the man can't expect us to live forever in Sparta, and I'm trying to build us a home now. It was a giant step in my

life, to move in with a man. A man I love. A man who's dangerous, powerful, elusive, giving, secretive, all of the above. A man
who, despite all that, I trust to protect me.

"I can barely get used to living here with you," I confess as I
admire my handiwork. The artwork over the stone chimney. The
trio of live plants, some taller than others, by the window.

"And I can't get used to the shit I need to live with in order
to live with you."

I laugh, then smile shyly as he follows me toward the bedroom area. "Don't pretend you don't like it because I've asked
your opinion on it all. And I'm not done yet, you know. I want to
paint the master bedroom royal blue and add some purple to our
living room. And then I plan—"

"Enough, baby."

We've reached the bedroom space, and he's tugging his tie
loose. Oh my . . .

Can he be any sexier, please?

Oh. *My.* He's very determined tonight. Tossing his tie aside.
Easing off his jacket.

"You can do anything you want with my apartment as long
as I get to do anything I want with you," he tells me in his most
sexy voice.

I don't stand a chance.

Nor do I want to.

I take off my heels—the black ones with the red sole he
bought me—and I carefully set them aside. "Make me any indecent proposal you want, the answer is yes, Mr. King."

"Right answer, princess." Eyes twinkling, he pulls my panties
out of his jacket and holds them out, then he crooks his finger
with his free hand. "Come here, princess," he finally murmurs—
the command sensual. Hot.

"I am here," I counter.

He tosses my panties onto a chair by the window. "You're over on the other side of the bed. And I want you here."

Oh my. *Really.* He wants me right where he is. He starts to unbutton his shirt and all that tan skin of his peeks out to tempt all of my fingers. I begin walking toward him, hearing him murmur—*that's right, princess*—his voice a shiver down my nape as he closes the last steps—the last steps—to me. I start shaking with adrenaline as I grab the back of his head and immediately trail my lips across his hard jaw, then I whisper in his ear, "Yes."

He groans hoarsely, running his hands up my back, holding me against his body—his impressive erection pressing into my pelvis. "You don't even know what I'm going to ask . . ." he huskily counters.

"It's yes, Greyson," I whisper, looking up into his hard face. "I want to feel you. I want nothing between us. We've already discussed it. I'm on the pill, and you're clean and you're mine. So it's yes, you perfect, sexy man. Fuck me, love me, fight with me, spoil me, just don't leave me."

"Melanie."

My name is whispered like a prayer. Within seconds, he pulls open the last buttons off his shirt and tosses it aside, and he's gloriously bare-chested and crushing me against him. He's so hot, muscled, strong, resilient, and buzzing like a live wire in my arms.

Suddenly I'm frantic. "Greyson, get me naked and get inside me."

I'm rubbing his strong muscles, eagerly dropping kisses on the corner of his lips, his throat, his shoulders as I unbuckle his belt and pull it off his slacks.

Tossing it aside, I bend to lick his nipple ring, using my teeth to tug on the smooth white gold hoop. He groans and sets me down on the bed, coming down with me. His mouth settles over mine. He frames my face in his big hands, and I hold the back of his head, both of us locking each other in place so our tongues can eagerly taste. Our breathing turns erratic, but we won't stop kissing.

He feasts on my mouth before he unlatches from me and slides his hands under my back to unzip my dress.

"Greyson, please," I whimper, trying to pull him back to me for more kissing.

"Shhh. Wait me out a bit." He tugs my dress down my body.

"It's going to wrinkle!"

"Shh. I'll fix it. I promise." He throws it aside as though he plans to make it all right by buying me a new one, then he takes my bare legs and kisses his way up my calves, my knees, my thighs. "I want to kiss every inch of your skin, from your toe to the back of your ears, to your lovely little head."

He covers one nipple with his mouth, trailing his tongue over the peak.

"Oh, please." Damn the dress. Who cares? Who cares about anything but this?

He runs his tongue over my other nipple, stroking his fingers up my sides, over my ribcage.

I arch my spine.

His teeth skim my ear, tugging my earlobe.

The tips of my breasts throb as he tweaks them between his thumb and forefinger. My blood is like a scalding fire in my veins.

His lips continue torturing me, relentless, hot, wet, covering my skin, tasting, nipping, teeth grazing. A haze of pleasure envelops me, every feeling in me exponential. He presses his lips against my clit, then takes it between them and gently suckles as he fills me with two fingers.

I can sense the way he needs this. The way he needs me. He nearly lost me. He nearly lost me twice—and forever. His eyes have been haunted, as if he's sometimes taken to that moment when he must've found me. Unconscious and almost gone to him.

I don't know if this has been harder for him, or for me, but I never want us to go through something like that again. And by the determination I see in his face when he looks at me, neither does he.

"Jesus, you ready, baby?" He stands and unzips his pants, and I watch his cock spring free. Pulsing and pink, ready for me. Eager for me.

No condom tonight. Every inch of him will be inside me.

Quivering, I sit up on the bed, my voice unsteady. "Don't make me wait this time, Greyson. I really crave and need—"

He presses a finger to quiet me, and I'm so starved, I suck it into my mouth.

Eyes smoldering, he watches me run my tongue up the length of his finger. "Hungry? Suck then," he thickly commands.

"Make me," I breathe.

He pushes his finger inside; making me. "That's right," he cooes with a soft smile, rubbing my tongue with his finger. "Your pleasure and need is mine to use and stir and mix until you're a fucking beautiful mess. *My* wet mess."

I'm hot enough to burst into cinders as I suck and I bite and nibble, tasting his delicious skin. As he slowly retrieves his lips, he lowers his head, the copper streaks in his hair shining in the lights as he comes closer.

Then my lips are under his, my mouth is his, my breath is his as I tilt my head back and melt into the fiercest, most delicious kiss I've ever had. Teeth nipping, biting, and then . . . our tongues.

His chest is warm, hard velvet under my fingers. Ripples of pleasure flow through me as his hands rub their way down to my bottom. My mouth throbs from his bites and I bite back, giving as hard as I take.

He spreads me out on the soft mattress beneath me, then he reaches between us and rubs his thumb over my sex. Moaning deep in my throat, I can hardly stand it as he slides down my body and kisses my pussy lips, lifting his head to look at me for a wild, frenzied heartbeat, his eyes shining like gemstones, then he bends down again and kisses my pussy some more.

"Stop me if anything hurts."

"My pussy hurts," I groan, locking his face between my thighs as I writhe from the intense pleasure. "My pussy hurts for you."

"That's all right, gorgeous, I've got just what you need." He pushes his long finger inside me. I clench and almost can't keep from coming.

He notices how close I am, my hands grabbing a fistful of sheets, and he surges forward and kisses me on the mouth, tasting of me. "Your smell, when you're hot for me, intoxicates me. And you're always hot for me, aren't you?"

I can hear the heat in his words, his voice carrying a unique, but gentle force. "Yes," I pant.

His deliciously hot kisses are driving me insane. Love, lust, need courses through me as he brushes his lips over my eyelids. "I want these lively green eyes, Melanie. I need these on me right now . . . when I'm in you. Just you and me."

He's on top of me, bare skin to bare skin, with only the necklace like some mark of his resting between my breasts. He smiles; he likes it. He watches me as he cups my nipples in his hands and I tease his nipples with my hands, one pierced, the other bare. Both of mine pucker for him. He groans when he looks at them and takes one in his mouth like something precious. He sucks so hard, my sex clenches around his finger.

I moan and rub my hands over his skin. "Ohhh." I reach out to stroke his erection; he's leaking and hard as rock for me. "Oh, god, here you are," I breathe.

He pulls out his finger and brushes my clit with my own wet-ness as he licks my chin, my jaw. "Yes?" he rasps. Asking *you okay?*

"Yes," I gasp, caressing his cock. I brush my thumb over the drops of semen already on the tip. He's tense above me and his chest vibrates with a delicious rumble as he turns his head and sets his hot lips on mine. Wet. Our mouths are wet and hungry and our breaths fast and eager. We're both bare naked and he's so perfect. His erection long, thick, pink. I hungrily bend over and grab the base and kiss the tip.

"Awww, hell, Melanie," he rasps as I savor him and carefully suck.

He takes a ragged breath, pulls me up with a gentle fistful of hair, and says, "Come the fuck here and let me put my cock where we both want it most."

I press my nose to his throat and tremble knowing I'm going to feel him without a condom for the first time. "I want you." I can barely get the words out, I'm so aroused. "You don't know how I want you. I want this cock in me. This guy. This man. In me."

Speaking my name in a gruff tone, he rolls to his back and pulls me down to his lap. I gasp when I feel him—hard and throb-bing—at my entry. I spread my legs over him, lowering myself to his erection with a little rock of my hips and a gasp of excite-ment. He watches me with smoldering hazel-green eyes, and the LOOK, how I love the look.

I kiss the corner of his eyes and wrap my arms around his neck as the head of him stretches me. Another, deeper groan rum-bles out of him and he clenches me in his arms and rolls me down onto my back, and when he rears up, he grabs my head with both his hands, fucks his tongue into my mouth as he thrusts his hips and shoves his cock deep inside. A cry escapes my throat and my breath catches. He's in me, to the hilt. *God.* Bare. I feel him pulsing inside me. The pleasure is so exquisite, my eyes roll into the back of my head. I make a gurgling sound as my body writhes for more, starved as never before. Greyson is thrusting me, all the while kissing me, and my body knots up on every breath-stealing, heart-stopping plunge.

He viciously nips at my throat, wrapping my legs around his hips. "Hold onto me," he says, voice husky in my ear.

I groan, undone. He's just as lost. Groaning too. Pushing. Pumping. Swiveling his hips. Claiming. Taking. "I need you," he hisses, "So fucking bad, *I need you!*"

I'm trying to keep up with him, clinging hard as my hips meet his in every movement, every frantic thrust. Over and over, like he's trying to blend us into one. I've got both of my hands and my mouth all over his muscled body as I take in as much of him that I can, my fingers busy, my tongue busy, my hips rocking. *Greyson Greyson Greyson*, my heart is pounding his name. I shiver under the heat of his skin as he glides his scarred palm up my arm. He moans my name and rolls his tongue over my nipple, his mouth knowing and tasting me, fingers trailing and exploring my curves. My back arches. Head to toe, I throb and burn. I can't believe the sounds we make in the dark. The way he feels. The way he smells. The way he wants me.

The passion in his eyes as he watches me. I suck on his earlobe. He shivers as I pull the ear and tug, and I whimper into his ear that I love him, I love him, I love him.

When I start to come, shockwave after shockwave hit me. With a soft cry, I tremble beneath him, feeling Greyson hold still and clutch me tight as he growls and jets off inside me. Warm. Wet. My king . . . filling me with him. It's all so very yummy and so very intimate my eyes sting.

I quickly swipe at two runaway tears, and he murmurs my name, gently placing his thumbs over the corners of my eyes.

"Pinch me so I believe it's really happening," I suddenly whisper.

He kisses each of my eyelids instead and tenderly rubs the wetness dry with his thumbs. "Yeah, that's not happening. I'm not ruining—"

I pinch his nipple ring. "Ouch! That's not nice, Melanie," he chastises, cupping my butt and giving me a light spank.

"Hmm. That *was* kind of nice," I tease, and his smile fades and his eyes grow dark with renewed lust.

"It felt so good being inside you, baby. You feel me?" he huskily asks as he pulls me closer.

"Yes," I breathe. My body hones in on the way he feels inside me, still as hard as before, and I swear I don't want him to pull out.

As though thinking along the same lines, he pins my arms up over my head, and then he's moving inside me again, murmuring slowly, tenderly, huskily as he makes love to me again. "Say you love it," he cooes.

I moan and close my eyes. "God, you know I do."

"Say you want it."

"I do, I do."

"Say it's me, it's always been me, say it, princess."

"Always you, just you. You may be zero in your world . . . but you're everything to me."

Our bodies are straining and moving together, our chests rubbing and his piercing brushing against one of my breasts as he kisses me. And he kisses me until our mouths are swollen and red and our need and want and emotions have gnawed at us, and he's mine, and I'm his.

Finally, the one for me.

ACKNOWLEDGMENTS

Thank you with all my love to my husband, my children, and my parents for their incredible patience, love, and support during all my processes—from creating, to writing, to editing, to endlessly, endlessly talking about "it."

To Stacey Suarez, for being the best trainer, and friend, and for being such a good sport she actually talks to my characters with me.

To my very beloved writer friends, so supportive, encouraging, and all around amazing, always ready to read, talk, cry, or laugh with me, and that means you Monica Murphy, Jen Frederick, Lisa Desrochers, Christina Lauren, J. A. Redmerski, and my dear VP girls Kim K, Kylie, Kim J, Renee, and Joanna, thanks for being true friends.

To CeCe, I have professed my love and gratitude to you at length by e-mail, but I needed to do so again. Thank you for reading *ROGUE* in its roughest form and becoming true Mel and Greyson fans.

To Kati Brown, you are not only an inspiring woman with always amazing input for me, but I want to pick your lovely brain apart and borrow it, I love your brilliance so much!

To wonderful Angie, Dana, Milasy, Neda, and Margie, thank you for your reads, your support, and your truly valued friendship. I adore you girls!

To Megan, thank you for making sure I delivered this in the shiniest way possible to my very amazing team at Gallery.

To Anita S. for the excellent proofreading, as always.

To Lori and Gel, you're angels, always helping me keep up with my own frantic pace!

To all the bloggers who've been beyond supportive of my characters and stories, I don't even have the words to thank you. But thank you for opening doors where they were previously closed before. Thank you for encouraging writers to express themselves in any form. And thank you for hooking us up with the best readers in the world.

To my agent, Amy, who is all wisdom, support, candor, encouragement, and patience, and whom I admire so much, I feel blessed to have found her. Or more exactly, I'm very blessed she found me!

To my genius editor, Adam, for his insightful input and support of my books and career; to my publicists Nina Bocci, Jules, and Kristin; and to the lovely Jen Bergstrom and her stupendous team at Gallery Books—I am both blessed and grateful to have such talented minds to work with. Thank you for all that you do.

And last, to you readers. Your support of me and this series has meant the world. Thank you!

XOXO!

ABOUT THE AUTHOR

Hey! Thank you so much for picking up *ROGUE*. I'm Katy Evans, and I'm happily married and live with my husband, two children, and three dogs, and I spend my time baking, walking, writing, reading, and taking care of my family. I'm so honored and grateful for the time you've spent with my beloved characters and me. Since the release of *REAL*, it's because of you and your incredible support that I've been able to watch my dearest, wildest writing dreams come true. I hope you enjoyed Greyson and Melanie's story as much as I did, and I can't wait for the next REAL series release! Coming up is Pandora's story, *RIPPED*, and it will be available soon from Gallery Books.

If you enjoy my books and would like to leave a review, I greatly appreciate you taking the time to share your thoughts with others. I love all my readers, and I love hearing from you too.

You can find me at:

Website: www.katyevans.net

Facebook: https://www.facebook.com/AuthorKatyEvans
  /521052267929550

Twitter: https://twitter.com/authorkatyevans

E-mail: authorkatyevans@gmail.com

Happy reading and stay real!

XO,
Katy